SPITFIRE STORM

AJ BAILEY ADVENTURE SERIES - BOOK 16

NICHOLAS HARVEY

Printed in the United States of America

First Printing, 2024

ISBN-13: 978-1-959627-27-2

Cover design by David Berens

Author photograph by Lift Your Eyes Photography

This book is dedicated to the memory of the brave men and women of the Air Transport Auxiliary who valiantly did their part during WWII.

1

PRESENT DAY

Captain Nolan Conrad checked his chartplotter and radar then lifted his gaze beyond the glass of the wheelhouse. From the tall cabin structure at the stern, his cargo of shipping containers stretched like building blocks to the bow, where the vast expanse of glistening Caribbean Sea filled his view.

But the waters ahead were not his primary concern. The nor'wester building in his wake gave him far more to worry about. He glanced over his shoulder through the rear windows where beyond the stern of the 100-metre-long container ship, the pale blue sky met the darker blue water. The storm was several hundred miles astern, so well out of sight, but the reports continued to speak of escalating winds. Conrad took a sip of his coffee and told himself to relax. *They were safely clear of the storm.*

The cautious decision would have been to remain in the Yucatán Peninsula port of Puerto Progreso and let the storm pass them by. And Conrad considered himself to be a logical and cautious captain. But several factors had urged him to press on and take refuge at their destination in George Town, Grand Cayman. Staying put meant facing the oncoming weather in the poorly protected Puerto Progreso, which was little more than a sturdy cruise ship pier with a small commercial section. He'd also felt quite uncomfortable in the unfamiliar port. It was the first time he'd made a detour to Mexico from his regular Miami to Grand Cayman route, and the unsavoury characters hanging around the dock had made him nervous.

His concerns had been realised when he'd walked into the small town for breakfast, and a young man had tried snatching Conrad's backpack. The captain had prevailed, grimly keeping hold of a strap, but when the thug had given up and let go, the backpack had slammed to the ground, smashing his company laptop. Conrad had hurried back to the ship, and once the dozen containers they were picking up had been loaded, he'd been more than keen to move on.

"I'm grabbing lunch," he said, stepping from the helm. "Be back in fifteen minutes, Enrique."

His second in command nodded and took the captain's place. "Take your time, Skipper. We're well ahead of the weather."

Conrad grunted his reluctant agreement and descended the steps to the galley two levels below. He certainly wasn't opposed to the idea that their trip could go smoothly, but his job was to foresee all potential hazards and delays, and the presence of the storm greatly increased the penalty for encountering either. His first mate was an optimistic man, and Conrad a realist, which made them a good pairing in the captain's opinion.

Lunch was a packaged salad from the fridge and another cup of coffee. His wife had taken to sending him on his way with a stack of healthy eating options. He'd mentioned his increasing weight had begun to concern him, and apparently his wife had agreed, as without hesitation she'd laid out a food plan. The pounds had stopped going on, but he'd yet to add in enough exercise to persuade his surplus mass to retreat. Spending fourteen hours a day in the wheelhouse, the maximum by regulation, wasn't conducive to a rigorous gym program, but Conrad was a diligent captain who felt displaced when not at the helm.

The piercing screech of the alarm sent Conrad to his feet and the salad bowl skittering across the galley table. Taking them three at a time, he bounded up the steps to the wheelhouse, where he was about to ask what was wrong, but there was no need. Smoke billowed from the control console and Enrique was trying to find somewhere to aim a fire extinguisher hose.

"Wait!" Conrad shouted. "Shut everything down!"

Enrique whirled around and the relief on his face at the captain's presence was clear.

"The smoke just started coming from underneath," Enrique cried, putting the fire bottle down and taking the ship out of drive so they could switch off the big diesel engines before cutting electrical power.

Conrad snatched up the radio mic and pressed the intercom button to broadcast over the entire ship, taking his brief opportunity before power was shut off to all systems.

"All crew, all crew, this is the captain. We have a fire on the bridge. Repeat, fire on bridge. Shutting down engines, then electrical power. Stand by."

Releasing the button, he ran to the main electrical box for the wheelhouse, opened the cabinet door, and turned to look at Enrique. The low rumble of the engines faded away and after flicking a series of switches, the first mate nodded to his captain. Conrad shut off the main power and the console screens immediately went blank.

"We need to pull the access panels," he ordered.

By the time he reached the console, Enrique had already produced two cordless drills with Phillips head bits from a storage cabinet, handing one to Conrad. Smoke still emanated from every seam and vent around the console and the two men coughed and spluttered as they removed the screws holding the panels in place. When Conrad peeled the first rectangular section of sheet metal away, a plume of smoke and heated air vented into the wheelhouse and he jumped back.

"Hand me the extinguisher!" he yelled.

Enrique abandoned his drill for the moment, picked up the fire bottle, and after a quick look inside the console, squirted the dry chemical powder at the flames he saw.

"That's enough," Conrad warned, knowing the powder could cause nearly as much damage to the instrumentation as the fire. The stuff got everywhere and was impossible to clean up.

Two more crew members, Hal and Tico, arrived, and the captain directed them to open all the doors and windows, letting the fumes out of the confined space.

"What a mess," Enrique muttered as he double-checked he'd put all the fire out.

"We need to get this smoke cleared so we can see what happened," Conrad said. "There's a couple of fans," he added, pointing to the row of cabinets below the back windows and looking at Tico. "There are also two emergency power banks in there somewhere. They can run 120 volts for a while, but we'll need to be conservative."

Hal joined Tico in searching for the items.

"We can turn on the emergency generator if we can isolate the problem area," Enrique said, setting the fire bottle aside. "But unless we can repair the controls, I don't know how we can run the engines."

Conrad ran a hand through his brown hair, which he'd noticed was turning lighter lately as more and more grey hairs appeared. This situation would certainly add more.

"Let's pull all the panels so we can to get a better look at what we're dealing with. We can't start the backup generator until we know it won't create another fire. First priority is to assess the damage, and second is to find the cause. With this weather up our ass, I need to know we can get back underway."

His first mate let out a long breath. "And if we can't?"

Conrad shook his head. "Then I need to make that call with enough time to get airlifted out of here. We could probably ride out that storm without power if it remained at its current strength, but I have a bad feeling it's going to keep building. I won't put the crew's lives at risk. But let's see what we've got here first, and then I'll use the sat phone to notify the authorities in Cayman."

Enrique nodded. "At least we'll have nav from the ECDIS on the laptop."

Conrad stared back at his first mate, shaking his head.

"Or not," Enrique realised. "Damn. It was on the laptop that's busted."

The electronic chart display and information system was independent software which relied on its own, self-contained satellite network to provide navigation and weather information in just such situations. Conrad cursed the young man back in Puerto Progreso. His opportunistic attempt at making a quick buck had potentially created a perilous situation the thief would never know anything about. Or care. He was probably too busy stealing some poor woman's handbag. But Conrad knew this was no time to dwell on such things.

Enrique began systematically removing screws which held any panel without screens, gauges, or switches attached.

"Damn, it stinks," he said as one by one the panels came off.

It was quickly becoming sweaty work. The hot, humid Caribbean air consumed the wheelhouse where the four men laboured. The fans helped clear the fumes, but after a while were doing little more than blowing hot air around, and Conrad turned them off to save the power banks. After thirty minutes, the captain lay with his upper torso inside the long cabinet-like console from one side, while Enrique had squeezed his smaller frame all the way inside the other end. They both swept torches around, examining the fire damage.

"This main cluster of wires is pretty bad," the first mate pointed out, covering his nose from the stench. "We won't know how many need splicing until we pull it all apart."

"Shit," Conrad muttered.

"I know, but it's all we can do, Skipper."

"No, Enrique," Conrad replied. "Look where I'm shining my light."

"Oh. Shit."

"Rat shit, to be precise," the captain confirmed.

Enrique eased back and winced. "Where do you think they've gone?"

"Down the conduit holes, I suspect. They'd have left in a hurry once the fire started."

"Except for one," Enrique said, and circled his light in an area amid a cluster of wires. "That explains the smell. One fried rat."

With a rag in his hand, Conrad reached into the mass of control cables and wires and picked up the dead creature, tossing it across the floor behind him.

"Burial at sea, please Tico."

"Aye, aye, sir," the crewman replied, and used the same rag to carry the barbecued rat outside and fling it into the ocean.

"Okay," Conrad continued, with his torch back on the fire damage. "Looks like the little bastard chewed through a power supply then arced itself to the back of the console. I think we've found the cause, so now it's all about repair."

He shuffled himself out of the console and stood, accepting a bottle of water from Hal. Enrique emerged from the other end.

After a long sip and a moment to think, Conrad gave his orders. "I'll call in our status on the sat phone. Enrique, identify which of the damaged wires are from the engine and steering controls. They're our first priority. We need power and the ability to manoeuvre. I'll get a weather update while I'm on the horn, so we know what time we have to work with. Tico's our best wiring man so use him to help you under there, and have someone else come up to join Hal as runners and helpers. Keep the others off the bridge, or we'll be tripping over each other. Sound good?"

"Aye, sir," Enrique replied. "I'll start by getting the wiring diagrams out, but I'll admit most of that stuff is Chinese to me."

"Tico can help decipher until I'm back," Conrad replied.

With a plan in place, the captain picked up the sat phone and walked outside to the gangway running behind the tall cabin structure. The big ship had already slowed to a crawl and would soon be at the mercy of the swells. Despite being a relatively small container ship, at 100 metres, or 328 feet, it was still big enough that the gentle open ocean's two-to-three-foot seas barely moved the vessel around. But that would change if the storm caught them. In large swells, if the unpowered ship turned sideways, it could be disastrous.

As Conrad looked up the emergency number to reach the Cayman Islands Coast Guard, he truly hoped they'd be back underway long before then.

"Ready?" Conrad asked, looking at Enrique, who was covered in sweat and grime.

It had been over four hours of hard toil, cleaning up the mess, stripping wires, and splicing in new sections from the limited repair supplies they carried on board. What at first had appeared to be a relatively simple patch job had turned out to be far more complicated.

"*Sí*," Enrique replied, but the captain noticed the man had his fingers crossed at his side.

Conrad threw the master switch and waited for the console to spring into life, but all he heard was a long groan from his first mate.

"Sorry, Skipper."

"Okay," Conrad said. "Let's figure it out. I'll leave the power on, so be careful. Use the voltmeter to trace the power. Where's the first place it goes in the console?"

Enrique went to speak, but the captain interrupted him.

"Wait. Did we check all the breakers? The ones downstairs?"

The next twenty minutes were spent studying the diagrams then running down five flights of steps to the engine room, where the power originated from the generators run by the diesels. They discovered more circuit breakers and emergency switches than they knew existed. Finally, they found the culprit and returned to the wheelhouse, where Hal stood by the console. Which was still dead.

"It didn't come on?" Conrad asked in exasperation.

"It came on," Hal replied. "But something sparked under there, so I turned the master back off."

Enrique's shoulders dropped, and Conrad looked at his watch. The weather report had not been good. As he'd feared, the nor'wester was gathering speed and strength as it funnelled between the Yucatán Peninsula and Cuba. What he'd thought to be an eight-hour margin was more like six, and they'd lost over five already. His eyes moved to the horizon, where the sky had grown ominously darker. The gentle ocean breeze had already become a steady wind as the gathering storm pushed air out front of its path.

"We don't have time for subtlety, Enrique. Stick your head under there and I'll throw the switch. Shout when you see where the problem is, okay?"

Enrique nodded and crossed himself, then squatted on his hands and knees, nervously sticking his head under the console. Conrad threw the switch and they all heard electrics arcing.

"Off!" Enrique called out, and the captain shut the power to the console down.

"It's the power to the instrumentation, Skipper. I must have missed a chewed wire."

"Can you get to it? We have a few minutes, but that's about it."

Enrique stood and pointed to the section housing the radar and chartplotter. "It's up in behind the instruments. We need to pull the lot of them out. It'll take hours, not minutes, Skipper."

Conrad returned his attention to the main electrical box, searching the labels on the wheelhouse breakers. He flicked off anything which he hoped wouldn't prevent them from starting the engines and steering the ship. When he was done, he tried the master switch once more. Enrique squatted to look underneath, and everyone listened carefully. A set of gauges and dials came to life, and several beeps emitted from computer systems booting up, but Conrad couldn't hear anything arcing.

"Seems okay," Enrique reported.

The ship rocked, and Conrad looked out the back windows. He could now see white caps and a wall of dark, menacing cloud filling the horizon.

"Try starting the engines," he barked, aware their time was done.

Any options of being airlifted were gone. He'd gambled on them fixing the problem, and all in, it was time to show his cards. The captain held his breath to see if they'd be wiped out or live to fight another hand.

"Come on, baby," Enrique muttered as he went through the start-up procedure.

The beautiful, low rumble of the diesels vibrated through the ship and they all cheered.

"South-east, Enrique," Conrad ordered. "Maximum power, please."

He turned and looked out the windows again as his first mate coaxed the big ship into motion.

"Can we outrun the storm?" Hal asked, gathering up all the loose panels from the floor of the wheelhouse.

Conrad picked up his sat phone, but paused to answer the question. "No. I don't think we can."

The ship had begun making good speed at 24 knots, but as the winds built and the seas became more and more tumultuous, their pace declined. The storm was moving faster than their 21 knots, and although the winds were creating following seas, the gusts and swirls formed confused swells which rocked and yawed the ship, slowing its progress. At 25 miles from Grand Cayman, the front of the nor'wester caught them, bringing gale force winds and serious waves.

Leaning against the helm seat in a wide stance, hanging on to the small wheel, Conrad focused on the compass as the cargo ship pitched and rolled. He cursed under his breath. About the same time he'd spotted the handful of tall buildings on Grand Cayman, the cloud and rain had consumed them, blinding him to any useful reference. All he could rely on now was the compass, his watch, and the marine chart he had spread across the console covering the useless screens of technology which had failed him.

"I have to give the island a wide berth," he shouted to Enrique.

His first mate leaned against the second chair, no more than six feet away, yet they both had to shout to be heard over the raucous wind and rain.

"We should get cell service soon from the island," Enrique yelled, optimistically checking his phone for a signal. "Nothing yet."

"That's how we'll know we're close!" Conrad replied. "We'll still be several miles clear of land when we pick up a cell signal."

"I'll keep checking," the first mate said. "And let's hope their cell network doesn't go down."

The two men shared a look. The way their day had gone so far, Conrad figured anything that could go wrong, and probably would, so he knew to be cautious relying on his cell signal theory.

Rain lashed against the glass, giving them glances and peeks of the outside turmoil as the wipers momentarily swept the water away before a fresh swath of rain rendered them blind once more.

"Hang on!" Conrad screamed as the wipers cleared his view for a brief moment.

He couldn't be sure, but what appeared to be a far larger wave was building ahead of them. His only reference in a wall of dark green and blue were the white caps whisked away from the tops of the waves. The ship rose alarmingly from the stern and appeared to yaw slightly as they rode the swell, before the bow picked up and they were pressed against the seats.

"Damn!" Enrique yelled as the bow dropped violently and the ship smashed into the ocean with a jarring hit.

Conrad barely kept his feet under him and grabbed at the chair, bracing for another swell, but the ship settled. They were back to being rolled and rocked by the heavy seas, nothing like the violence of what they'd just survived.

"Rogue wave?" Enrique asked, rubbing his elbow and checking his phone again.

"Maybe," Conrad muttered, and stared through the window.

As the wiper cleared a brief view, he knew something was different. It took five more swipes of the rubber blades until he realised what had changed.

"We lost some," he shouted, and looked over at his first mate.

"Lost what?" Enrique asked.

"Containers," the captain replied. "Must have been that crazy wave. We've lost some containers."

2

PRESENT DAY

Annabelle Jayne Bailey leaned into the fierce wind, holding the hood of her rain jacket, keeping it from blowing from her head as she squinted across Governor's Creek.

"This seems a bit worse than advertised," she yelled to be heard over the wind and rain.

Her sarcastic English understatement wasn't lost on her friend and mentor, Reg Moore. He swiped water from his shaggy salt-and-pepper beard and double-checked the stern line he'd just secured to a dock cleat.

"I've a bad feeling this ain't the worst of it," he shouted back in his gruff London accent. "Is the bow secure?"

"Yeah, yeah," AJ replied. "Let's do the last one."

Reg owned three Newton custom dive boats and AJ owned one, plus a rigid inflatable boat or RIB as they were commonly called. Unless they planned to spend a week diving the North Wall, they usually moored on the west side of Grand Cayman, offshore from the pier they operated from. But like most dive trip businesses on the island, they also rented slips in the Cayman Islands Yacht Club marina on the east side of the narrow stretch of land behind the famed Seven

Mile Beach. Inside the expansive and shallow North Sound, the marina offered far better protection from storm swells. And this nor'wester had escalated substantially since the warnings began a few days ago.

While Reg carefully made his way to the bow of AJ's Mermaid Divers' boat, *Hazel's Odyssey*, AJ untied the single bow line and moved it to the cleat on the far side of the finger pier. Fighting against the wind and driving rain, she then moved around the boat to the next finger pier to secure a second bow line, again using the farthest cleat available. Lengthening the lines allowed play for the rise and fall of the water level the incoming swells would bring. Reg played out and adjusted the lines before re-securing them to the bow cleat on the Newton. Moving to the stern, they repeated the exercise, but with criss-crossed lines made possible by the square shape of the rear of the dive boat.

"What are we forgetting?" AJ asked, looking over the long cockpit of her boat where dive tanks sat in racks behind the bench seats running down both sides.

"I'd say that's best we can do," Reg shouted back. "But I dare say we should check some of these other boats along the dock. Just in case someone's away."

Dive boats were on the third of four main piers stretching out into the bay known as Governor's Creek. The marina had worked with the operators to install a compressor at the head of number three jetty. Air lines plumbed underneath the pier ran to each spot, allowing the captains and crews to refill their dive tanks with whip hoses from a connector on their dockside pedestals. Most of the spots on pier three were rented by the dive companies or charters who also offered a diving option. They were generally a tight group who all mucked in to help each other when needed, so if anyone happened to be off island with the storm approaching, they'd need their lines taken care of.

Reg and AJ had seen most of the regulars during the hour or so they'd been prepping their lines, but Reg paused by a centre console with twin outboards.

"Chris hasn't been down yet," he called out to AJ, who was looking over their own Newtons for a final time.

AJ looked towards the shore. "He's arriving now," she shouted back, spotting the man cinching his hood tightly around his face as he exited a van.

Reg waited for Chris to reach his slip. "Need a hand, mate?"

"Wouldn't mind," Chris replied with an American accent. "We've been doing work on the house and could've done without this storm. I had to leave Kate fixing plastic around all our building supplies."

"Strong winds and a bit of rain, they said," AJ complained as she joined them. "I think someone took a tea break instead of checking their maths."

"Maybe it was the intern's turn at predicting," Chris joked. "Gimme a minute and I'll grab my extra lines," he added, stepping aboard his boat.

It took them less than ten minutes to adjust the existing lines and add two more in a similar fashion to how Reg and AJ had done theirs. The only difference was at the stern, where the outboards stopped them crossing over the lines. Chris thanked them both, and all three made their way through the gate in the security fence to their vehicles.

Reg started his old Land Rover and the little wipers did their best to clear the glass while the electric motors whirred noisily.

"Will we make it home?" AJ ribbed, slipping her hood down and running a hand through her damp shoulder-length blonde hair highlighted with purple streaks.

"Don't start," Reg groaned, putting his beloved Landy in reverse with a crunch from the gearbox.

"I was just wondering as I know it has Lucas electronics," AJ continued, picking on the infamous British company.

Reg shook his head and water droplets flung around the front of the vehicle.

"Did you know, Lucas holds the patent for the short circuit?" AJ said, trying not to laugh.

Reg moaned as he drove them from the marina, rain lashing down the windscreen. "Really? These bloody Lucas jokes are older than you."

"And yet still pertinent today," AJ rebutted. "In fact, did you know, Lucas invented the first intermittent wiper? Just not on purpose."

This time AJ couldn't stop herself from laughing.

"Where did you come up with this rubbish?" Reg asked, peering out the glass in the dim evening gloom.

"The internet," AJ replied proudly. "I thought I should be prepared for my next adventure in your ancient vehicle."

"It's a bloody classic," Reg replied defensively.

"You both are."

"I *wish* I was only 54 years old," Reg grumbled.

"Did you know," AJ continued between laughs, "that Lucas invented the single-position three-function switch? Handles dim, flicker and dead."

"Are you done?" Reg asked.

"I think so," AJ admitted, unable to recall any more from the long list of internet abuse aimed at the Lucas company.

"When do you think we'll be back in the water?" she asked instead.

Reg shrugged his broad shoulders. "Normally I'd say in two days, but I don't know about this one. Nor'westers are unpredictable. The island ain't used to being hit from that direction."

"I feel awful for my customers," AJ reacted. "This'll ruin their holiday."

"Doesn't help our income too much either," Reg commented as he crossed the bypass roundabout and headed north on West Bay Road.

"Better have another check at the dock, don't you think?" AJ said, although the idea of heading straight home for a shower and a glass of wine was far more appealing.

"Yeah," Reg agreed. "Glad we pulled the boards or we'd be scrambling right now."

The reason they'd been later than many of their fellow captains getting to the boats was the unenviable task of unbolting and removing many of the planks from the jetty they shared. If heavy waves made it to the usually calm western shore, they could easily swamp the low pier and, as they crashed against the ironshore coast, rip the boards from the framework. Removing a third of the planks let the water pass through the jetty without destroying it.

Night fell early with the dense, dark clouds blanketing the island, and their automatically activated floodlights were already on by the time Reg pulled into the little car park by their dock.

"Blimey," AJ muttered, watching the waves exploding against the shore and the pier, spraying water across the tarmac towards the Land Rover. "This could be as bad as a hurricane."

"Might be," Reg agreed. "I hope no one got themselves caught out there on the open water."

AJ cringed at the thought. It never ceased to amaze her how the most tranquil and beautiful waters could become such a terrifyingly tempestuous maelstrom.

"If it's this bad here, I can't imagine how bad it must be around the point."

Reg turned the Land Rover around. "Let's have a look."

Turning left out of the car park, he wound his way along North West Point Road, past waterfront homes and condo complexes on their left. The rain hammered against the windscreen and the little wipers struggled to keep up. Reg drove slowly and AJ noticed they hadn't seen another vehicle on the road since leaving their dock. The road curved to the right and the rain intensified even more.

"Strewth," Reg muttered, leaning forward to see through the glass.

Silver thatch palms, casuarina trees, and sea grapes whipped in the swirling winds and the Land Rover rocked and swayed while the raindrops sounded more like pellets peppering the aluminium body. Reg turned into the entrance to Lighthouse Point, a condominium building which also housed a small restaurant and a dive shop. Their pier was the perfect shore diving spot to visit the

Guardian of the Reef, a magnificent 13-foot-tall bronze statue by world renowned sculptor Simon Morris, set at 50 feet underwater. But not today.

Seawater washed up the driveway beside the elevated building, and Reg braked to a stop. The Land Rover's headlights struggled to pierce the intense rain and gloom of the storm, but from what they could see, it appeared the ocean was consuming the shoreline and pier. A car parked against the building rocked violently as another wave crashed and the water pummelled the driver's side.

"Nothing we can do," Reg said, shaking his head as he slowly backed the Landy up the driveway.

Driving south and then east on the road was remarkably different from their arrival. With the winds and driving rain to their rear, the wipers could finally clear the water from the windscreen and they could see more of the road ahead. Small branches and rubbish blew across their path, and Reg had to drive around a plastic dustbin tumbling along the edge of the road.

"Want to stay at our place?" he offered as they approached West Bay Road.

"Thanks, but no," AJ replied. "I'd better check everything's okay with the house."

"I can help you look around if you want to grab a change of clothes," Reg said.

AJ could hear the concern in his voice but she was ready to crash out in her own space.

"I'll call you if I get worried," she replied, and Reg didn't push the issue.

AJ's tiny cottage was a guest house in the grounds of a large waterfront home on the north end of Seven Mile Beach. The owners, a wealthy couple from Atlanta, Georgia, came to the island three or four times a year for a few weeks at a time. They were more than happy to have AJ living on the property to keep an eye on the place, and hadn't raised her rent in the many years she'd lived in the cottage. She offered them free dive trips in return.

Reg stopped outside the wooden privacy fence extending along the side of Boggy Sand Road from the large garage. AJ pulled her raincoat hood back up and braced herself for the onslaught as she watched the fence rattle and shake.

"We'd better do a round of checks in the morning," AJ suggested, poised ready to grab the door when she opened it to stop the wind wrenching it away.

"Pick you up at six," Reg replied. "And shout if it gets too sporty tonight."

AJ groaned at the early hour. It was actually about the same time she had to be up every morning to prepare for her customers, but she hated early mornings.

"Fine, but we're stopping for coffee."

"Right, because they'll be open after this mess," Reg laughed.

AJ groaned again, before grimly keeping a firm hold of the door as she got out and faced the storm.

3

MAY 1942, ENGLAND

Green fields and hedgerows whistled by only 300 feet below the wings of the Miles M.19 Master II trainer. With the short hop from White Waltham Airfield in Maidenhead to the Miles factory at Woodley Airfield near neighbouring Reading only being 10 miles, there was no reason to climb to a cruising altitude. Pilot Second Officer Parker with the Air Transport Auxiliary had drawn a cushy chit that morning. Deliver the Miles for repairs, meet the ATA driver for a ride back, then another, far more interesting delivery of a Hawker Hurricane fighter to RAF Tangmere in Sussex.

The River Thames wound through the fields on the port side and the airfield was already in sight on a pretty spring morning. Blue skies dotted with wispy clouds and the low altitude meant Parker hadn't bothered with a heavy Sidcot flying suit. As spring slowly transitioned into summer, it was becoming warm enough for a flight jacket.

As ATA pilots were non-military, international law prohibited the guns from being loaded, and radio use, even if operational, was strictly forbidden. Parker's leather flying helmet wasn't even fitted with headphones or a microphone. The ATA pilots were charged with flying below cloud, using map and compass alone, so a keen eye for landmarks became second nature.

Ahead, a plane rose from the expansive grass runway of the airfield, taking off into the wind on a north-easterly heading. As Parker couldn't radio the aerodrome, a lap of the field would be the only warning of the Master's imminent landing. Banking, aerodrome personnel could be seen busily going about their morning business, and no other planes appeared to be taxiing or circling the field.

When the engine cut, Parker was facing north-west having just started a wide arc around the airfield. No warning, no hesitation or misfire, just a complete shutdown of everything electrical, including the 870-horsepower Bristol Mercury engine. The mechanic had told Parker the Miles had been grounded due to an electrical fault they couldn't find which had been causing the plane to momentarily cut out during training flights. He hadn't mentioned a comprehensive system failure, which was now catastrophic at only 300 feet and a speed not far above the plane's stall velocity.

Parker craned to see above the canopy covering the trainee pilot's empty front seat. At five foot four, sitting on a parachute pack wasn't enough to see particularly clearly off the nose of the rapidly slowing plane, which was quickly losing height. With only seconds to make a life-or-death decision, Parker dipped the nose to gather speed, figuring stalling would be a worse way to die than crashing on an attempted landing.

There was simply no time or altitude to complete the loop of Woodley Airfield, so the extensive and open grassland would have to be the pilot's saviour. Originally known as Hundred Acre Field, the runway was vaguely defined amid the sprawling meadow as running parallel to Headley Road and by the location of the hangers. Wind noise rushed over the cockpit in the eerie void usually filled by the comforting sound of the Bristol Mercury.

With a dead engine, the hydraulic pump had also stopped, so the only means of lowering the landing gear was the hand pump.

But Parker knew there wasn't enough time. Having the wheels halfway down would be far worse than a belly landing and would almost certainly send the plane tripping over onto its nose. With the left wing tip barely clearing the hedgerow lining Headley Road, the Miles Master whooshed past a Magister parked off to the side. Parker squared up the wings before holding on grimly to the stick as the underside of the plane met the ground.

The propeller buckled and bent under the cowling, its destruction drowned out by the raucous sound of the air scoop being ripped from the belly and the plywood skin splintering. Still travelling at a high rate of knots, the plane slid across the dew-laden grass, and with one eye peeking open and gritted teeth, Parker wondered if the Miles would ever come to a stop. Dirt flung from the prop, splattering on the windscreen and obscuring much of the pilot's view as the Master crossed the traditional runway at an almost perpendicular angle. The plane jostled and bounced over the rough ground unintended for anything but taxiing.

With a final spray of turf from the bent propeller, the Master came to a halt, accompanied by creaks and hisses from an array of damaged parts. Releasing the belts, Parker slid back the canopy, quickly hopped to the wing, and took the unusually short step to the ground. Within moments, a Standard 12 Tilly skidded to a stop and two uniformed men rushed over.

"Bloody hell, old chap," the first man exclaimed. "That was a close call."

Parker turned to face them, slipping off the leather flying helmet, and letting her long brown hair fall across her shoulders.

"I'd say," Pilot Second Officer Dotty Parker agreed.

Both men's demeanour instantly changed with a sour look on their faces.

"Oh, I thought it was a real pilot," the second man groaned. "What happened? Drop your make-up case in the cockpit and forget to put the wheels down?"

If Dotty hadn't been used to the unfiltered prejudice against the female ferry pilots, she might have torn a strip off the pair of them.

She could say with confidence that she and most of her fellow 'Attagirls', as the female pilots had been nicknamed, had more hours in their logbooks than the majority of their male ATA counterparts. More hours in fact than almost all of the fighter pilots taking off every day in the Spitfires and Hurricanes to duel with the Germans over the English countryside. But that was partly due to the limited life expectancy of an RAF pilot in 1942.

Holding back the adrenaline already pumping through her veins after the emergency landing, and despite neither man wearing a uniform, Dotty wisely kept her tone civil.

"Electronics and engine all gave up the ghost, I'm afraid. No time to hand pump the wheels down. Should be a car to ferry me back to White Waltham if you wouldn't mind giving me a lift to the Miles hangar."

"What are we supposed to do with this?" the second man asked tersely.

"I was ferrying it here for repairs at the factory, so I dare say we should tell the Miles folks where to find it." Dotty cast her gaze towards the hangars from where several more vehicles were now heading their way. "Looks like they're already on their way."

She retrieved her ATA pilot's notes from the cockpit, the ferry pilot's two-ring book of small cards with the critical statistics and notations necessary to ferry each aircraft, then lit herself a cigarette with shaking hands. This had been the closest call of her five-year flying career since her father, who was also a pilot, had agreed to her taking the Civil Air Guard pre-war flying training for sixpence an hour. Which had still been a stretch for her working-class family.

After a series of explanations and plenty more suspicious and critical looks and comments, Dotty made it to the front of the building where a Humber Snipe waited for her.

"That took a while," the Women's Auxiliary Air Force driver said in a friendly tone when Dotty climbed in the passenger seat.

"You very nearly had a coffin to take back with you," Dotty replied. "That Master tried to kill me."

"Gosh, are you okay?" the driver asked as she pulled away, looking her passenger over.

"I'm fine," Dotty said, letting out a long breath. "But I had to fill out a blasted report before he'd sign my chit."

Dotty explained her ordeal to the driver on the twenty-minute ride back to White Waltham, and her nerves began to settle as she spoke to a sympathetic ear. Once back, she found the news had travelled fast, as usual.

"I could have dropped it on its belly and shoved it off to the side here, Parker," the Sergeant greeted her. "Saved the petrol if you'd told me you planned to spear the kite into the runway."

"Sir," she greeted him. "Engine quit on approach, sir. Not much to be done."

Dotty knew Flight Captain Harold Ellis was stuck between a rock and a hard place. As an ATA officer, he was supposed to treat the female pilots with the same respect he gave the men, but if he was seen doing so by the men, he'd never hear the end of it. His compromise was to adjust his manner according to whoever was within earshot. As several male pilots were gathered in the lounge, he gave her a hard time.

"Still up for another delivery?" he asked, his voice challenging more than concerned.

"On my way to get my chit, sir," Dotty replied.

He nodded and smiled. "Be careful," he added quietly as she passed by.

"Parker," a voice called out as Dotty had almost reached the operations room.

She turned and saluted Commander Pauline Gower, who returned the gesture.

"What happened, Dotty?" the commander asked in a gentler tone.

Gower, a flyer and daughter of a British member of Parliament, was the person responsible for persuading the authorities to allow female pilots into the newly formed ATA at the outbreak of war.

She took her role as commander very seriously, keeping her women in line, but also vigorously supporting them when appropriate.

"Everything shut down, ma'am," Dotty replied.

She was tired of telling the story over and over, but knew if only one person believed her, Pauline Gower was the most important officer to have in her corner.

"I was circling the field when I lost power."

"Did you try cycling the ignition?" Gower asked.

"I was at 300 feet on the downwind side of the field at the time, ma'am, so I chose to focus on a dead-stick landing."

Gower looked thoughtful for a moment. "Pilots are worth more than the planes we fly, Dotty. Good choice."

Dotty felt the knot she hadn't realised had been gripping her stomach release, and let out a sigh.

"Thank you, ma'am."

"Let me take you off the schedule for a few days, Dotty. Close calls like this take a toll."

Dotty paused. The thought of a few days away from the chaos felt appealing, but flying aeroplanes was her lifeblood. Picturing herself sitting in her billet brooding over what she could have done differently made her stomach cramp all over again.

"No, ma'am. I need to get back on the horse."

Gower nodded. "Good girl. What do you have up next?"

"Hurricane to Tangmere, ma'am."

The commander raised an eyebrow, but forced a smile. "Nice day for it."

Although a civilian, Marjorie McKinven had been the secretary in the operations room since the formation of the ATA, and handed out the daily chits to every pilot flying that day. Most were dropped by transport plane at various airfields around the country where their aircraft awaited to be ferried to another location, but occasionally their appointed aircraft was already at White Waltham. It was a complex and detailed game of constantly moving pieces which Marjorie and her superiors juggled every day.

The brand new Hurricane Mk IIC fighter had been ferried to

White Waltham from the Hawker factory in Langley, just 12 miles east, because after taking off a few days earlier, the ATA pilot had reported an issue with the landing gear refusing to retract. Heavy cloud moving over Langley had persuaded him to land at White Waltham rather than return to the factory airfield, and Hawker had sent over a mechanic by car to fix the issue. At least Dotty hoped he had.

Nerves made her fingertips tingle and her legs twitch as she ran through her pre-flight checks. With hand signals to the ground crew, Dotty fired up the Merlin XX engine and the mechanic removed the trolley accumulator used to supply external power to the starter. Screwing down the Ki-Gass priming pump once the engine was running cleanly, Dotty set the rpms to 1,000 and waited for the temperature gauge to move from the stop while she checked her other gauges and tested the flaps. Two ground crew sat on the tail to prevent the plane from 'ground looping', the issue of an aircraft tipping over onto a wing due to crosswinds and the torque action of the propeller.

Taxiing to the runway, Dotty weaved back and forth to see past the long nose blocking her view while the plane rolled along on its tail wheel. Once lined up for take-off, she came to a stop for the two men to drop from the tail and move clear. Winding up the 1,240 hp Merlin, she accelerated down the smooth grass using the markers either side of the runway to maintain a straight line. The tail wheel soon rose from the ground and the field came clearly into view a few moments before the Hurricane lifted from the earth and was airborne.

Dotty immediately moved the lever to raise the landing gear and held her breath. Two green lights made her smile, and as she banked to head south, she spread her map across her lap despite intimately knowing the countryside below. Looking out of the canopy, she picked up her first familiar landmark, and tentatively allowed herself a hint of the joy she usually felt being in the air.

4

PRESENT DAY

The rain finally stopped shortly after dawn and the winds settled, although occasional swirling gusts still blew the carnage around. Thomas, AJ's employee and friend, joined her and Reg for their early morning checks on the boats and then the dock. AJ was pleased to see their lines had all held, and apart from a variety of detritus floating in the water, all looked well at the marina.

Reg let Thomas drive the Land Rover when they backtracked to West Bay as he'd been dying to try his hand behind the wheel. The tall, lean local was one of the few Caymanians to work in the dive industry, despite their heritage as water people. His infectious smile and positive outlook were also the perfect balance for AJ's allergy to early mornings.

"I ain't too used to shifting da gears," Thomas laughed as he ground the gearbox from third to fourth. "I'm so sorry, Reg."

"She's stood up to worse in the past 54 years," Reg said despite wincing every time Thomas attempted a shift. "Just take a bit more time and make sure the clutch is all the way down."

AJ bounced along in the back, sipping her coffee she'd brought from the house, and looking at the mess by the side of the roads. It was mostly leaves, small branches from the trees, and rubbish which hadn't been secured before the winds hit. The community were already out there cleaning up, and she knew from past experience that the tourists arriving in a few days wouldn't even know they'd had a major storm.

They spent an hour tidying up their small car park and making sure all was well with their little hut which served as an office, bathroom, and storage, despite its diminutive size.

"We putting da boards back in?" Thomas asked after bagging the last of the rubbish.

Reg shook his head. "Not until the seas calm down a bit more."

AJ joined them at the head of the pier where sloppy seas still splashed water over the jetty's framework. The usually calm west side was a dark green with white caps spitting from the swells instead of the calm cerulean blue. Broken clouds and peeks of clear sky were just beginning to chase the dark gloom away to the southeast.

"I think you're right, Reg," AJ said. "This will take a few more days than normal to settle down."

"Did you hear that, Thomas?" Reg reacted, and AJ rolled her eyes, knowing what was coming.

"I believe I musta bin mistaken, sir," Thomas replied, grinning from ear to ear. "It sounded like boss lady say someting about you bein' right. But I ain't never heard such a ting from her lips before."

"Hell just froze over," Reg added, his broad shoulders and barrel chest shaking as he laughed.

"Sod you two," AJ muttered and started towards the hut. "Let's see if Divetech need any help."

"Divetech?" Thomas questioned, as they turned to follow her.

"Yeah, we went by last night and Lighthouse Point was taking a thrashing," Reg explained. "The north-west-facing shores took the brunt of it. We should see how they fared."

A few minutes later after loading into Reg's Land Rover – which he drove this time – they made their way a mile north and had the answer. The car they'd noticed being battered by the water washing up the parking area was perched on the steps to one of the condo buildings. AJ, Reg, and Thomas walked past the mess with their mouths agape.

"Can we help?" AJ asked one of the Divetech crew who was standing in front of the shop.

"Nothing we can do right now," the young woman replied. "Waiting on an insurance assessor to get here. Can't start cleaning up until then."

AJ looked through the open door to the dive shop. The interior was devastated. Most of the inventory of dive gear, clothing, and display items had been ripped from the walls and shelves and now lay on the floor in a huge pile. She glanced over to the little place next door, VIVO cafe, and it appeared to be wiped out as well.

"I'm so sorry," AJ sympathised. "This looks worse than when Hurricane Ian came through."

"Way worse," the woman agreed.

"Have Jo call us if we can help once you get the go-ahead," AJ said, referring to the owner of Divetech. "We're happy to muck in."

"Appreciate it," the woman replied.

Driving away, AJ considered how lucky they'd been not to have any damage. The reef system on the west side had almost certainly played a part, along with the direction from which the storm had arrived. Grand Cayman was the peak of an underwater mountain which barely reached beyond the surface of the ocean. The sandy sea floor sloped gently away to the shallow reefs between a few and 40 feet below. In most areas, another sandy patch extended to the outer reef, which started deeper before dropping off the side of the underwater cliffs into the abyss. Initially around 600 feet deep, the steep slopes of the mountain extended down to 6,000 feet within a few miles of the island.

With the winds and swells usually approaching from the northeast and the well-spaced double reefs, the west side enjoyed tranquil waters, perfect for diving year round. But the unusual storm had thrown up waves in new patterns which shifted sands and stirred up the sea floor, so the water clarity would take a few days to return to its gin-clear norm.

"I reckon it's a good day to check and service gear," Reg announced as he headed south. "Can't see there's much else to do until we can move the boats."

"It's that or go to the salon for a mani-pedi," AJ replied.

Reg frowned at her. "When was the last time you did that?"

AJ looked at her short, work-worn fingernails. "When my mum took me as a mother-daughter bonding experience."

"So you're saying you're due?" Reg asked.

"No, you silly bugger. I'm saying we're servicing gear."

"That's what I thought you meant," Reg muttered, and kept on driving back to the marina.

Eight hours later, after dropping Thomas off at his parents' house in West Bay, Reg told AJ she was coming to his place for dinner. That was his wife Pearl's orders when he called her on the way, and AJ didn't complain.

As they walked through the door, Reg's dog, Coop, flew around the corner from the living room and skidded to a halt in front of them, dropping his backside to the floor while his tale swished side to side. Reg just looked at him for a few moments, driving the poor mutt crazy in anticipation.

"Hello, boy," he finally said and reached down.

Coop was beside himself with joy, spinning around and nuzzling Reg's arm as the big man scratched behind his ears. After a few seconds, Coop moved on to his second favourite person, AJ, and rolled over on his back at her feet. She scratched his tummy and made a big fuss of him.

The Cayman brown hound, as the locals called the crossbreeds which all seemed to come out some shade of brown, would normally have spent the day with Reg, but with the chaos on the island Reg thought it best to leave him at home.

"Take all your dirty stuff off by the door," Pearl said as she came to greet them.

"That'll be your mind she's talking about," AJ quipped, slipping out of her boots.

"Nah," Reg grinned. "Pearl don't mind that part at all."

He leaned over and kissed his wife.

"TMI!" AJ yelped. "I should never have said anything."

Pearl moved over to AJ and gave her a hug.

"We're old but we're not dead yet," she said with a laugh.

Reg and Pearl smiled at each other as they walked into the kitchen with a glint in their eyes like a pair of newlyweds. They were AJ's island parents with Bob and Beryl Bailey so many miles away in the UK, and in many ways she was closer to Pearl than she'd ever been to her own mother. A barrister and a stern, businesslike woman, Beryl had never quite understood AJ's passion for diving, and certainly didn't approve of her purple-highlighted hair and colourful full-sleeve tattoos.

AJ's father, Bob, who was the CEO of a large company, was more easy going, and had long ago accepted his little girl marched to the beat of a different drum. And that was okay. Bob and Reg kept in regular touch and had become firm friends over the years, strengthened when they'd teamed up to help AJ get started in her own dive operation after working for Reg for many years.

"Nothing special for dinner, I'm afraid," Pearl announced. "I've been getting the accounts straightened out while I had the time, and rehearsing a few new songs for Friday night."

"Your throw-together meals are a million miles better than anything I'd cook for myself, so I'll love whatever you have," AJ said. "Can I help with anything?"

"Set the table, if you don't mind," Pearl replied while she gathered items from the kitchen. "And there's a Chardonnay open in the fridge if you fancy wine."

"What new songs have you got?" AJ asked as she laid knives and forks out on the dining table.

"You'll have to wait and see," Pearl replied with a wink.

Pearl was an amazing singer with a raspy rock-'n'-roll voice which drew a big crowd a couple of Friday evenings a month when she played at the local pub. A few years younger than Reg, she was still a beautiful woman with a full, busty figure that the male crowd didn't mind being entertained by.

AJ placed the wine on the table and was about to sit down when Pearl's mobile phone rang.

"I'll call whoever it is back after dinner," she said, but glanced at the caller ID. "Hmm, maybe I should take this."

"Who is it?" Reg asked.

"Says it's the Port Authority," Pearl replied, and answered the call, putting it on speaker. "Pearl Moore."

"Mrs Moore, this is Brian Watler with the Cayman Islands Port Authority. We've met a few times at the Fox and Hare, and I know your husband."

The man spoke with a hint of the local island accent.

"Oh yes, I remember you, Brian," Pearl replied.

"Hey, mate. This is Reg, I'm here as well."

"Oh, good. I'm glad you're both on the line. Am I right in saying you are expecting a container shipment this week, Mrs Moore?" Watler asked, his voice remaining subdued.

"We are, and please call me Pearl," she replied. "My mother recently passed, and we organised to ship a few things over after her funeral. Is it here?"

Watler cleared his throat. "The ship has indeed arrived and we unloaded it this afternoon. But I'm afraid I have some bad news, Pearl."

"Why? What happened?" she asked, looking up at Reg, who moved closer.

"The ship was caught in the storm, and unfortunately, several containers went over the side. I'm afraid one of them was yours."

Pearl gasped.

"Obviously this is something you'll have to take up with the shipping company, but I recognised your name on the paperwork, and figured I'd give you a heads-up."

"Bloody hell," Reg responded, putting an arm around his wife who held her hands over her mouth.

"Everything I have of my parents was in that container," Pearl whispered. "Everything."

"I'm really sorry," Watler said. "I wish there was something I could do."

"Thank you for letting us know, Brian. We appreciate the call," Reg responded while Pearl was still speechless.

"Where did they lose them?" AJ blurted before Reg hung up.

"I'm sorry?" Watler questioned.

"Do the crew know where they lost them?" AJ repeated.

"They lost all instruments, so I doubt they can pinpoint the spot, but the captain told me they were probably ten miles or so from the island."

Reg and AJ exchanged a glance.

"The captain still in town?" Reg asked.

"For a few days I believe," Watler replied. "They have to effect repairs before they can leave."

"We'll be by first thing in the morning, Brian," Reg said. "Can you put me in touch with the captain?"

Watler hesitated a moment. "I guess I can, sure. But Reg, you know as well as I do that anything over the side ten miles out will be 6,000 feet down by now."

"You're probably right, Brian, but we'll be by in the morning all the same."

"Okay. I'll see you tomorrow," the man replied. "Once again, I am sorry to bring you this news," he added before hanging up.

Pearl couldn't keep the tears at bay and Reg pulled her closer.

"We'll see what we can figure out," Reg whispered.

"It's all gone," she said between sniffles. "Brian's right. Everything will be at the bottom by now."

"Doesn't hurt to take a look, now, does it, love? We'll go see tomorrow," Reg assured his wife.

But they all knew she was almost certainly right.

5

1942

Even at the reduced speed ATA pilots were limited to, the Hurricane covered the 45 miles to Tangmere near Chichester in less than 15 minutes. Delivering to an active fighter or bomber airfield always made Dotty nervous. *What if they scrambled just as she arrived?* She couldn't imagine the confusion she'd cause.

Circling the field, she saw no signs of activity on the ground or in the surrounding skies. Rows of Hurricanes and Spitfires lined up near the dispersal huts, but apart from ground crew working on one or two and pilots sunning themselves on the grass, all looked quiet.

Dotty touched down with a three-point landing which brought a smile to her face, then carefully taxied to where a ground crewman waved her into an empty spot in a row of planes. As she shut down the Merlin engine, she couldn't help but wonder if the space was vacant due to a loss on an earlier sortie. The strategic bombing campaign that had recently begun over Germany was experiencing an horrendous loss rate, but the fighter units weren't having it easy either. The life expectancy of an RAF pilot could often be measured in weeks.

As Dotty climbed down from the cockpit, a pilot approached the plane, slapping a mechanic on the back.

"How long do you need, Jimmy?" he asked.

The mechanic looked up at Dotty, giving her a double take when she slipped off her helmet.

"If she flew okay, then ten or fifteen minutes to arm and refuel, sir."

The pilot turned to Dotty and smiled. He had bright blue eyes. "She ready for duty, Pilot Officer...?"

"Second Pilot Officer Parker," Dotty responded. "Landing gear had a problem from the factory, but they fixed it yesterday, and it worked fine both ends for me. I didn't note any other issues. Of course, they discourage us from pushing the kites like you chaps have to do."

He looked at the mechanic. "Sounds like she's been test flown, Jimmy. Let me know when she's ready. I dare say we'll be scrambling again before too long. Too nice of a day for the Hun to leave us alone."

"Sir," Jimmy acknowledged without losing his dubious look about the test flight.

The pilot extended a hand to Dotty. "Flying Officer Richard Lovell, but everyone calls me Sandy."

The man had a boyish face with a handful of freckles and a mop of sandy blonde hair which Dotty assumed was the cause of his nickname. She guessed he was no older than her, and might even be younger.

"Pleased to meet you, Second Pilot Officer Parker," he said, releasing her hand.

"Dotty," she bumbled. "My friends call me Dotty. For Dorothy," she explained, and wished she'd kept her mouth shut.

Her cheeks flushed.

"Care for a cuppa before you head home?" Sandy offered.

Dotty nodded, not trusting herself to speak again. He was a nice-looking bloke with a warm, pleasant manner and a quiet, unassuming confidence. Which was a list of traits she considered herself to be void of. His accent was south-east England, but middle class rather than the posh pronunciation of so many RAF officers with their wealthy upbringing and exclusive schools.

After remembering her parachute, pilot notes, map, and small overnight bag, Dotty followed the pilot into the dispersal hut where the rest of Sandy's squadron sat around on an eclectic mix of furniture. Some read the newspaper, while a group played cards at an old dining table, and a few took the opportunity to catch up on sleep. All those awake turned and watched the female pilot walk in.

"Dotty here just delivered my new kite," Sandy announced. "She's joining us for a cuppa before heading to the train station."

Several of the men offered a greeting amid a series of murmurs. One pilot lowered his newspaper and grinned.

"I hope you took your lipstick and knitting needles from the cockpit, my dear. Hate to see old Sandy get a prick in the behind," he said in a distinctly upper-class accent.

He raised his paper amongst a sea of laughter. Dotty blushed.

"I should be getting back," she urged.

"Nonsense," Sandy insisted. "Ignore them. How many hours do you have in the air, Pilot Second Officer Parker?" he asked as he poured from a China teapot.

"I believe today puts me at about 480 hours," Dotty replied, unsure whether she should simply leave or brave out the chilly reception.

The pompous aviator lowered his paper and glowered at her. "Poppycock."

"I can show you my logbook next time I'm in Tangmere if you'd like your poppy uncocked, sir," Dotty found herself saying.

The men burst into hysterical laughter. All except one man, who returned to hiding behind his newspaper.

"Bloody good show, Dotty," Sandy said, handing her a cup of tea.

"I shouldn't have," she mumbled, blushing all over again.

A siren rang so loudly, she almost dropped her teacup and the men all jumped from their seats, grabbing life preservers and parachutes.

"Duty calls, I'm afraid," Sandy said, rushing past her. "Thank you. It was lovely to meet you," he added before hurrying out the door to the field.

Dotty wasn't sure what to do, so she put the teacup down and moved to the open door, watching the men scramble into their planes. How quickly the peace and quiet of the Sussex countryside had been transformed into a thundering rumble of engines and frantic action.

"What are you doing in here?" came a stern voice from behind her.

Dotty swung around to see a stern man with a thin moustache wearing a dark blue RAF uniform with the triple sleeve stripes of a wing commander.

"I just delivered…" Dotty began, but the man quickly cut her off.

"Move on back to your ferry pool and stay out of the men's way," he barked, surging past her to the airfield.

Stunned, embarrassed, and frustrated, Dotty quickly retreated through the dispersal hut and found her way to the airfield office. The young Women's Auxiliary Air Force secretary organised a car, and thirty minutes later, Dotty stood in Chichester railway station figuring out how she could navigate her way back to White Waltham in Maidenhead.

Sitting in the railway carriage as it bounced along the tracks, Dotty thought about her family and how devastated they would have been if her ordeal in the Miles Master had not ended with her walking away. Her father now taught new pilots at RAF Little Rissington in Gloucestershire, and her mother and younger sister lived in the relative safety of a family billet in the village.

Her father, Patrick, had been over the recruitment age for active duty at the outbreak of war, but his flying experience made him a natural choice for training the young men volunteering to protect the skies over Great Britain. Dotty imagined sitting across from him in their London terraced home living room and explaining her emergency landing at Woodley Airfield. She could picture his wrinkled brow as she talked him through the details and decisions she'd made in a blink of an eye.

Dotty would give anything for the opportunity to hear him tell her she did all she could under the circumstances. *But would that be his response?* Regardless, her father would be thoughtful and encouraging with his words, as he'd always been. For many children, their parents could be difficult and critical teachers who allowed their pride or concern to apply undue pressure, but Patrick had been incredibly calm and patient while flying with his daughter.

When he enrolled her in the Civil Air Guard pre-war pilot training program at seventeen years old, she'd already accumulated more than 100 hours at the controls of an aeroplane. The minimum age was eighteen, but her father looked the other way when Dotty filled out the application, and if anyone had ever figured it out, they hadn't said a word. Dotty graduated the course with a class C licence, which was the highest level allowed for women, regardless of their ability, and continued accruing hours, many solo, until civil flying ceased with the ominous approach of war.

Dotty was beside herself, unable to fly, but she joined the Women's Auxiliary Air Force, or WAAF, as a means of getting as close to airfields and aeroplanes as she could. During the Phoney War which lasted eight months from September 1939, she drove officers and important people around as Britain's young men trained for what was to come, and the country braced themselves. On 10 May 1940, the German forces marched into Belgium, the Netherlands, and Luxembourg, marking the end of the Phoney War and the beginning of the Battle of France.

In late 1939, Commander Pauline Gower was tasked with organising the women's section of the ATA and the carefully chosen first eight female pilots were accepted into service as No 5 Ferry Pilots Pool on 1 January 1940. Initially, they were only cleared to fly de Havilland Tiger Moth biplanes from their base in Hatfield, but by June their role was expanded to other non-combat types of aircraft such as trainers and transports.

Dotty applied from the moment she learned of the group, and in the spring of 1941 finally received a letter to interview with the ATA at White Waltham. Stunned to meet none other than Pauline Gower herself, she passed the flight test despite being rusty after several years on the ground, and entered the ATA's own training program.

As the train rattled down the tracks with the South Downs then the countryside of Surrey rushing past outside the window, Dotty thought about Sandy Lovell. She wondered if he'd made it back from the sortie she'd watched him leave for. She couldn't imagine how his squadron had all seemed so calm and relaxed while not knowing when the call to scramble would come. In moments of determination she'd often wished women were allowed to fight alongside the men. But having been in the dispersal hut and seen them run without hesitation to their Hurricanes, knowing they may never return, it highlighted their bravery. *Could she be that courageous?* It hit her with a mixture of relief and guilt that she'd never have to know.

Dotty wasn't certain, as she was usually uncertain of most things except flying a plane, but Fighter Pilot Sandy Lovell had appeared to be interested in her. *Or did he flirt with all the girls that way?* Perhaps he'd simply been courteous. Something the female pilots weren't accustomed to at the airfields. Tolerated was the most they could hope for. The Hooray Henry pilot and wing commander's attitudes were more in line with how the women were treated. Scorned or whistled at seemed to be the two options. But Sandy had been different.

When Dotty finally made it into the station at Reading, after changing trains in Guildford, she dragged her parachute and overnight bag along to the office in search of a telephone to call for a car. Sitting outside the station, waiting, she convinced herself that Sandy had merely been polite. Nevertheless, with the hope that the young, blue-eyed man would still be alive, she decided she'd mention to Marjorie McKinven that another ferry job to Tangmere would be gratefully received.

6

It was as though there had never been a storm. Blue skies, wispy clouds, and calm seas greeted AJ, Reg, and Pearl as they pulled into the tiny port in George Town. Most of downtown's waterfront area had been swept free of the foliage and rubbish washed ashore by the waves and whipped up by the winds. Cruise ships would be arriving in a day or so, depositing sunburnt tourists into the streets, like any other week on the island.

A large – by Cayman Islands standards – container ship sat moored alongside the main dock with its load already removed and carried away to the distribution area on the other side of town. Port workers busied themselves with clean-up and organising outgoing containers ready for Miami.

"Here to see Brian," Reg told the woman at the reception when they walked into the office.

"Let me see if Mr Watler is available," she replied politely from behind the counter. "Your name, please?"

"Reg Moore. He's expecting us."

Before the woman took a step, a man appeared from the back. He wore dark trousers and a pressed white shirt with the port authority logo emblazoned on the left breast. AJ guessed him to be in his forties.

"Hi Reg, Pearl," he said, coming around the counter to shake hands.

"This is our friend, AJ," Reg replied, and once all the introductions and greetings were handled, Watler led them outside.

"I'm sure you saw the ship," he began. "I texted with the captain this morning. He's aboard while they're hard at it on repairs. Let me call him and let him know you're here."

Watler made the call and after a brief conversation began walking across the docks, beckoning the three to follow. "I'll escort you to the ship. He can't leave, but he's invited you aboard. I told him you ran a dive op and know the local waters as good as anyone."

When they reached the ship, it towered overhead and the stern protruded into the open water beyond the concrete dock. A gangplank led from a door in the side of the hull to the pier, where a man stood waiting for them.

"I'm Tico. I can take you to the bridge," he said as they approached.

"I'll leave you in his hands," Watler told them. "Call me if you need anything."

"Thank you," Pearl replied, and they followed Tico into the ship.

"Couldn't have been much fun in the storm," AJ said as they walked down a long passageway, their footsteps echoing around the metallic walls.

"Been in worse," Tico replied. "But we lost all our instruments, which made it more challenging. Good job our captain knows his stuff or it might have been a disaster."

"You were blind in that mess?" AJ questioned.

She couldn't imagine being at sea in a ship this size without anything but a compass these days. Throw in the storm and it would be terrifying. Plenty of vessels had fallen foul of the low-lying island and treacherous shallow reefs.

"Lost the engines for most of the day. Got them back online as the storm caught us," Tico explained as they began scaling steel steps. "Made it to the lee of the island and rode it out."

Entering the bridge, AJ took in the fantastic view from the high elevation, reaching across the west side of the island to the North Sound.

"Captain Nolan Conrad," a man in jeans and a T-shirt said. "Forgive my casual attire; it's all hands on deck for repairs."

Reg shook his hand. "Appreciate you taking a minute to see us."

The captain offered his hand to Pearl then AJ.

"I'm very sorry about your container. It was a bad storm," he explained. "But we were fine until we encountered a rogue wave. Very unfortunate. Our office in Miami or our representative here on the island can help you with a claim."

"We'll speak to them," Reg replied. "But we were hoping you might be able to give us an idea of where you lost them."

Conrad nodded towards the console which had been stripped completely apart.

"As you can see, we're working on our electrical system," he said, then glanced at his watch. "In fact, we have a specialist flying in this morning to sort all this out before we can get underway again. We were sailing blind the other night. I had no GPS or I would have marked the spot." He took a moment before continuing. "But as I'm sure you know, the majority of containers lost at sea tend to sink very quickly. It would be very unusual for one to float for very long unless it was empty, or full of something very light and buoyant."

"Ours had my late mother's possessions," Pearl offered. "Solid wood furniture and boxes of heirloom-type stuff. A lot of family photo albums and such."

"And a few Land Rover parts," Reg said.

AJ kicked his foot and scowled at him.

"Which are unimportant in comparison," he quickly added, scowling back.

"I'm truly sorry for your loss," Conrad said to Pearl with an expression of sympathy. "Both for your mother and your goods, but I'm afraid I can't be of much help."

"Okay, thank you anyway. I appreciate you meeting with us," Pearl replied, and turned to leave.

"A rogue wave?" AJ said, questioningly. "Did you have a rough idea of where you were at the time?"

"Rough, yes," the captain replied. "But as I said, without GPS or a visual reference, I'd be guessing within a few miles."

"Could you show us on a marine chart?" AJ persisted.

"We shouldn't waste any more of the poor man's time, love," Pearl urged, pointing her thumb towards the steps. "What's done is done."

Reg held up a hand to his wife. "I reckon I know what AJ's thinking, Pearl." He turned to the captain. "Could you show us?"

Conrad smiled. "Sure, but like I said, it'll be a rough estimate at best."

The captain stepped to a long chart table at the back of the bridge and opened the upper, full-length drawer. Pulling out two charts, he spread them across the table, one on top of the other. The first showed the upper part of the Caribbean Sea from Florida down to the bottom of Honduras, and he began tracing his approach to the island with his finger.

"We ran into trouble up here," he said indicating open ocean north-west of the Cayman Islands but well south of Cuba. "I used a heading of 242 degrees, but when we neared the island, the storm caught us, and just as I picked up a visual reference, visibility closed down." Conrad slid the second chart out and placed it on top. It covered Grand Cayman and the surrounding ocean in greater detail. "I estimated our position as being here," he said, once again placing his finger on the spot. "Continued on 242 until I'd halved the distance..."

"Based on speed?" AJ asked.

"Correct," he replied. "We were hoping to pick up a cell signal and use a phone as navigation, but I turned us south on 196 out of an abundance of caution before that happened. We couldn't risk the signal being down. I kept heading south until I was confident I'd cleared the island before cutting straight west. The seas calmed a noticeable amount when we reached the lee of the land mass, and then we picked up a cell signal and could see where we were on a map. We rode out the night until visibility picked up in daylight."

"Okay," Reg said, rubbing his scraggly beard. "Where did the wave hit you?"

"Before we turned south, back here," he pointed out.

Reg looked at AJ.

"It's the long shot of all long shots but worth a look," AJ commented.

"What are you thinking?" Conrad asked.

"See here," Reg said, tapping a finger on the chart. "That's Twelve Mile Bank. You can see everything around it drops off quickly to hundreds of feet and then 6,000 feet. But the bank has a flat top, several miles long and only 120 foot down. Because of the steep slope, even that deep, the bank can affect the surface in rough weather."

"There's a chance the rogue wave happened when they passed over the edge of Twelve Mile Bank," AJ spelt out for Pearl, who moved closer to the table.

"Really?" Pearl questioned. "You think the container could be sitting on top of the bank?"

AJ put her hand on Pearl's arm. "I wouldn't get your hopes up, but it's worth taking our boat out and scanning the bank for a day or two."

"A hundred and twenty feet deep doesn't usually affect the surface that much," Conrad pointed out. "I'm telling you, this was substantial wave action."

"Was it taller than you'd seen?" AJ asked.

"Enough that I noticed it, and visibility was barely farther than the bow," the captain replied. "But it was the timing that did us in. We were in following seas but this was like something hit us bow on. It was very strange."

"Locals have reported similar things for years," Reg said. "It's a popular spot for sport fishermen as the tuna, mahi, and wahoo feed over the bank."

"The currents can run hard too," AJ added. "We usually drift dive from one side to the other. It all adds up to a big, fat mess on some days."

Conrad nodded. "Then I hope this has been of some help, and I wish you luck in your search."

"Thank you for giving us the time, Captain," Pearl responded, shaking the man's hand. "You've been very generous."

"I'm sorry we lost your precious cargo on my watch," Conrad replied, shaking hands with Reg and AJ. He took out his wallet and produced a business card. "My cell number and email are on here. If you think of it, please let me know how you get on with your search."

"We will, thank you," Reg said, taking the card, and Tico led them from the bridge.

Once to the dock, they walked across the yard to the office, where Brian Watler met them.

"Thanks for arranging that," Reg said. "Captain's a nice bloke."

"He's a very nice fellow," Watler agreed. "Nolan's been running this route for a few years now. Was he able to give you any insight?"

Reg nodded. "He was. It's probably a wild goose chase, but we'll head out and take a look around once the seas settle a bit more."

"I hope you're able to recover some of your belongings," Watler replied, smiling sympathetically at Pearl.

They thanked the port authority officer and returned to where they'd parked.

"Do you really think it's worth looking?" Pearl asked, her hand in Reg's big paw.

"I do," he replied thoughtfully. "I don't think we should get our hopes too high, but we'll always wonder if we don't at least try."

"There's another good reason to look," AJ said, pausing by the Land Rover.

"What's that, love?" Pearl asked.

"If the container happens to be reachable, and we don't get to it, it'll be open to salvage," AJ replied. "Anyone could claim it."

Pearl's shoulder's slumped, and Reg frowned at AJ.

"Sorry," AJ muttered. "But it's true."

7

Dotty had heard horror stories from other girls about their billets, so she was relieved the family she'd been placed with were nice enough. The Ramsays' son was somewhere in Libya with the Eighth Army from where reports in the newspapers talked about a fierce battle had begun against German and Italian troops led by Generaloberst Erwin Rommel. Vera, the mother, tried her best to put a brave face on her fear of losing her son, but if Dotty made it home late at night she sometimes found Vera crying alone in the kitchen. The woman would wave off Dotty's bumbling attempts to console her landlady, and Dotty always wondered how the husband, Stan, could let his wife suffer in solitude while he slept upstairs.

Opening the front door with the key she'd been given, Dotty felt worn out from the emotion of the day, and looked forward to whatever meal Vera had scraped together from rations, followed by a hot bath.

"You're home!" the daughter, Rosie, greeted her before she'd had a chance to close the door. "What did you fly today? I saw a Spitfire go over this afternoon and wondered if it was you."

Dotty smiled. This close to White Waltham and several other

airfields which had been created or expanded for the war effort, she had no doubt a hundred aeroplanes had passed overhead during the day.

"Wasn't me," Dotty replied. "No Spitfire today."

"Oh," Rosie responded sounding momentarily deflated.

At fourteen, the girl was old enough to understand the dangers and consequences of war, but couldn't help being swept up in the romance and excitement. Dotty prayed a telegraph boy wouldn't knock on the door she'd just walked through one day and hand the family a telegram that would shatter any taste of adventure the war held for the teenager. Losing the brother she idolised would change her life forever.

Exhausted, Dotty dreaded facing a million excited questions, but seeing the girl disappointed seemed worse. "But I crash landed a Miles Master then delivered a Hurricane in one piece," she said and quickly hung up her coat and made a beeline for the kitchen.

"You crashed!" Rosie enthused, giving chase.

"Leave the poor woman alone," Vera said, buttering bread on the counter. "And set the table like I asked ten minutes ago."

"Yes, Mum," Rosie glumly acknowledged. "But I must hear all about it over supper."

"Sorry, dear," Vera said after Rosie left to complete her chore. "What's she talking about? Crashing?" she asked in a whisper.

"Crash *landed*," Dotty emphasised. "My first delivery this morning to the Miles factory decided to more clearly identify its previously intermittent issue by clapping out altogether. I had to put down dead stick with no landing gear."

Vera looked at her with some concern but mostly confusion.

"The engine stopped running," Dotty clarified.

"Oh, my. You must have been terrified. You couldn't, you know, jump out? What do they call that?"

"Bail out," Dotty replied.

"That's it," Vera said, waving the butter knife in the air.

"I was too low."

Vera shook her head. "I don't know how you do it, dear. I'd be beside myself even if everything went as it was supposed to. I'm not sure we're made for such things. Best left to the men, if you ask me."

Dotty wasn't sure how to respond. It was one thing having men doubt a female's ability to fly planes, but the number of women who thought the same way was astonishing. Unladylike was a term Dotty and the other female pilots often heard, despite the break-throughs women like Amelia Earhart and Amy Johnson had forged. Although they had both died while flying aeroplanes, so perhaps not the best examples to use.

Amy Johnson, a record-breaking aviation pioneer, joined the ATA in 1940 with more flying hours and experience at the time than almost any other pilot the organisation recruited, male or female. On 5 January 1941, while delivering an Airspeed Oxford from Prestwick via RAF Squires Gate to RAF Kidlington, she was caught out by rapidly declining weather and trapped above the thick, low clouds to avoid running into the hillsides. Likely out of fuel, she bailed out, only to land in the frigid waters of the Thames Estuary near Herne Bay. Spotted in the water by the crew of HMS *Hasle-mere*, and calling for help, their captain, Lieutenant Commander Walter Fletcher, dived into the Thames after ropes fell short of reaching Johnson.

Amy's body was never found, and Fletcher, unconscious from hypothermia when pulled from the water, died several days later in hospital. Dotty remembered reading about the incident in the paper like it was yesterday. She'd been devastated. Her hero was then second-guessed, blamed, mourned, and celebrated in an avalanche of press amongst the other news of war. The one thing the tragedy did not do was deter Dotty from wanting to become an ATA pilot.

"Can I help with anything?" Dotty asked, rather than engage Vera in further discussion of her suitability to deliver aeroplanes for the war effort.

"Here, take the bread in with you, dear," Vera replied. "Then have a seat. It's not very exciting I'm afraid, but all I could scrounge up at the butcher's today."

Vera turned to the oven, so Dotty took the plate of thinly sliced bread with even more thinly spread butter into the dining room.

"Good evening, Mr Ramsay," she said to Stan, Vera's husband, who was already seated at the table. He nodded an acknowledgment.

Stan struck Dotty as being a cold and unsympathetic man. Partly concluded from Vera's solitary breakdowns, but also by the manner in which he appeared to let his family life happen before his eyes with minimal involvement. She couldn't be sure if he'd always been this way, if it was a result of the war, or perhaps his son's deployment, but Vera and Rosie continued as though life was somewhat normal. They talked, made plans, and even laughed while Stan chewed his food in stern silence.

"I must hear about your crash today," Rosie insisted, once everyone was seated and Vera served the limited slices of ham with boiled potatoes and cabbage.

"Don't pester her, Rosie," Vera chided. "Let her eat her dinner in peace."

Dotty smiled. "I don't mind," she said when Rosie looked crestfallen.

Which was a lie, as she really didn't want to relive the experience all over again.

Vera shrugged. "You know Rosie, she won't leave you be until bedtime."

"Not so," Rosie complained, pouting before turning her attention back to Dotty.

"White Waltham to Woodley in a Miles Master," Dotty began, then relayed her harrowing story between bites of the food which she knew Vera had done her best to make more appetising than her ration book allowed.

When dinner was done and the plates cleared, Dotty helped Vera and Rosie with the dishes while Stan returned to his chair in the living room to smoke his pipe.

"Why won't they let you use the radio?" Rosie asked, just as

Dotty was hoping to slip away for a bath before writing letters in her room.

"Because we're non-military," she replied. "Same reason our guns can't be loaded."

"What if a German plane attacks you?" Rosie asked. "You can't defend yourself."

Dotty thought for a moment before answering. It was a difficult subject. Truth be told, the ATA pilots were in as much danger from overeager English anti-aircraft gunners as they were from meeting a German in the skies. The bombers and their fighter escorts were coming over at night when ATA pilots weren't allowed to fly, but fighter attacks near the coasts were taking place every day. There had been stories floating around about ATA pilots being shot at by enemy aircraft.

"I've never seen a German plane while I've been flying, and the hope is that we never will while delivering aircraft, but we're told to avoid any contact with the enemy."

"That's all well and good until the Hun decide to come after you, right?" Vera said.

Dotty took a moment to reply. Her landlady made a good point. One which had been discussed at length amongst the ATA pilots.

"We're flying mostly around the Midlands and sometimes down to Sussex," Dotty replied. "The German fighters only have fuel to cover the southern part of the country."

Which was somewhat true. The advanced airfields of the Luftwaffe in France, Belgium and the Netherlands gave the Germans farther reach, but the RAF's early warning defences were alerting the coastal squadrons in time for them to intercept over the channel or the southern counties. Most of the time. But that was the Focke-Wulf FW-190 and Messerschmitt Bf 109 fighters. The Messerschmitt Bf 110 heavy fighter often used for bomber escorts had a far greater range. A stray pilot separated from his squadron, making his way to the channel, would be the most likely problem.

"It would be an unlikely stroke of bad luck to run into the Luftwaffe," Dotty added. "And if we did, they'd probably be high-tailing it home and happy to avoid a confrontation."

Vera looked at her sceptically. "Let's hope so."

"Although it would be rather exciting," Rosie added, putting the last of the dishes away.

"Don't be a stupid girl," Vera uncharacteristically snapped. "This isn't a bloody game. They're shooting real bullets and dropping those awful bombs, blowing innocent people like your Auntie Grace to pieces."

Rosie's face turned bright red and her lips quivered. "I know," she stammered.

"Vera," came Stan's voice from the kitchen doorway. His tone was calm and even but clearly reprimanding.

Vera reached out and pulled her daughter to her chest. "It's alright, love. I'm sorry. This war has us all on edge every moment of the day."

Rosie's head nodded against her mother's shoulder and Dotty glanced over at Stan. His expression was unreadable. Whether he asked for a cup of tea or told the family his sister had been crushed beneath the rubble of her own house in London's East End, his face never changed. His eyes momentarily met Dotty's and for a brief second she caught a glimpse of the pain, fear, and concern behind his stoic facade.

"I have letters to write," Dotty said, and hurried for the stairs, leaving Rosie still clutched in Vera's arms and Stan returning to his chair in what she now believed to be his tortured silence.

Dotty's bath was traded for a good wash with soap and a flannel as she couldn't wait to be alone in her room with the door closed, shutting the war with all its misery outside. But of course it didn't work that way. Her mind drifted to the Miles Master, and then to the men at Woodley Airfield whose accusing looks told her they assumed she'd made an error. And the wing commander at Tangmere who'd chased her from the dispersal hut where the real airmen had lounged and pretended to be relaxed just moments before.

But then she thought of Sandy once more, and felt a flutter in her stomach. Despite her lack of self-confidence when it came to social situations, Dotty knew men had shown interest in her at times. She'd occasionally felt a reciprocal interest, but never beyond a few cinema trips and an ice cream afterwards. Any budding romance soon withered when all she wanted to talk about was aeroplanes and flying. Men didn't seem to know what to do with a pretty young woman whose goal in life wasn't to darn their socks and prepare their meals.

By the increased pace of her heart beats, Dotty knew she was smitten with the youthful fighter pilot, and quickly reminded herself that he probably didn't feel the same way. But hope was the life raft that all of Allied Europe was desperately clinging to, and Dorothy Parker couldn't stop herself from holding on to a little hope for the airman with sandy blond hair to like her in return.

8

Hazel's Odyssey crested the swell and plunged into the valley on the backside of the wave. AJ throttled up the twin diesels and ran hard until the bow rose up the next wave, funnelling into the gap through the reef guarding the North Sound. The cut could be challenging on calm days, but on the heels of the storm with winds now shifting from north-west to the usual north-east, the confused seas made the run treacherous. If she didn't keep the bow of the Newton heading straight into the swells, the boat could be turned sideways. Once that happened, they'd be swept over the reef which reached the surface on either side of the cut like the jagged teeth of a thousand sharks.

Back in the marina, the other dive operators sat on their boats, keenly waiting for a report from the first eager captain to risk the run. They knew if they stalled long enough, AJ Bailey from Mermaid Divers wouldn't be able to resist for long.

"I told you we should have waited until this evening!" Reg yelled as they crested another swell.

The dive tanks rattled in their racks as the 36-foot dive boat plummeted once more with AJ opening up the throttles.

"Piece of cake," she yelled back, and stole a glance over her shoulder.

They were a hundred yards clear of the reef, and she grinned. They were almost there. The bow rose one more time and AJ throttled back, but could already tell the swell wasn't as tall or powerful as the last few. As they dropped over the other side, she cut west and rode the Newton down the trough, turning to crest the four-foot wave that seemed petty after what they'd just come through.

"Radio in and tell them it's fine," she said, grinning at Reg.

He shook his head and picked up the mic, clicking the button open.

"Securité, securité, securité. This is *Hazel's Odyssey* at Big Channel, North Sound. Conditions still sporty. Advise wait. Over."

AJ laughed. She knew he wouldn't tell them it was okay, and if she'd called in she would have told them exactly what Reg had. The custom-outfitted twin diesels on *Hazel's Odyssey* and all of Reg's three Newtons gave them a significant power advantage over the average dive boats. And waiting until that evening cost nothing but inconvenience, which was cheaper than losing a boat.

"Did you guys turn around, Reg? Over," came a man's voice over the VHF.

"Negative, negative. We're heading west. But I'll be waiting to move mine. Over."

The man's voice came over the speaker again, but he was laughing this time. "I bet AJ said it was a piece of cake. Over."

"That's affirmative. Over," Reg replied, and hung up the mic.

He still clutched the aluminium framework on the fly-bridge as it would be a bumpy ride around the north-west corner of the island, but they were out of danger.

"Think Pearl will be okay?" AJ asked.

They had dropped Reg's wife at home after leaving the port authority office, and she'd been putting a brave face on things, but AJ knew it had to be devastating for her.

"It's been a rough few months," Reg admitted. "What with her mum getting sick and then passing. All the back and forth to England to see her, then the services. Now this."

The big man shook his head and pulled his rain jacket zipper up to his chin. It was a tropical summer day, but the cool winds from the storm still lingered and the salty spray occasionally whipped through the air, peppering the two of them.

"Honestly, there's a lot more stuff in that container than we have need or room for," Reg continued. "But as you know, Pearl's an only child, so it was bring it all over or throw it away. We didn't have time to sort through everything over there, so we said bugger it, ship it all and we'll sell off the furniture we don't want and Pearl will have time to go through all the family stuff."

"Which of course are the things that'll be ruined," AJ said. "Photo albums and whatnot."

"Unfortunately," Reg agreed. "But there's a safe in there too. One of those fireproof jobs. I don't know all that's in it as we didn't have time to look, but Pearl thinks there's all kinds of family birth and death certificates, as well as her dad's war medals. He was in the army for the last few years of World War Two. The safe might be dry."

"When did she lose her dad?" AJ asked.

"Twenty-five years ago. He had a stroke in 1999. He smoked for most of his life, which probably did him in. Lovely bloke. He could sing and play piano, which is where Pearl gets it from."

"It's horrible to think she's lost all those irreplaceable things," AJ said as she deftly guided the Newton through the lumpy seas. "She has to be heartbroken."

"She is, but Pearl's one tough lady," Reg replied. "We'll get through this."

AJ scanned the open water. "I reckon we can give it a go tomorrow, Reg. It will be a lousy dive day out on the bank, but should be okay to troll around and scan with the sonar."

Reg nodded. "Chances of finding these things are about zero, but I agree, we have to look. Tomorrow should be calmer." He scratched his beard and pointed to the horizon. "That's one of the fishing charters, isn't it?"

"Looks like it," AJ responded, taking her binoculars out and handing them to Reg.

He raised them to his eyes and did his best to focus on the fishing boat as their own vessel rolled and pitched. "Yeah, it's either one of the charters or a private sport fisher. That's a good sign."

It took another thirty minutes for them to round the north-west corner, where they looked over and saw the repairs beginning at Lighthouse Point. As they made the west side, the seas quickly relented in the lee of the island with the shifted winds, and the last ten minutes were far more comfortable.

AJ dropped Reg at the dock, where Thomas and Reg's crews had reaffixed the boards, then idled out to the mooring a hundred yards offshore in twenty feet of water, taking a kayak with her. With practised skill, she secured the Newton on her own, then paddled back in to where Reg sat with his legs hanging over the side of the pier.

"One down, three to go," she said, carefully standing up in the kayak before levering herself onto the pier next to Reg.

He looked at his watch. "Sunset's at seven. Reckon we'll leave the marina at six. Winds should lay down some when the sun gets low."

"I'll ride with you," AJ offered.

"Don't have to," he replied.

"You rode with me."

"Only so I could give you a hard time."

AJ grinned. "Exactly. And I plan to return the favour."

Reg chuckled like the rumble of a far-off thunderstorm. "I might have you drive one of mine."

AJ winced. "That'll piss off the boys."

"That's the point," he replied. "Got one thinks he's the dog's bollocks. Needs knocking down a peg or two."

AJ raised her fists like a boxer. "Put me in, coach."

Reg chuckled again, then heard his mobile ring and fished it from his pocket. "Pearl Divers. Reg speaking."

His brow creased as he listened to the caller.

"Hold on a second, mate. If you don't mind, I'm going to put you on speaker so someone else can hear this too. We're doing this together."

Reg put the call on speaker and held the phone out for AJ to hear as well. She looked at him quizzically, but he just nodded to the phone, telling her to listen up.

"Okay, sure," a Englishman's voice said. "So as I was just telling Mr Moore, my name's George Cook, and the fellow at the port authority gave me your number. He said you might take a boat out to look for the missing containers."

"Yeah," Reg said tentatively, waiting for the man to say more.

AJ wondered if the guy was a reporter who'd got wind of the problem. In which case this would be a short conversation. The last thing they needed was a reporter tagging along trying to make a story out of nothing. Pearl wouldn't want that at all.

"Well, I'm interested in being involved," George said.

"Is that right?" Reg countered dubiously. "Why's that then?"

"Because the other two missing containers belong to me."

"Oh, blimey," AJ muttered, feeling bad for pre-judging the man as Reg had.

"But you do understand this is needle in a haystack stuff, right?" Reg explained. "The containers will have sunk, and most of the ocean around here is 6,000 feet deep."

There was a pause.

"To start with, we're going out to check one area that isn't that deep on the chance they happen to have gone overboard there," Reg added. "If they're not, which is probably the case, then this whole search will be over the same day it starts."

"I see," George said. "And when are you going for a look?"

"Hopefully tomorrow," Reg replied. "The seas are starting to calm down, although they'll still be rather unfriendly 12 miles out, but we'll go take a look."

"What's in them?" AJ mouthed to Reg.

"You ask," Reg mouthed back.

AJ shook her head. She'd learnt men liked to talk salvage with other men.

Reg rolled his eyes. "George, can I ask what's in these containers of yours? Is it something that's salvageable if it's been underwater?"

"Tyres," George replied. "I'm a tyre importer and we distribute to all the garages and automotive stores here on the island. As long as we bring them up in a timely fashion, they'll be perfectly fine."

AJ held up both hands. "Insurance?" she mouthed.

"Aren't you insured?" Reg asked. "Surely you'll be reimbursed the value and save the salvage cost."

AJ cringed when she realised the question was rather impertinent, but she still wanted to know the answer.

"Yes, I am insured, naturally. But there's a tyre shortage on the island and part of my shipment from Mexico is missing. If I can recover them and fulfil my orders I'll have the insurance company cover the salvage costs and we'll all come out better off."

"Plus we won't have oily rubber on the sea floor," Reg added.

"That too. We all need to do our part for the environment," George replied. "Can you give me an estimate on what the cost would be to bring my cargo up?"

Reg looked at AJ and shook his head before speaking. "I think you're getting the cart so far ahead of the horse, he's stopped to graze and soak up the sun, mate. Let's see if we find anything to begin with, and then we'll go from there. I promise we'll help you out if indeed we find any containers."

"That's very generous of you, Mr Moore, thank you."

"Reg is fine, and my troublesome compatriot here is AJ."

"Then thank you, Reg and AJ," George responded. "And you're saying there's nothing to be done if they're in the deeper water?"

"That's submersible territory," Reg explained. "Just getting one out to the location would cost ten times more than your tyres are worth, mate. And that's before they ever splash in."

"Then let's hope your hunch is right and the containers sank in your shallower location," George said. "Please keep me apprised of your progress tomorrow. You can reach me on this number day or night. Do you need funds for this initial reconnaissance trip? I'm happy to help cover expenses."

"We have the first trip covered, George, and we'll let you know whether we find anything or not," Reg replied. "We'll speak tomorrow either way."

"Thank you both," the man said, and ended the call.

Reg and AJ sat side by side on the dock and didn't say a word for several minutes.

"You know what would be pretty naff?" AJ finally asked.

"If we found his containers and not ours," Reg replied without hesitation.

"Yeah. That's exactly what I was thinking," AJ said. "That would be *really* naff."

9

Rain and low, dense cloud kept all of White Waltham's ATA pilots on the ground the next day. With the taxi plane unable to take off, ferrying was thin even in the parts of the country with clearer weather, as there was no one to fly the planes to their destinations. But adhering to the strict ATA rules and without radios, poor weather crippled the system. The following day began in the same way, but by mid-morning, the clouds lifted to a workable altitude, and a few patches of blue sky showed through the grey cover.

With a bustle of activity, pilots scrambled to the taxi aircraft as flight control announced a weather window opening. Dotty took her chit she'd been given by Marjorie McKinven and boarded the Avro Anson bound for the satellite Spitfire factory at Castle Bromwich. It was a bumpy ride. The weather window was more of a tiny porthole, with scattered banks of cloud as low as 600 feet and a ceiling of under 1,500 feet. The pilot dodged and weaved between the cumulus, following a combination of roadways, railway lines, and a compass heading.

Across the cramped, boxy cabin of the Anson sat an older man with the left sleeve of his uniform jacket pinned to the body of the coat. When he nodded to Dotty, she noticed his right eye focused on her while his left eye appeared to be staring towards the cockpit.

"I'm one of the reasons they call the ATA the 'Ancient and Tattered Airmen'," he joked.

"Dotty Parker," she said as nothing else came to mind. She extended a hand which he shook.

"Stewart Keith-Jopp."

Dotty knew the name but had never met the man before. He'd lost his arm and sight in one eye while flying in World War I. She was fascinated by how the man could still fly a plane with only one hand, but blushed and looked away.

"It's alright, Miss Parker. You can ask," he said with a grin on his face. "You're wondering how this works, right?"

"I am curious, sir," she bumbled, barely audible above the drone of the engines. "I seem to need both hands for flying."

"I use my knees," he replied, "and I make sure I do everything in a very specific order."

"As long as we get them there, right?" she responded. "We don't have to be perfect; we just have to deliver the planes in one piece," she added, quoting one of the ATA guidelines.

"Whenever the aeroplane lets us," he replied, and Dotty froze for a moment.

Was she now the laughing stock of the ATA because of the Miles Master incident? Knowing she didn't deserve to be wouldn't stop a cruel rumour spreading and being repeated as fact.

"You heard about my landing at Woodley?" she dared ask.

Keith-Jopp looked amused. "Word gets around. From what I heard, you did well to set her down and walk away in one piece."

Dotty breathed a sigh of relief and looked over her shoulder out of the window as the Anson descended towards the airfield at Castle Bromwich.

Her chit, like everyone else's on the taxi plane, was for a Supermarine Spitfire. Great Britain's pride and joy of the air. Dotty had flown them many times before, but each time she saw the name on her chit butterflies tickled her stomach in anticipation.

"I was hoping for one closer to home," one of the other girls said as they walked from the Anson towards a row of new Spitfires. "I have a date tonight with an American chap who's awfully dishy."

"Where are you going," Dotty asked, overhearing her.

"Chichester," the woman replied. "I'll never make it back in time with this late start."

"Tangmere?" Dotty blurted.

"That's the one."

"I have a Spit going to the 140 Squadron at RAF Northolt. I'll trade with you," Dotty quickly offered. "You'll make it back from South Ruislip in plenty of time."

"Do we need to get permission?" the woman asked. "I've never done anything like this before. Are we allowed to swap like that?"

"I've traded before and never heard a word about it," a male pilot called back as he walked to his plane.

The woman looked unsure.

"Here," Dotty said, holding out her chit. "He said it's fine."

The woman scoffed. "It's fine for him, but we don't get judged by the same rules. I don't need to get in trouble."

Dotty thought about the Miles Master and wondered whether she was already on a sticky wicket. But the draw of Tangmere was too strong.

"No problem then," she said, withdrawing her chit and trying another tact. "I hope you make it back in time. Train took nearly four hours for me the other day. Kept stopping and waiting to let priority trains pass at the intersections." Dotty continued walking, looking for the tail number on her piece of paper.

"Wait," the woman called out. "To heck with it. I'll trade. But if we get in trouble make sure to tell them one of the blokes told us we could do it."

Dotty knew that wouldn't carry any weight and would probably bring more trouble than aid, but she smiled and switched chits. She double-checked the tail number and destination on her new assignment with a flutter in her tummy when she read RAF Tangmere.

A man in civilian clothes hurried down the line of planes, shouting at the pilots, men or women, as he went. Dotty heard him once he was close enough.

"Only flights south or west are cleared to take off; north and east on a weather hold!"

Dotty looked to the sky and caught the mechanic doing the same.

"Been lifting some, but reckon we're in for a spot more rain this afternoon, miss," he said as she strapped herself in the tight confines of the fighter plane.

"If I stay east of the Cotswolds, I can pick a way over the Chilterns," Dotty thought aloud. "Then keep clear of Haslemere and I'll just have the South Downs to worry about."

The mechanic looked as though he was about to comment further, but kept it to himself. "Ready when you are, miss," he said instead.

"One minute, please," Dotty replied, reading through her pilot notes although she knew the Spitfire procedures by heart.

This was no time to rush things and make a silly error. She was about to fly 125 miles at several hundred miles per hour pinned between clouds above and the English countryside below. In places they would be squeezing together, forcing her into one or the other if she couldn't find a way around. Finished with the notes, she secured them beside the seat and studied her map, picking out the main landmarks. Oxford and Reading would both be good waypoints with airfields nearby if the weather forced her to land.

The raucous sound of Merlin engines drowned out any chance of further discussion, so Dotty gave the mechanic a thumbs-up before running through the start-up sequence. After priming the fuel and switching the starter magneto to the on position, Dotty glanced at the mechanic for a final okay that everyone was clear of the prop before she pressed the starter button. The engine instantly roared into life, causing the whole plane to reverberate. She flicked the main magnetos on and watched the temperature gauges, which soon moved from the stops.

In quick succession, so the volatile engines didn't overheat, the planes which had been cleared for take-off taxied, then followed each other one by one into the air, turning in the direction of whatever airfield they were destined for. For Dotty, she made a 180-degree turn across the Spitfire factory and picked up a southerly heading of 160 degrees, keeping the Mk Vb at an altitude of 800 feet. Which was about 500 feet above the fields of the West Midlands, and a few hundred feet below the dense cloud.

Grey and subdued, the lack of sunshine took much of the contrast away from the ground below, and the endless green fields and small villages all looked the same. At Banbury, Dotty spotted the railway line and followed its curving path to Oxford and continued tracking the rails towards Reading. The Chilterns loomed, with low-hanging clumps of cloud nestled against the hilltops. But the railway had been built alongside the Thames river which cut a valley through the slopes, and by dropping to a few hundred feet above Lower Basildon and Pangbourne, Dotty cleared her first major obstacle.

Low enough to see faces turn to the sky and people wave as she buzzed over their heads, Dotty wondered what their expressions would be if they knew it was a woman at the controls. With little time to ponder such trivialities, she spotted the larger town of Reading and continued over the tracks as they turned south-east. Fifteen miles later, just past Farnborough, the line split, heading east or west, and she was forced to leave the comfort of the tracks and return to a compass heading.

Ahead loomed the chalk hills of the western reaches of the North Downs, their peaks above Haslemere lost to the cumulus. Aiming the Spitfire to the western side of the slopes, Dotty flicked her eyes between her map and the horizon. Her next landmark was critical, and below, the countryside was nothing but an endless sea of farmland. Fields bordered by hedges and small lanes which zig-zagged about, following centuries old pathways linking farmers' properties.

With the land only 150 feet above sea level, Dotty was sure the cloud ceiling had dropped. Her window of navigable air space seemed smaller and as she approached the hills of the South Downs, the green slopes loomed like a wall rising to meet the dense clouds. There was one valley through to the south coast, and if she missed it, a pilot could wander back and forth along the countryside, lost, and soon searching for any available airfield to set down.

"There you are, my lovely," Dotty breathed as she spotted the railway line.

Coming from the north-east, the tracks turned due south and ran through a narrow valley formed by the river Arun. The stone parapets and turrets of the eleventh-century medieval castle were a welcome sight as Dotty raced over the little town of Arundel, before banking west to follow the railway line along the foot of the South Downs towards Chichester.

Tangmere came into view a mile or so north of the tracks. As she was about to bank right, she checked out the port side of the cockpit for air traffic. Five miles south over the English Channel the muted steel blue of the water met the grey of the clouds as though most of the colour had been drained from the world. Dotty noticed a handful of dots growing larger in the dim sky.

Having always dreaded getting in the way of her own fighters, a knot formed in her stomach. Then the idea that the planes weren't British caused a moment of panic. Torn between landing as soon as she could or getting out of the way, Dotty flew past Tangmere and circled towards the coast. Two planes peeled off from the others and climbed until they kissed the clouds.

Although she couldn't make out their paint schemes, Dotty thought the dark silhouettes were those of Hawker Hurricanes. Her eyes shot back to the squadron, where a trailing plane spewed smoke from the engine while two others flanked the wounded fighter, escorting him to safety. They were definitely friendlies.

Now, the question was whether the RAF pilots had recognised her as one of their own.

The two Hurricanes dived from above and Dotty quickly dipped the nose of the Spitfire, hoping they'd see the roundels before opening fire. Her instinct was to take evasive manoeuvres, but she forced herself to maintain her circling bank over the West Sussex countryside. If she acted like prey they'd be more inclined to think of her that way. The two Hurricanes pulled out of their dive and flashed over her cockpit so close Dotty felt like she could've slid the canopy open and touched them.

The rest of the squadron passed by below her, and she saw flames begin to lick along the fuselage of the damaged plane. Completing her turn and following the group towards the airfield, Dotty stayed well back to give them room. The pilots dropped to the ground, landing two and three abreast, and the pair of escorts shot ahead of the wounded Hurricane as the pilot cut the engine.

Dotty was glad she'd given them plenty of room. The rest of the squadron landed on the field, leaving the straggler to glide in dead stick. The orange and yellow flames had disappeared but a small trail of smoke still emanated from the cowling as the pilot expertly touched down.

Dotty breathed a sigh of relief as she lined up the Spitfire to land, staying slightly left of the Hurricane. In a flash, colour returned with a vengeance as the slowing Hurricane burst into flames. Dotty gasped in horror as she passed by the stricken plane which lazily veered left, crossing behind her.

Instantly, she knew the dark outline of the pilot fighting to pull back the canopy amid a raging cockpit of fire was a sight that would live in a haunted part of her mind forever.

10

The farther from the island they motored, the more the swells grew, but were still nothing like yesterday's charge through the North Sound cut. Leaving at daybreak helped as the breeze was barely a tickle, keeping the surface smooth and rolling. On the other hand, leaving early didn't help AJ's mood. But after forty-five minutes, a large travel mug of coffee, and Pearl's refusal to accept her grumpiness, she was in a better frame of mind.

AJ had a charter group with her all week, who'd decided to give their last day a miss as the visibility underwater probably wouldn't be that great. With the storm, their number of dives had been severely compromised, but no one could control the weather.

AJ and Reg had decided to take *Hazel's Odyssey* for the trip. Reg had one of his boats free, but AJ's Newton had a newer and better combination fishfinder and chartplotter she'd recently purchased, with a 12-inch screen. Fishfinders weren't nearly as effective or detailed as a towable side-scan sonar, but they did have some advantages. Namely, a high-end fishfinder was a small percentage of the cost of a towable, and the number one reason was that AJ had one.

"We're over the bank," she announced, and switched from the GPS screen to sonar.

A three-dimensional map of the sea floor appeared in shades of yellow and green with the depth reading 130 feet.

"How do you want to do this?" Reg asked, looking over AJ's shoulder at the screen.

AJ used the touchscreen to split the picture with half on sonar and the other half back on GPS. It took her a few tries as the rolling boat made her finger bounce on buttons she didn't intend. After swearing under her breath, she leaned back against the helm seat.

"I'd like to run the perimeter, then move in, but it'll be trickier to navigate than if we do straight lines down the length."

Reg thought for a moment. "I like your perimeter idea. If one of us drives and watches the GPS, the other can watch the sonar screen. Keep our recorded track on the screen and we'll run inside it once we start the next lap."

"I can do whatever you need, too," Pearl volunteered.

"We'll all rotate," Reg said. "'Cos believe me, this'll be tedious."

"Alright, I'll start off the side of the bank then," AJ said and turned *Hazel's Odyssey* to port, watching the depth until the slope became apparent on the sonar.

When the depth read 200 feet, she turned to starboard and moved her eyes to the GPS, aiming the bow along the depth line on the map. Twelve knots felt like a good compromise between speed, comfort, and getting a good look at the sea floor without missing anything. AJ settled in for the long day she expected ahead.

The topography of Twelve Mile Bank is not unlike Grand Cayman itself, just smaller, and 120 feet below instead a few feet above the ocean's surface. Nearly five miles long and about a mile wide, the underwater peak is relatively flat with occasional coral heads, known as bommies, peppering the expanse of sandy sea floor. The edges slope away steeply, reaching a depth of 6,000 feet within a mile or two of the bank.

AJ linked her mobile to the Newton's stereo and put on her 'beach mix' playlist. It felt a bit like a nice island cruise on the water, but she knew it wouldn't last long. The gentle roll of the seas would turn to chop when the winds picked up, especially when she turned the boat east into the swells.

"There!" Pearl yelped, and AJ backed the throttles off.

"That's a bommie, love," Reg said.

"Are you sure?" his wife questioned. "It's bigger than the others."

"Yeah, but it's a bommie," AJ agreed, and picked up the throttles once more. "Believe me, if we find a container, you'll know it."

"See how rounded the ends are on that?" Reg pointed out as the object moved toward the back edge of the screen. "If we find a container it'll be perfectly angled with sharp corners. It'll look like a big Lego brick."

"Hmm," Pearl mumbled, clearly not completely believing them. "And it's when, Reg, not if."

Reg offered her a forced smile and AJ focused extra hard on the screen to avoid acknowledging. Pearl couldn't help herself. She was an optimist who always tried to look on the bright side and see the good in everyone and everything. Despite their warnings, she'd let her hope overtake the reality of the situation. But AJ couldn't blame her. The idea that all those mementoes and heirlooms were lost to the depths was devastating.

"What's that?" Pearl said and pointed to the screen again.

"Sushi," AJ replied.

"It's what now?" Pearl replied, then gave AJ a playful pat on the shoulder as she realised what her friend meant. "Oh, you silly bugger. That bunch of moving blobs are tuna?"

"Probably," AJ replied with a grin. "Or a school of big jacks."

They'd reached the south-west corner of the bank and the depth on the screen began to plummet. AJ turned to starboard and found the 200-foot point again as they traversed the rounded far end of the bank. She checked her watch to see it was almost 10:00am.

"Want to switch?" Reg asked, holding onto the frame as the Newton rocked.

The swells were now hitting them broadside.

"Yeah, ta. I need to pee," AJ replied, and slid from the helm seat.

Reg took over driving while Pearl stepped up to watch the sonar.

"I'm nervous now I'm officially in charge of monitoring this thing," Pearl said, cringing. "If we never find them I'll be convinced I missed the bloody things."

"Big Lego bricks," AJ called out before scampering down the ladder to the deck below.

After using the marine head in the bow cabin, she washed her hands then grabbed three stainless-steel water bottles and filled then from the big, round, insulated water cooler. She selected a handful of energy bars and stuffed them in her pockets. With the carabiners for the water bottles looped through a finger, they clanked together as she scaled the steps, before handing them out on the fly-bridge.

"Good job," Reg told her, setting the water aside and ripping into the energy bar. "Hungry work sitting around watching a 12-inch telly."

Nudging farther and farther to starboard, they were finally facing west-north-west and running along the top side of the bank. The drop was steeper along the north-facing slope so the depth varied quickly between 160 feet and 240 feet as the underwater mountain curved in and out. The swells were now hitting them on the starboard bow, shoving the Newton to port and knocking it off the desired path. AJ watched the sonar while Reg wound the wheel back and forth in a dance with the rolling swells.

They continued the search with the breeze picking up and the music playing, each lost in their own thoughts until AJ broke their silence.

"You're an only child, aren't you, Pearl?" she asked without taking her eyes off the screen.

"I am, unfortunately."

"You wished for a sibling?"

"Honestly, I didn't know the difference, but I meant unfortunate for my mum and dad," Pearl explained. "She had two miscarriages before me, so they'd given up, figuring it wasn't to be. Seven years later, me showing up was a bit of an accident and they were terrified she'd miscarry again, but it all went fine."

"And they didn't try again after you?" AJ asked.

"My mum was thirty-five when I was born, and back then, that was considered getting on a bit to have kids. I suppose they decided not to push their luck."

"Dolphin!" AJ yelled, pointing off the port bow.

"Oh, lovely!" Pearl exclaimed, as they watched the fins arc out of the water.

"Look," Reg said, nodding at the sonar screen.

A series of elongated blobs seem to be along for the ride under the keel of *Hazel's Odyssey*.

"I didn't think we had dolphins here," Pearl said, smiling as she peered over the console to watch them play off the bow.

"We don't," AJ replied. "Except for the poor buggers they keep in the pens for the tourists. Bottlenose aren't native to this part of the Caribbean."

"I've only seen them a handful of times," Reg agreed.

"And never this close," AJ added, right before she screamed, "Stop!"

Reg startled and looked at her. "What?"

"Turn around, Reg," AJ said excitedly, unsure whether she'd imagined something below the pod or not.

As Reg began to swing the Newton to starboard, they watched the edge of the bank disappear.

"What the heck?" AJ muttered.

"We're right at the north-east corner," Reg commented, continuing to turn the boat around.

They soon passed over the edge and the depth shot back to 140 feet. To stay on the top of the slope, he had to go north-west for a hundred feet before following the edge around the corner to retrace their path.

AJ began questioning herself more and more. It was probably a glitch or an illusion, but she thought she'd spotted a very straight line on the screen. *Could it have been several dolphins all lined up in some way?*

"What did you see, exactly?" Pearl asked, and AJ could tell the poor woman was doing her best to contain her excitement.

As they passed back over the area they'd just been and nothing stood out on the sonar, AJ felt embarrassed. It had been a lot more enjoyable to play with dolphins than stare at empty sea floor, and now she'd got Pearl's hopes up for nothing.

Reg pushed the throttles back. "Bloody hell."

Pearl gasped and put her hands to face.

AJ laughed. "Lego brick!"

Moving slowly, the boat rocked and rolled in the swells as Reg began circling what had to be a container resting on the very edge of the bank.

"I suppose there's always the chance this has been here a while," Reg said, and AJ smacked him on the arm.

"Don't ruin the moment, you old goat," she told him and laughed again, but the idea that it might be one of George Cook's containers full of tyres was not lost on her.

"See that!" she blurted. "Deeper. Off the side, Reg. We barely grazed it."

Reg cut hard to port and turned the Newton around, gently opening the throttles and driving from sonar. When the depth read 180 feet, he turned parallel to the bank again.

Appearing smaller than the first container, a second one came into view, its straight lines and sharp corners distinctive over the surrounding natural terrain. AJ reached over and recorded a GPS waypoint into the chartplotter's memory.

"Feeling lucky?" Reg teased.

"Gotta be close by somewhere, right?" AJ responded, and squeezed Pearl's shoulder.

Pearl hung on the back of the helm seat and didn't say a word.

Reg circled deeper and checked at 200 feet then another pass showing 250 feet on the depth reading.

"It would get pretty serious below that depth, love," he said over his shoulder to his wife.

She nodded, which he couldn't see, but AJ had learnt over the years that the two of them seemed to know what the other was thinking most of the time, regardless of whether they could see or hear each other.

Reg cut in closer to the bank, passing over the first container once more, and AJ logged another waypoint. Circling in the vicinity, Reg made eccentric circles, moving wider each time. On the second lap around, they crossed over the third container.

"Stone the crows," he muttered. "I don't believe it."

Pearl reached over the back of the seat and wrapped her arms around him.

"Thank you," she whispered with her face buried in her husband's shoulder. "Thank you both."

11

Dotty sat in the cockpit of the Spitfire with the canopy slid back, feeling the cool breeze brush her face. She dare not get out. Somewhere behind her, across the airfield, ground crew fought the fire, or might have already extinguished the flames – she didn't know and couldn't look. After three years under its dark cloud, the war had finally come to meet her. She'd seen the bombed-out homes. The devastation of neighbours and friends losing loved ones. The newsreels at the cinema, the figures and articles in the newspapers. It all felt surreal, distant, and while terrifying, it was happening to other people. But watching a man being burnt alive had changed everything.

"Sir?" came the voice of a mechanic.

Dotty braced herself, pulling her nerves together as she knew she had to. Gathering her pilot notes and bag, she stepped from the plane with parachute in hand. She slipped her helmet off.

"Oh, sorry, miss," the mechanic said as she stepped down from the wing.

"That's quite alright," she replied, relieved her voice functioned.

"Everything okay with the Spit?" he asked.

Dotty nodded. "Yes. All good. I'll just get my delivery chit signed," she mumbled, walking away trying desperately not to turn around and be drawn back into the disaster.

Inside the dispersal hut for the Spitfire squadron, men glumly sat around. No one had been outside watching. One young pilot, who she didn't think was more than eighteen years old, appeared pale, his lips quivering. Dotty was sure she looked the same way.

"I need to get my chit signed," she said. "Who should I see?"

"Wing commander," one pilot replied. "He'll probably be…" the man trailed off for a moment, pointing to the airfield. "He's usually with the Hurricane squadron when he's not in his office."

Dotty stood in the middle of the dispersal hut, paralysed. Her whole reason for trading destinations was to run into Sandy once again, but until that moment, she hadn't considered the possibility that the inferno could have been *his* Hurricane. Her feet were anchored to the floorboards, and for a few seconds she thought she might pass out.

The Spitfire pilot looked at her quizzically. "Are you okay?"

Forcing her legs to move, Dotty nodded, heading straight for the door. Her pace quickened once outside, and her heavy parachute pack bounced off her thigh as she broke into a run. Across the field to her right, service vehicles and a fire truck surrounded the smouldering wreckage, but Dotty kept her eyes ahead, focused on the Hurricane squadron's hut.

As she burst through the open door, a group of faces turned her way. The remaining pilots from the squadron were huddled around a table with the wing commander. Dotty knew after every sortie the pilots conducted a debrief, and so apparently, the routine continued while the charred remains of their comrade were hauled from the wreck.

Dotty searched for Sandy's locks of blond hair and confident smile. But she couldn't see him amongst the crowd.

"Wait outside," the wing commander barked.

Dotty held up her chit, although she didn't know why. Getting a signature was the furthest thing from her mind. Perhaps to justify her presence, she wondered, blushing.

"Outside!" the wing commander repeated angrily.

She quickly retreated, dropping her parachute by the door and fumbling for her cigarettes and matches. Her legs were shaking, so she sank into an armchair. The furniture seemed absurdly out of place on the grass outside the dispersal hut. Dotty closed her eyes and inhaled her cigarette, but all she could see was RAF Flying Officer Sandy Lovell's innocent young face and the silhouetted figure in the burning cockpit. Her eyes blinked open, desperately trying to escape the inescapable images her mind cruelly clung to.

"That was you in the Spit?" came a voice she recognised.

Dotty leapt from the seat, tossing her cigarette aside. Sandy stood before her with a dirty face and grimy uniform smelling of smoke. She stepped towards him, reflexively ready to wrap her arms around the man she barely knew, but abruptly stopped. He was indeed a man she barely knew, and a fighter pilot on duty.

He smiled, but it wasn't the easy, relaxed smile from the first time they'd met. It was a relieved, momentary break from the horror he was living through. But all Dotty could think about was the fact he was still living. Somewhere, suppressed beneath her relief, was the guilt of feeling elated based on another man's violent death, but she couldn't help herself.

"Thank God," she murmured. "I thought it was you."

"I'm not sure God has any bearing on what the world is doing at the moment," he replied softly. "He certainly wasn't with Graham today."

Dotty didn't know who Graham was, but hearing a name attached to the tragedy brought her guilt closer to the surface.

"He's the fellow who gave you a hard time the other day," Sandy said. "Was," he corrected himself.

"I'm sorry," was all Dotty could think to say.

While she hadn't been enamoured with Graham's chauvinist treatment of her, she certainly didn't wish him dead. Especially in a manner she wouldn't wish upon her worst enemies. Well, perhaps that wasn't completely true, she considered. Hitler and his Nazis deserved such an end. And if God were to become involved at some point, she suspected a fiery exit to hell may await them after all.

"All for nothing," Sandy fumed under his breath. "Never even saw the Huns they sent us after, but the flak over the coast of France tore us apart. Nowhere to bloody go under this cloud."

Sandy turned towards the dispersal hut door and saluted. The wing commander did the same before glaring at Dotty, holding out his hand.

"Needed that plane this morning."

"Weather, sir," Dotty replied shakily, handing the man her chit.

"The war doesn't stop for a bit of cloud," he snapped in reply, signing her piece of paper. "Should've put a man at the controls and had it here this morning."

"They can't fly either," Dotty heard herself say. "Sir."

The wing commander glared at her. "What?"

"ATA rules, sir. They apply to all the pilots, male or female," she explained in a more subservient tone.

"Ridiculous," he fumed. "Be on your way," he added with a wave of his hand before striding back inside the dispersal hut.

Dotty worried her legs would give out once again. Too distraught to be angry, she felt overwhelmed with everything that had happened during the afternoon.

"Don't take it personally," Sandy said. "Wing Commander Harrington is tough on everyone, but he means well."

"I don't think he means me well," Dotty replied, managing a hint of a laugh.

"Do you have to return to White Waltham right away?" Sandy asked.

Dotty's first thought was how the pilot knew where she was based. *Had he taken the time to find out?*

"I have to call and see if there'll be a taxi flight or if I'm supposed to take the train again."

Sandy glanced at his wristwatch. "I suspect we're done for the day now the weather is closing in again. I'd be surprised if there's a taxi plane making it across the South Downs."

Dotty thought about her own squeeze through the valley over Arundel. "I expect you're right, so it'll be the train for me."

"Would the ATA mind if you had dinner before returning home?" he asked.

"They like us to get straight back," she replied before realising what his question implied.

She felt her face blush yet again and wished her body wouldn't so easily give away the turmoil she always felt inside.

"Perhaps another time," Sandy said, nodded, and walked into the dispersal hut.

Dotty wasn't sure whether to slap herself in the face or chase after the pilot, but she did neither. Instead, she hurried to the airfield office behind its rows of sandbags stacked against the outside walls covering the windows and waited for the operators to connect her to White Waltham.

"ATA, Marjorie McKinven speaking."

"Hello Marjorie, it's Dotty. I'm in Tangmere. Is there a taxi plane or should I take the train?"

"You're in Tangmere?"

Dotty had completely forgotten about trading assignments, but the Operations Room secretary's question brought it all rushing back.

"I'm so sorry," Dotty said with a wince, "I traded with another pilot."

"I know, I've already spoken with her. I'm amazed you made it to the coast. Just about everyone else set down wherever they could see an airfield, or turned back to West Brom."

"Really?" Dotty responded. "It was a bit woolly over the hills but I went between or around them."

"Well, I'm glad you made it safe and sound," Marjorie said, and Dotty's mind flashed to the man she now knew was named Graham.

"Oh, and Dorothy," Marjorie McKinven continued, "If you'd wanted more trips to Tangmere you should have said. It does mess up things a wee bit when you pilots start trading around. I don't know who ends up where, so I put the wrong name on the next assignment."

"I did mean to ask you about it, but this just sort of happened. Another girl needed to be home earlier than me. I am sorry for any trouble I've caused."

"We can't run the ATA around you girls' dating calendar," Marjorie said in an officious voice.

Dotty was slightly taken aback. "I really am sorry."

Marjorie laughed. "No, that's what Commander Gower has to say about the matter. But I don't mind as long as it doesn't make too much more work on this end. I'm all for the pilots getting to visit their family or a beau if the opportunity arises. If I know, then I can steer you that way when possible. Do you have family down that way?"

"No, well, something like that," Dotty stammered.

Marjorie chuckled. "I see. I believe I understand. Well, if you're brave enough to face Wing Commander Robert Harrington, then I'm game to send you there whenever it works out. I've heard he's not a fan of ferry pilots, especially the female variety."

"Thank you, Marjorie," Dotty replied, looking at the WAAF secretary to make sure she couldn't hear the conversation. "And I can confirm your second point. I've received a prickly reception on both deliveries so far."

"In that case, I hope he's worth it," Marjorie joked. "Oh, I almost forgot. Commander Gower asked to see you first thing in the morning. I've taken you off tomorrow's schedule."

"Am I in trouble?" Dotty asked, thinking the whole trading business had been swept under the rug.

"No, no. You're up for training, I believe. She wants you certified for Class 4 advanced twin-engined aircraft."

A burst of nervous excitement shot through Dotty, leaving her speechless. It was a nod of confidence from Gower and an amazing opportunity to fly bigger planes, which not all ATA pilots were chosen to do.

"Safe travels," Marjorie signed off. "We'll see you tomorrow."

"Thank you," Dotty said, then hung up. She looked over at the secretary who was busily typing something. "Could I get a car to the station, please?"

The WAAF smiled. "Waiting for you out front, miss."

"Oh," Dotty said in surprise. "Thank you."

As she headed out the door, it dawned on her that she might not be back this way for a while. If she remembered correctly, the training lasted at least a week. Dotty felt a strong urge to run back to the dispersal hut so she could explain to Sandy why she'd be absent for a while, and that she was an idiot for not staying longer today. But the car was waiting. And she'd never been one for boldness and spontaneity, unless it involved an aeroplane.

The trip home to her billet dragged on and the trains seemed extra slow in the late afternoon and early evening. A steady rain set in from the low grey cloud which enveloped all of southern England, and when Dotty finally walked in the front door, she was dripping wet and ready for a bath.

The Ramsays had all gone to bed, but a few minutes after Dotty went into the kitchen to find ham sandwiches waiting for her, Vera came downstairs in her dressing gown.

"I can warm something up for you, dear," she offered.

"This is perfect," Dotty replied, holding the thin sandwich up. "Thank you for thinking of me."

"Thought you'd be home early today," Vera said. "What with the weather and all."

"Managed to deliver a Spitfire down south," Dotty replied. "But the trains were slow coming back."

She looked up at her landlady who she could see was tired, crow's feet wrinkling the edges of her eyes. Dotty would give anything to share the burden of the horrors she'd seen that day, but the last thing Vera needed was to listen to a story about a young man cruelly taken too soon.

"Goodnight, Vera, and thank you again," she said instead.

12

The ride home was into the swells, although the seas continued to settle, and AJ found a steady speed for the Newton that didn't beat them up too badly. Reg sent text messages to Brian Watler at the port authority and Captain Nolan Conrad, letting them know the containers had been located. Both were excited and amazed. Not wanting to shout over the sound of the wind and the waves, he waited until they docked before calling George Cook.

"Mr Cook, this is Reg Moore."

"Good afternoon, Reg. Are you back already?" the man asked, and AJ listened to the call on speaker as she unwound a hose to wash down *Hazel's Odyssey*.

"We are. Just tied up," Reg replied. "We're pretty sure we found them."

"Really?" George enthused. "That's fantastic news. Where? How deep are they? Please give me all the details. This truly is great news."

"East end of Twelve Mile Bank between 120 and 160 feet down," Reg explained. "That's a diveable depth, so we'll start coming up with a salvage plan."

"How soon do you think?" George asked.

Reg looked over at AJ, who shrugged her shoulders before speaking.

"Maybe tomorrow for a first dive. But I have to see what I have for customers."

"We'll get back out over the weekend and do a reconnaissance dive," Reg added. "From there we can decide how best to proceed. I presume your containers have locks on them."

"They do, and a customs seal from Mexico. They're combination locks and I can give you the code, or simply cut them off. You can cut the seals but please keep hold of them so we can show the customs officials here."

"Alright, text me the codes we'll need. The locks should still be functional as it's only been a few days," Reg replied.

"We'll secure a way to moor to the site and film each container showing its position and orientation," AJ said, sitting on the aft deck bench next to Reg. "Then next week we can return and look at getting inside them."

"At that point," Reg added, "we'll probably need to hire a larger vessel to transport everything to shore. But, like AJ said, let's make sure we can access them first."

"But you said you can dive to that depth, right?" George asked, sounding concerned.

"We can, but it's at and beyond recreational diving limits, so we'll be decompression diving the site," Reg replied. "It's considered technical diving and we'll be limited on dive time and number of dives we can do in a day. Efficiency and safety will be the name of the game."

"Well, I can't tell you two how chuffed I am that you found the containers. Keep me posted every step of the way, and as I said before, I'll gladly help with the expenses. Perhaps I could come out to the Twelve Mile Bank with you when you start bringing my tyres up?"

"No problem, George, we'll keep you updated, and it'll be boring topside, but you're welcome to ride along. We'll talk to you over the weekend."

Reg hung up, and AJ looked over at her friend and mentor. It had been a noisy and bumpy ride back, so they hadn't had a chance to talk much yet about a plan.

"How many boats are you running tomorrow?" she asked.

"One, maybe two," Reg replied.

Saturdays were usually slow as most people flew in or out that day.

"I'll check what I have," she replied. "I think I have three or four clients, but maybe we can consolidate on one of yours and take *Hazel's Odyssey* back out tomorrow."

Reg lifted his eyes in the direction of their little hut, where Pearl had hurried off to once they'd docked.

"She's checking email and bookings now. Let's get cleaned up, then this afternoon figure out what you have, and we'll come up with a plan this evening."

"Sounds good," AJ said and leapt to her feet.

Grabbing the hose, she triggered the sprayer and began washing down the deck, making sure to douse Reg's feet in the process.

"Oi!" he grumbled and quickly stood up.

"Get off my boat," she told him, trying to hide her grin. "I have work to do."

The afternoon flew by. AJ grabbed lunch at Heritage Kitchen on her way home to catch up on emails and phone calls. Three customers were still keen to dive on Saturday so she texted Reg to see if he had room. He was happy as it made sending a second boat out worthwhile, so she called her clients and explained they'd be on Reg's *Blue Pearl* in the morning. They were residents who often dived on Saturdays knowing it was a quieter day and didn't mind at all.

Sunday would be a different story as she had a full boat of eight divers from a new group arriving, so she'd have to take them out in the mornings, but should be free in the afternoons.

Next on the agenda was getting gases sorted. Their compressor at the dock could fill air in the tanks, but to allow them to stay longer at deeper depths, they'd need custom blends. She picked Thomas up in her 15-passenger van, and drove into George Town to Island Air, the main supplier to all the dive operators on Grand Cayman.

"Want to come out to the bank with us, or work on Reg's boat?" she asked Thomas after filling him in on the morning's discovery.

"Dat's easy," he grinned. "Da bank."

"No tips on that trip," she pointed out.

"You pay me so good da tips are just pocket money," Thomas replied.

AJ looked over at her friend, and they both burst out laughing.

Working as a dive guide meant a uniform of shorts and T-shirts, endless diving for free, the ocean as your office, and usually being around fun people having a good time. It also signed you up for six days a week of long hours, lousy benefits, if any, and crappy pay. This was true anywhere in the world. Running a dive boat business was a tough and unreliable way to make a living, so most owners weren't earning their fortune either. Weather cancellations, boat troubles, and rising costs of everything made competition fierce and profits low. But AJ treated Thomas more like a partner than an employee, and he understood she'd always do whatever she could for him. He was salaried rather than day rate, so he knew he'd be paid even when the boat couldn't go out, and at the end of the year, she always gave him a bonus based on Mermaid Divers' net earnings.

Which was why they could both joke about it.

"Okay, get your phone out and double-check me," she said as they drove down the bypass on the way to town. "The deepest container we think is around 160 feet, so I was thinking 26% nitrox. That's 170 feet max depth at 1.6 ATA, right?"

AJ had the tables memorised, but it was always wise to have

someone else verify her plan. Thomas pulled up a dive app on his phone and found the depth charts for various mixes of nitrox, the name given to an oxygen and nitrogen blend different to regular air.

"Dat's right, boss. 145 feet at 1.4 ATA."

"Good," she replied. "The other two are around 120 to 140. 28% is 156 feet max, right?"

"Yup. 132 at 1.4 ATA."

Oxygen, in the volume breathed at increased pressure matching the weight of water above a diver, became poisonous at a given point, so staying above the maximum depth for the mix was critical. The 1.4 ATA was the recommended max depth, and 1.6 ATA was the absolute maximum. Going deeper could cause the diver to go into convulsions, seizures and drown. It wasn't a line in the sand to take lightly. The trade-off was breathing more nitrogen, which was the limiting factor on how long they could stay down. The human body has no use for the nitrogen we all breathe and disposes of it through our blood system and tissues. When absorbed at the elevated volumes of divers under greatly increased pressures, the body can reach saturation – the point at which it can no longer dissipate the incoming nitrogen loading. The diver is then required to perform decompression stops at shallower depths to allow the body to catch up before surfacing. The downside of not doing that is as potentially fatal as oxygen poisoning. It is why one of the main rules of recreational diving is to stay well within decompression limits. Tech divers go through extensive training to learn how to safely go beyond those boundaries.

"Let's plan on three dives," AJ thought aloud. "We'll go to the deep one first, then try to stay at the other two on the subsequent dives. And we'll take 50% nitrox for deco tanks."

"What if da deep one is da container wit Mrs Moore's stuff inside?" Thomas asked.

"Hmm," AJ grunted and considered the idea. "Good point. It'll limit our bottom time, but this is just a reconnaissance trip. We'll take enough tanks and mixes to cover all options for two divers in the water at a time, so six dives total."

"I can't go 160, boss," Thomas pointed out.

He'd recently completed his first certification into tech diving, but his training limited him to 150 feet.

"We can figure that out in the rotation," AJ assured him and grinned. "You'll get to use that shiny new cert of yours."

"Sounds like a plan, boss," he replied with a broad smile.

The Fox and Hare pub was already packed when AJ arrived at quarter to eight. Pearl's first set usually started at 8:00pm, and Reg gave AJ the stink eye for being late. Pearl didn't mind at all and wrapped her up in a hug.

"Get him a drink, love; you know how he gets all fussy setting up my gear."

AJ laughed and Pearl gave her a wink. It was good to see Pearl with a smile on her face again, although AJ couldn't help still worrying about what they'd actually be able to salvage from the container. Anything paper or fabric would be ruined.

"You look gorgeous," AJ said, stepping back and admiring her friend.

Pearl wore a summer dress which accentuated her feminine curves, revealing just enough cleavage to be sexy in a teasingly classy way. Her hair hung in long blonde waves and she wore her stage make-up, which was a little heavier than her usual eyeliner and lipstick.

"Thank you, love," she replied. "And you always do."

AJ ruffled her own hair which was still damp from the rushed shower she'd stepped from fifteen minutes ago. Leggings and a Mermaid Divers tank top had been clean and within easy reach, finished off with her nicer pair of flip flops. On her best days, AJ considered herself to be pleasant in appearance, but nowhere near Pearl's head-turning league, and she blushed at the compliment.

"Break a leg," she told Pearl. "I'll get Mr Grumpy a drink and distract him for a bit."

As she wiggled through the crowd to the extensive oak bar, she exchanged greetings with most of the patrons who she knew at least in passing or from being regulars in the pub. The bartender, Frank, spotted AJ from the far end and with a brief exchange of hand signals understood her order. With the efficiency of experienced bartenders all over the world, he had a Strongbow cider and a Seven Fathoms rum over a cube of ice in front of her within a minute, while concurrently serving two other customers.

"Cheers, Frank," she said and made her way back to the table Reg always commandeered for Friday nights.

He accepted his drink with a nod and a brief lift of the glass before taking a sip.

"We have a plan for tomorrow," AJ announced as she took her seat. "Thomas is coming with us and I have tanks in the van. Just have to load them on the boat in the morning, so let's leave at 9am."

Reg turned and frowned at her. "Nine? That's practically the morning shot. Eight."

AJ rolled her eyes and sighed. "I can't have a decent lie-in? Fine. Eight."

Reg nodded and took another sip of the smooth local rum.

Pearl's voice boomed over the speakers, greeting everyone, and the crowd cheered loudly. As the drums started into a cover of 'It's My Life' by Bon Jovi, AJ couldn't hide the grin on her face.

If she'd said eight, she knew Reg would have pushed for six or seven. But she could handle eight in the morning.

13

Dotty sat at the little table in her room wearing her dressing gown and a towel wrapped around her wet hair. She'd been staring at the piece of paper with pen in hand for more than fifteen minutes, unable to decide how to start the letter. *Dear Sandy? Was that too informal?* But Dear Flying Officer Richard Lovell sounded like an official government notice. Dotty hated moments like this. Flying a plane, she had an uncanny knack of knowing what to do, or at least had a system for processing, deciding, and taking action. Skills built upon training, repetition, and her natural ability. But when it came to social situations with the opposite sex, none of the physics and aerodynamics applied, and she felt like a broken machine constantly in freefall.

Finally, in frustration she threw all caution to the wind, forced her hand to the parchment, and began the letter.

Dear Sandy,

I hope you don't mind me writing, and I hope even more that you're safe and well. I am sorry I had to leave Tangmere in such a hurry today, and I wish I'd delayed my return. I would be delighted to have dinner with you.

Unfortunately, I won't be ferrying any planes to Tangmere in the next week or so, as I'm being sent away for training on advanced twin-engined aircraft. Which I'm excited about, but disappointed I shan't be seeing you again sooner. Perhaps we could have dinner when the next opportunity arises?

I hope you don't think I'm being too forward, and if I've completely got the wrong end of the stick about all this, please forgive me and let me know. You have far bigger things to worry about than a silly girl bothering you.

Yours sincerely,

Dotty Parker

She reread the letter three times and cringed at her words on each occasion. Dotty addressed an envelope while she tried to reconfigure every sentence in her head. She got as far as placing a fresh piece of paper in front of her, but in the end, folded the letter she'd written and stuffed it into the envelope. Too tired to torture herself over her lack of poetic and romantic proficiency, she changed into her nightgown and settled into her single bed.

Her alarm ringing woke Dotty from a deep sleep she'd finally managed after tossing and turning most of the night, wracked with nightmares of burning aeroplanes. Vera placed a cup of tea and a slice of toast and jam in front of her when she made it downstairs, still somewhat in a daze.

"Need me to post that for you?" her landlady asked, pointing to the letter Dotty had brought down with her.

"No, that's alright," Dotty replied, and stared at the envelope addressed to the Tangmere airfield. After a few more moments of indecision, she slid the letter across the kitchen table. "Actually, that would be lovely. Thank you."

Vera whisked the envelope away, looking at the recipient before dropping it into her handbag.

"Found yourself a young man, have you?"

Dotty felt her cheeks glow. "Just a friend. A penpal. Perhaps," she bumbled.

But releasing the letter into the world didn't feel as completely terrifying as Dotty had expected. There was some element of relief, and a dangerously elevated amount of hope attached to the correspondence.

High cloud and brief appearances of the elusive sun meant White Waltham was abuzz with activity when Dotty arrived. On one hand, she felt proud of the fact that she'd been selected for the next step in her training, but on the other rested a sense of exclusion as the ATA pilots loaded into taxi aircraft.

"Time to get you certified on advanced twin-engined aircraft, Dotty," Commander Gower said, getting straight to the point. "Report to Flight Captain Ashcroft at Advanced Flying Training School here at White Waltham."

"Yes ma'am, thank you," Dotty replied.

Gower looked at her with an expression that softened. "My gut tells me you're one of the good ones, Dotty, but I'll be honest with you, not everyone feels the same way. Between the Miles Master business this week and your risky flight into Tangmere yesterday, I had to personally vouch for you."

Dotty was stunned. "Risky flight, ma'am?"

"You were the only one who made it to the southern coast yesterday. Two others turned around, saying it was unsafe."

"The squadrons weren't grounded at Tangmere, ma'am," Dotty replied defiantly. "I never lost visual and never flew in or above the cloud, ma'am. They should know where to slip between the hills."

The Commander held up a hand. "All things I pointed out, Dotty. You're preaching to the choir. But we're all still stinging from the loss of Amy Johnson last year. Some, like me, by the loss of a friend and a marvellous pilot. Some from the negative press the incident brought on the ATA and the choice to allow female pilots."

"More men have pranged planes than women, ma'am," Dotty quickly pointed out.

"I know the numbers better than anyone, Dotty, but I'm not the one stopping our girls flying more planes."

"Of course not, ma'am. I'm sorry."

"Look, Dotty, you're a great pilot and Ashcroft's a tough but fair man from what I've seen," Gower explained. "Do as he says, learn all you can, and you'll get your Class 4 rating and another champion in your corner."

"I'll do my best, ma'am," Dotty replied.

"I'm confident you will," Commander Gower said, before dismissing Dotty to begin her training.

Dotty had hoped for another female pilot in the training group, but she was alone amid four male pilots of varying ages and experience. Flight Captain Ashcroft, a seasoned pilot by wartime standards of thirty-one years of age, greeted them all with equal scepticism while he explained the plan for the week. They'd be flying a Bristol Blenheim light bomber which had been introduced before the war and used heavily over the first few years until being superseded by heavy bombers such as the Avro Lancaster. The Blenheim was slow, heavy, and produced some of the worst losses per operation for the RAF, but made an adequate training aircraft.

Usually crewed by three personnel, the Blenheim at White Waltham had a jump seat placed behind and offset from the pilot. It did not have co-pilot controls, so short of dragging the student from the seat, the instructor had to rely on verbal commands and the student's ability to keep them safe. A navigator's seat in the nose and the gun turret on the top of the fuselage halfway to the tail were the only other spaces for passengers, neither of whom could see what the pilot was doing.

"Kill me, and you will not pass this rating," Ashcroft told the class without cracking as much as a grin.

Dotty was relieved not to be chosen first when it came to their first flight in the twin-engined plane. Ashcroft wisely chose the most senior flyer amongst them, but made Dotty come along in the navigator's seat. She was given a headset and found listening in over the intercom to be useful information, but sitting in the mostly clear Perspex nose felt terrifyingly exposed even without Messerschmitts shooting at her.

Training consisted of a mixture of long sessions in the classroom followed by more pleasurable time flying the Blenheim. The days rolled by without incident apart from one scary moment when Dotty was riding along in the nose once again. One of the male pilots confused the emergency fuel cut-off for the pitch control, which were both located very close together behind the pilot's head. If Ashcroft hadn't spotted the mistake immediately and corrected the controls, the momentary engine cut and subsequent dive would have been unrecoverable.

From the clear nose of the plane, plummeting at an alarming speed out of control towards the earth was an experience she didn't care to repeat. Her own fingers became very familiar with the two controls after that. That was not a mistake she'd be making.

Gower had been right: Ashcroft was tough but fair. Towards the end of the week, without saying as much, he focused more on those who needed the extra time, and demanded excellence from all five pilots. They all passed, and the Flight Captain looked Dotty square in the eyes when he shook her hand and told her she was now rated to fly advanced twin-engined aircraft.

Dotty was proud of herself, but glad when the week was over. She always found flying a new type of aeroplane exciting and rewarding, testing her skills, but having a rating on the line and under critical scrutiny at every moment was exhausting. Regardless, she walked through the front door of her billet with a Class 4 rating, which meant she could fly almost everything the ATA ferried except for heavy bombers and seaplanes. She was also promoted to the rank of Pilot First Officer.

"Hello, dear," Vera greeted her, wiping her hands on her apron as she appraised the chicken meat on the carving block.

"Did you pass your testing?" Rosie asked excitedly, hurrying down the stairs.

"I did," Dotty replied with a feeling of pride puffing her chest out a little.

"Now, what is it they'll let you fly after you passed this training test?" Vera asked. "I can't keep it all straight."

"Advanced twin-engined aircraft," Dotty explained. "Like the Blenheim we flew this week, but others such as a Beaufort or a Wellington."

"I don't know all those names, but I'm sure I'd be terrified if they put me in any of them," Vera commented, chopping the chicken into portions.

Rosie drilled Dotty with questions during dinner while Stan didn't say a word and Vera oohed and aahed occasionally.

"Oh, Dotty, I almost forgot," Vera said, carrying the dishes to the kitchen. "A letter came for you today. I'd say it's from your *penpal* in Sussex."

Ignoring her landlady's cheeky implication, Dotty raced from the dining room to the little table in the front hall where post and keys tendered to be left. She couldn't believe she'd walked past the letter and that Vera had taken this long to tell her about it.

"Thank you for dinner. I'll be back down to help with the washing up," Dotty called out as she took the stairs two at a time.

Closing her bedroom door, she sat down in the desk chair and turned the envelope over in her hands. It was addressed to Miss Dorothy Parker and the postmark was from Chichester. Dotty's heart raced. Opening the letter could change her life. One way or another. Against her wishes and willpower, she'd allowed herself to dream about a romance with Sandy, and all that could bring to her future. Leaving the letter unopened left that hope alive. Breathing, blossoming, and full of joy. Dotty didn't want those feelings, which had been stirring and causing her heart to beat faster all week, to end.

But, like pulling a splinter from a fingertip, it was surely better to tear into the envelope and know?

Dotty remained motionless except for the envelope rocking back and forth in her grasp, staring at Sandy's handwriting on the address as though the slant of the words could give her a clue. With all the pain, misery, and gloom surrounding the war, clinging to a ray of optimistic bliss didn't seem so bad. But all things must come to an end at some point, and she'd need to tell Marjorie McKinven in the morning whether to send her to Sussex when possible or avoid Tangmere as though it were Germany itself.

With her hands shaking, Dotty ripped the envelope open and took out the single sheet of paper, holding her breath.

Dear Dotty,

I was so pleased to receive your correspondence. Thank you for taking the time to write to me. I hope your training is going well. You seem like you're a topping pilot, so I'm sure it is.

My dinner invitation still stands for whenever you're next in Sussex. We are not blessed with a wide variety of choices near Tangmere, but I'd be overjoyed to eat sandwiches from a picnic basket as long I'm in your company.

Please write again soon if you're unable to visit.

Sincerely yours,

Sandy

Dotty jumped up from the chair, spilling it over backwards, and danced around her tiny bedroom, reading the letter over and over.

"Everything alright up there?" Vera called from downstairs.

"Yes, yes," Dotty replied, opening the door enough to poke her head out. "Quite alright, thank you."

Vera broke into a wide smile. An expression Dotty had never

seen her landlady manage in the whole time she'd been staying with the Ramsays. For a few seconds, the two women shared a moment of delight where they both forgot about the chaos surrounding their lives. Then Vera turned back to her kitchen and her dread about her son's wellbeing, and Dotty went back inside her room.

Where no war could wipe the smile from her face.

14

With the seas settled back to normal after the storm and a following breeze from the north-east, the ride out to Twelve Mile Bank took less than an hour at a comfortable speed. AJ used her GPS waypoint to quickly find the containers, which appeared on the screen like building blocks in shades of yellow and green.

"Surface current doesn't seem too bad," AJ commented after taking the Newton out of gear and watching the ocean floor below them on the screen.

The boat slowly moved south-west along the edge of the bank.

"What's the chances the current will be the same down there?" Reg asked with a grin, looking over the side at the deep blue water.

"Pretty low," AJ scoffed. "But you never know. We'll hang a weighted line first and take a look."

Thomas nodded and headed for the steps. "How deep, boss?"

"Thirty," AJ replied, glancing over her shoulder. "And use a five-pounder."

"Got it," Thomas replied.

His tall, lean figure disappeared down the ladder.

"Usually runs south or south-west," Reg commented, watching

the image of the container slide from the screen as *Hazel's Odyssey* was pulled away from the location.

"I'll hop in and take a quick look at the hanging weight," AJ said, dropping the Newton in gear and idling back over the dive site. "Then we'll see how far over you need to drop me so I drift to a container. I'll put a line on whichever of the two shallower ones is the easiest to reach."

Reg scowled at her.

"What?" she asked.

"Why don't we both go?"

"Because that's a waste of gas, and the fills are expensive," AJ replied. "And no reason for two of us to get the nitrogen loading. All I'm going to do is tie the line to one of those thingies in the top corner of the container."

"Corner casting."

"I'm sorry?" she questioned.

"Those blocks on the corners with the holes in them are called corner castings. They're used to align the containers when they're being stacked."

"As I said, all I'm doing is tying us into a corner casting."

"So how come you're tying in the line?" Reg persisted. "It's your boat. You drive and I'll dive."

"You're absolutely right," AJ declared. "It's my boat and I'm captain; therefore I'm calling the shots."

"Flip a coin and sort it out, bosses!" Thomas shouted up from the deck. "Lines in da water."

"Fine," Reg grunted, digging a coin out of his pocket.

"Fine," AJ grinned, waiting.

Reg flipped the coin, but missed catching it, and they both stepped back to let it fall unimpeded. AJ leaned over.

"It's heads!"

Reg picked it up. "Which would be great if you'd called heads, but as you didn't call anything, you forfeit."

"Bollocks! I would have called heads."

"I would have bought Apple stock in 2008 if I was smarter, but I didn't, just like you didn't call heads," Reg grinned. "Forfeit."

"Flip again and I'm calling heads," AJ urged.

Reg laughed, but flipped the coin in the air and caught it this time. He slapped it down on the back of his beefy hand.

"Heads!" AJ yelped in glee. "Steer the boat, old man, I'm going diving."

"Fine, but don't bugger it up. I don't feel like driving all over the place trying to find you when you get swept off the bank."

AJ stuck her tongue out at Reg as she descended the ladder.

While Reg idled farther north-west with the depth on the screen dropping away to 400 feet, AJ geared up. She grabbed her Dive Rite backplate with the smaller recreational wing and a single tank which she used every day for guiding her customers. A standard 32% nitrox fill would work fine for what she hoped to be a short stay at 120 feet to handle the line, keeping well out of deco. She'd switch to her twin-tank rig for the exploration dives. AJ double-checked the gas setting in her Shearwater Perdix wrist-mounted computer, and did the same with the Teric she wore on her right wrist for backup.

"Ready!" she called out as she waddled towards the stern with fins in hand.

She heard the Newton clunk out of gear, but the engines still idled. She gazed around at the Caribbean Sea, stretching to the horizon in every direction. A handful of Grand Cayman's tallest buildings were just visible to the east. It was an eerie feeling knowing they were alone, a long way from anywhere.

"Clear to dive!" Reg shouted from the fly-bridge.

AJ moved to the corner of the swim platform, donned her fins, and pulled her mask in place. Thomas handed her the weight on the end of line which was tied to a forward cleat so it didn't get caught in the props while they'd been idling.

"Thank you," she said, popped the regulator in her mouth, then took a diver's giant stride off the port side into the Caribbean Sea.

With gas in her wing she bobbed on the surface with the line taut in her hand. She quickly dumped the gas and began descending into the vast ocean surrounding her in all directions. Everywhere she looked was dark blue. Except above. *Hazel's Odyssey* was her only contact with civilisation.

It took a while to drop to 25 feet as everything was moving. The boat was drifting with the surface swells, and a slight current seemed to be following the same direction underwater. But it was stronger than the surface, as the line wouldn't hang straight down; it was leading the boat, hence her depth being five feet short of the length of the line. She knew that could easily change again when they went down to the bank. AJ let go of the weight and drifted with it next to her for a minute. Below her, the dark blue gradually darkened and took on a greenish hue. They'd drifted over the bank.

Slowly ascending, AJ surfaced behind the boat where Thomas had dropped the aluminium ladder. She removed her fins then stood on the bottom step, handing the fins to Thomas and taking her reg out.

"Bit stronger than up here, but at thirty it's the same direction," she called up to Reg.

He gave her an okay hand signal and waited while Thomas hauled the weighted line in. AJ stepped up the rest of the way, then swung the ladder up, fastening it in place.

"Good, big boss," Thomas shouted once the weight was back aboard.

"Moving," Reg announced and returned to the helm.

AJ heard the clunk of the transmissions going in gear, and hung on tightly to the ladder rails. Reg motored a hundred yards in a north-west direction while AJ slipped her fins back on, and Thomas prepared a line for her to take down.

"Dis is 160 feet long, boss," he told her. "Got a loop both ends."

"That should work," AJ replied, taking the coiled up line and wedging it into the waistband of her harness.

Using a stainless-steel carabiner, she hooked one loop to a D-ring on her shoulder strap, just in case the line slipped out. The boat clunked out of gear.

"Clear to dive," came Reg's booming voice, and AJ stepped back into the water.

Beyond kicking with her fins, she was now at the mercy of the current, and there was no time to waste. She descended, with her eyes flicking between her Perdix and the deep blue ahead. Occasionally, AJ turned to check where the boat was, just to keep herself orientated. Otherwise, there was nothing to do until she picked up visual references on the bank.

At 60 feet, the hue down and ahead changed as it had before. At 70 feet, she could make out the slope of the side of Twelve Mile Bank, and at 80 feet she knew something was wrong. Nowhere in her field of vision was a shipping container. Levelling off at 90 feet, the top of the bank was now passing by 30 feet below her, and she could make out coral bommies, schools of fish and even a nurse shark hugging the sea floor. AJ made a quick 360-degree turn, but there was nothing that resembled a container. She immediately began ascending.

The current at depth was far stronger than at the surface and she was covering a lot of ground in a hurry. Taking out a reel, she clipped on her SMB, or safety marker buoy, and blew air from her wing's dump valve into the bright orange tube, making sure to only partially fill it. She let the reel begin spinning in her hand, unravelling as the SMB shot up towards the surface. Because she'd traded gas in her wing to gas in the SMB, which she still held, AJ had traded buoyancy between the two mediums, keeping her ascent under control.

At 60 feet, she looked up to see the SMB on the surface and began winding the reel in as she continued up. The SMB was no longer creating buoyancy, but after a few fin kicks, she was back to bleeding gas from her wing as the surrounding water pressure lessened. By the time she reached 40 feet, AJ could no longer make out details on the bank below, and all she could see all around her was deep blue once more. If Reg and Thomas didn't see her SMB, bobbing in the two-foot swells, she'd be lost at sea, and as she scanned the surface as far as she could see, there was no sign of the Newton's hull.

"Should have called tails," she muttered into her regulator.

Her dive had been very short, but 90 feet was deep, and although she was nowhere near close to requiring a decompression stop, good practice was to always perform a safety stop at 15 feet for three minutes. This not only allowed more nitrogen to be processed by the body, it also gave all the body's air pockets time to equalise properly to the lower pressure. The downside in her current predicament was it would be three more minutes until she was on the surface. Potentially, three more minutes away from where Reg and Thomas expected her to be.

AJ levelled off at 15 feet with the SMB tugging and slackening on her reel line as the swells rolled through. She checked her Perdix to see the countdown ticking away painfully slowly. Just as she contemplated surfacing, figuring *found and a longer surface interval before diving again* was better than *lost and never diving again*, she heard the drone of the Newton's engines, and the white hull came into view.

The next two minutes crawled by, until AJ finally surfaced and grabbed the ladder. Thomas took her SMB and fins, so she could climb aboard.

"What did I tell you?" Reg growled, standing on the deck with his hands on his hips.

AJ spat out her reg and lifted her mask. "Fine job dropping me nowhere near the bloody containers, mate!"

Reg grinned. "Did you see them?"

"Nope," AJ laughed. "I was off like a rocket as soon as I dropped below about 60 feet. Which way did I drift? South?"

"Yup," Reg confirmed. "We were tickling our way south-west, then Thomas spotted your SMB due south. Lucky he did. It was at least 200 yards from where we'd drifted to."

AJ grinned at Thomas. "Thanks. Maybe I should tip you after all."

Thomas laughed. "Maybe so, boss. Big boss here offered me a

raise to come work for him if I forgot I seen dat SMB, but I told him you threatened to give me a big old tip for dis trip."

AJ dropped her jaw. "The cheek of him!"

"To be fair," Reg said, as AJ dropped her kit in a rack, "it was more about scoring the boat, but I didn't think to offer him halves on it until we found you."

"I would've taken dat deal," Thomas said with a serious expression.

"I'm never choosing heads again," AJ muttered as the other two couldn't keep from laughing.

15

It was a good job Dotty wasn't keen on avoiding Tangmere as Marjorie McKinven had been true to her word and scheduled Dotty for a flight south on her first day back in the ferry pool. High cloud and clear blue skies meant every pilot was assigned somewhere, with planes being moved around the country. The mood was buoyant in the Anson taxi flight, as in general, the ATA pilots loved their work. Serving their country and getting to fly the latest aircraft with no one shooting at them wasn't a bad way to spend the war.

Dotty was the last to be dropped off at RAF Newmarket, and it was late morning by the time she walked to the Westland Lysander she'd been assigned to deliver. Suffolk to Sussex could be just over one hundred miles if she could fly straight there. But the direct route meant flying over London and risking being shot at by friendly anti-aircraft guns as well as dodging barrage balloons. Dotty would happily add fifteen miles to the trip and avoid such risks. Going the east side of the capital put her closer to the coast, the Thames estuary, and the docks, so she'd prefer to fly west where she'd be over more familiar territory near Maidenhead.

The plane was painted matte black instead of the usual brown and green camouflage of the RAF.

"Ready to go?" she asked the mechanic who had the cowling off the 890 hp Bristol Mercury XII radial piston engine.

"Bit of a hold-up, I'm afraid," the man replied, giving her the seemingly obligatory look over and eyebrow raise. "Oil leak."

Dotty looked at her watch. It was already close to midday.

"Take long to patch up?" she asked.

"Trying to find a fitting we could use now, but I don't know that we can even get to it without pulling the engine out," the mechanic replied.

"Oh, that doesn't sound good."

"I'd say get yourself a bit of lunch then come back and see how we're doing, love."

Dotty nodded and walked towards the airfield office in search of somewhere to leave her gear for a while. She felt deflated. Her nervous anticipation had been building during the taxi ride, which had felt like it would never end as they dropped pilots all over the place before landing at the little base at RAF Newmarket. Now she was on an indefinite delay.

"You the ferry pilot?" a man asked as she opened the office door.

Dotty noticed the sergeant stripes on the arm of his coveralls and his field service cap was tilted at an angle on his head. Oil and dirt smeared his cheeks.

"Yes. Here for the Lysander," Dotty confirmed.

A young WAAF sat behind a desk with the phone to her ear. She had a pained expression on her face.

"Wing commander down at Tangmere is up my arse over the bloody thing," the sergeant ranted. "'Scuse my language. Apparently its needed for an operation this evening. Like I can control when the bloody oil fitting decides to leak. 'Scuse my language, miss," he added, and turned from Dotty to the secretary. "And miss."

"I've met Wing Commander Harrington, Sergeant," Dotty sympathised. "He doesn't strike me as a patient man."

The sergeant scoffed. "Can say that again. He certainly doesn't have any sympathy for how bloody hard it is to find a British Standard Fine thread oil fitting in the middle of Suffolk at the drop of a hat. Couldn't be Whitworth like everything else, could it?"

Dotty had no clue what the man was babbling about but she nodded as though she did.

"Could I drop my things here while I get a spot of lunch and leave you chaps to get on with it?"

The sergeant waved a hand around the office. "Anywhere is fine, but you'll want a ride to the pub, girl. There's bugger all close by."

"You're excused," Dotty said with a smile before the harassed sergeant had time to apologise. "And don't worry, I'll sort something out. We're used to finding our way around places."

Placing her helmet, parachute and bag on a chair, Dotty walked outside the front door and looked around. Ferry pilots were often left to their own devices at airfields, which tended to be in out of the way spots. There were very few advantages to being a female pilot, but one was that it was usually possible to find an obliging man somewhere to give her a lift.

Lunch, sitting outside a delightful pub which had meagre but palatable food, soon passed by, and so did the afternoon. And into the evening. With everyone glancing at their watches at regular intervals, the mechanics grunted, moaned, and swore at the Lysander as more pieces seemed to be removed than bolted back together. Dotty was asleep on the grass with her head on her parachute when the sound of the Bristol engine startled her awake.

The sergeant and the other mechanic were pointing, looking, and waving back and forth to each other, any chance of speaking drowned out by the noisy engine. Dotty couldn't tell if their gesticulations were celebrating success or commiserating disaster. But when they shut the engine down and began reaffixing the cowling, she took it as good news.

It was now 7:15pm. Only a month from the longest day, sunset would be around 9:30pm so daylight wasn't an issue, and if the matte black paint scheme was a clue, the Lysander was needed for a night mission over occupied France. As Dotty climbed into the front seat of the cockpit, the sergeant marched across the field from the office.

"I talked to Wing Commander Harrington," he called up to Dotty, who had the side window slid open. "He says he doesn't care what the ATA rules are, you'd better fly as fast as the plane will go or he'll have you scrubbing floors of the barracks from now until the end of the war."

Dotty scoffed. "Which would be sooner than Hitler thinks if we had a few thousand Harringtons to drop on the French coast. They'd have the Hun running in all directions."

Her cheeks glowed red as she realised what she'd just said about a senior RAF officer, but the sergeant laughed.

"Too, bloody right. If you'll 'scuse my language."

"Clear?" Dotty called out, trying to settle the nerves in her stomach.

"Clear," the sergeant shouted back. "Good luck, girl."

Dotty wasted no time. The engine was warm and the gauges all looked good, so she taxied across the field and opened up the throttle as soon as she turned onto the grass runway. She slid the side window closed and after a few moments the Lysander with its unique fully automatic wing slats lifted off the ground and Dotty banked south before she'd even cleared the hedgerow surrounding the field.

By the standards of the modern fighters, the Lysander was a slow beast with its non-retractable landing gear and larger frontal area, but Dotty soon had it humming along at its maximum 200 mph. Her next dilemma was whether to risk flying over London or taking the longer route and skirting the city's hazards. She could picture Harrington standing outside the dispersal hut, tapping a foot impatiently while he eyed the skies.

The time for a final decision came quickly at the plane's top speed, and Dotty stayed on course, knowing she'd at least keep west of the city centre by a few miles. Using Wembley Stadium as a waypoint, she breathed a sigh of relief when Twickenham Stadium passed by under her port side and she was leaving the suburbs of London. Until a black puff exploded ahead of the Lysander.

It took Dotty a moment to realise it was anti-aircraft fire, the British equivalent to the Germans' flak which she could now see bursting all around her. The gunner had well-timed the fuses of the shrapnel shells, estimating her altitude, which she swiftly needed to change. Dotty pulled back on the yoke while banking to starboard, wishing the Lysander had more power. The tinging sound of metal hitting the canopy came from behind her head and she gritted her teeth.

Maybe it was the matte black paint, or perhaps a trigger-happy gunner, but finally someone must have told the man that he was shooting at one of his own as the flak stopped as quickly as it had begun. Dotty turned back on course and spent the next few minutes swearing like a sailor as her heartbeat gradually returned to normal.

Clearing the South Downs, Tangmere soon came into view. Skipping the standard circling of the airfield, Dotty sat the Lysander down, dropping to the grass deep along the grass runway to save taxiing time. With a ground crewman waving his arms above his head, she brought the plane to a stop in front of the now familiar Hurricane squadron's dispersal hut. Wing Commander Harrington was already barking orders when she shut the engine down and slid the canopy back. Three men stood to one side, only one of them wearing a uniform. The other two wore dark-coloured civilian clothes with parachute packs at their feet.

Dotty dropped to the ground as the mechanics hurriedly topped off the fuel in the Lysander and checked her over.

"It's you again," Harrington muttered as though the thought uncontrollably fell out of his mouth. "Well get out of the way so the men can get on with it."

Dotty looked at the ground and began walking away, feeling her cheeks flush with a mixture of anger and humiliation.

"There's holes in this canopy, sir," a mechanic called down, standing in the rear seat of the Lysander. "Couple of pieces of metal stuck in the fuselage, too."

"What the bloody hell happened?" Harrington blasted, and Dotty stopped in her tracks.

"Anti-aircraft fire, sir," she replied.

"Our lot shot at you on the way here?" the man in what Dotty now noticed was an army uniform asked.

He was older than most of the pilots she was used to seeing outside the ATA.

"Near Twickenham," Dotty confirmed. "Gave me quite a scare."

"Lucky they didn't take your head off," the mechanic said with a whistle.

"Can it fly?" Harrington demanded.

"I flew it here, so I'd say so, yes," Dotty retorted and immediately wished she'd kept her mouth shut.

The mechanic stifled a laugh and Harrington whipped around in her direction, venom in his eyes.

"Your job was to have this aeroplane here this morning in tip-top condition which you've failed to do in every regard," he seethed. "Now get out of my sight."

Dotty couldn't breathe. She forced her feet forward until a hand on her arm stopped her.

"Thank you for getting our plane to us," the army officer said quietly.

Dotty looked up and the man gave her a nod. Next to him, the other two men, who were blackening their faces with boot polish, both gave her a brief nod as well. The officer released her arm.

"God speed and be safe," she whispered in return.

As Dotty walked away, she lifted her chin and held her head high. A tear finally escaped down her cheek, but instead of demoralised humiliation, her emotions were now driven by a sense of pride. While one man tried to beat her down, three more had lifted her up. And those three brave souls were the ones about to fly over enemy-held territory under the cover of darkness to perform a perilous and critical mission. Men who may well never return.

Dotty was exhaling a deep sigh of relief when she rounded the corner of the dispersal hut and ran straight into a pilot. Her notes and maps flew and she dropped her parachute to the ground.

"Rumour has it I'd run into you out here," Sandy said in amusement, "but I hadn't planned on being so literal about it."

Dotty had just swept through too many emotions in the past twenty minutes to stave off the one she now felt overwhelmingly consuming her. She threw her arms around the fighter pilot and kissed him on the lips.

16

It took an hour to map out a new plan, get together all the lines they needed, reset the boat's position, and gear up. Anticipating a longer dive during which they'd accomplish more than just tying in the first line, AJ switched to her Dive Rite backplate set up with double 80-cubic-foot tanks and a full-size higher lift wing. Reg donned exactly the same kit, and they both carried a 50-cubic-foot deco bottle with 50% nitrox.

"Ready, Thomas?" AJ called up to the fly-bridge.

She heard the Newton come out of gear, followed by Thomas's voice from above. "Good to go, boss."

AJ waddled unsteadily to the corner of the swim step with 100 pounds of equipment hanging from her 125-pound frame. Using the ladder rail as support, she slipped her fins on one foot at a time.

"Okay, eagle eyes, watch for the SMB. There'll either be a line or two divers attached to it."

"Got it, boss," Thomas shouted back. "Now hurry up or I'll need to reset the boat."

A loud splash from the opposite corner of the swim step let AJ know Reg was in the water, so she followed suit. Usually, they'd perform a final round of buddy checks on the surface, verifying their preparation one more time, but the current took that option away, requiring them to immediately descend.

Kicking towards each other, they made sure to stay in close contact as they quickly dropped, equalising their ears as they went. With the mass of the three full tanks and no gas in their wings, the pair fell swiftly through the water column, slowing their descent when they reached 90 feet. This time, the edge of the bank came into view along with one of the containers, which sat precariously perched near the drop-off.

Continuing to drop, they kicked towards the steel block, which looked to be the size of a house with the lens effect of their masks. Levelling off at 135 feet, AJ scooted around the lee side of the container, and began removing the first line from her waistband. Reg was yet to join her, but she had a good idea what he was up to. Finning to the top corner of the container, AJ peeked around the edge and immediately felt the tug of the current on her mask. Its full strength was clearly evident now she was stationary and mostly hidden from the effects. Reg clung to the lock mechanism, and AJ realised that the container was actually on its side.

Focusing on her task, she pushed the end of the line through the large holes in the corner casting, and began pulling the other end of the 160-foot line through the loop to secure it in place. Reg drifted around her then kicked to fall in behind. Once AJ had the line through the loop, she took out her SMB and clipped it to the loop at the opposite end. With a burst of gas from her backup regulator, she filled the orange tube about one quarter full, knowing the gas would expand on ascent as the water pressure lessened. Before it could drag her up with it, she released the SMB and watched it head for the surface with the line.

The original plan had been to secure the rope to the shallowest container, which sat south of their current position. In theory, its top corner would be at around 112 feet, which meant 160 feet of line had plenty of slack to handle the swells and drag from the current.

AJ held up her wrist level with the top of the steel, checked her Perdix, and noted the rope was now connected at 128 feet. Less ideal, but she figured it would work. Once Thomas saw the SMB, he'd switch it for a buoy, then secure *Hazel's Odyssey* to the loop, giving the boat a mooring and the divers an ascent line.

AJ turned and saw Reg had moved to the far end of the container, where he'd attached a second line. What came next was tricky. They planned to connect the three containers with lines, but one was somewhere below them on the slope, and the other was down current. Tackling one each would be the most efficient way to proceed, but would result in them being separated if something went wrong. For which there remained a high probability. Reg looked over and put his index fingers from both hands together, signalling that they should stay together, then pointed towards the shallow container. AJ returned an okay sign and beckoned him her way.

As best she could tell, the current was running about 20 degrees farther west than a straight line between the containers. They needed to start as far east as they could and swim in an easterly direction while they drifted. Reg kicked her way, and AJ checked her computer. They'd been down for 11 minutes already. They'd planned on no longer than 30 for this dive, at a maximum depth of 130 feet. They'd already been deeper. Once Reg arrived, AJ nodded, and they set off.

With Reg carrying the line, he was effectively tethered to the first container, so he led the way, angling himself east and finning as the current pulled him south-south-west. AJ fell in behind, kicking in the same way, ready to grab hold of Reg if anything went awry so she'd remain tethered too. It was as though they were flying in the ripping current. It was all about to happen very quickly.

Their first problem approached almost immediately. A large bommie lay in their way, and a choice had to be made. If they went around it to the east, the line would likely be pulled against the coral once they made the second container. West meant surrendering a chunk of hard-earned distance offsetting the angle of current. They could easily miss container two. Over meant more exposure to the current, but AJ considered it to be the best option. Reg must have come to the same conclusion as he rose when they approached the bommie and drifted a few feet clear of the top.

AJ looked down at the myriad of life occupying the outcrop of reef as they raced by. Colourful juveniles of all kinds of species darted under coral shelves and a chain moray eel followed the diver's movements from a crevice, sensing their presence. In the blink of an eye, the bustling scene was behind her, and Reg quickly dropped deeper in the lee of the bommie, where their drift slowed for a short while. AJ kicked hard, taking advantage of the brief respite and clawing back some of the ground they'd lost. Looking over her right shoulder, she could see the container looming ahead and was sure it wasn't enough.

They were about to miss container two and be forced to haul themselves back to the first container. If they could both hang on to the line. Reg knew it too, as he was kicking hard with long, sweeping leg movements, maximising the power of the dive fins. AJ watched him reach out. His fingertips brushed the end of the steel container, rubbing along the sheet metal until they fell upon the vertical locking bar. It was mere inches out of AJ's reach, and just when she thought they were being swept away, she crashed into Reg with a clank of tanks.

She heard his disgruntled snarl on impact, but somehow the big man managed to hold on with one hand, and AJ grappled hold of some part of Reg's harness. The pair hung like waving flags off the end of the container, and AJ knew there was no way Reg would be able to keep them both in place for long. She clawed her way forward along the top of his tanks, dragging her deco bottle along with bangs and scrapes of metal until she too could grab one of the bars.

From there, she moved to her right and gripped the corner casting, before pulling herself as far forward as possible. With a couple of swift fin kicks, she was able to scoot into the lee of the container where she sucked down a few hard breaths and thanked their good luck. If that container had fallen to the sea floor the other way around, they wouldn't have had anything to grab hold of.

A moment later, Reg joined her. The look in his eyes was enough to let her know the grief she had coming once they were topside, and AJ laughed into her regulator. In response, Reg handed her the rest of the line he'd been carrying.

AJ checked her Perdix. They'd been down for thirteen minutes. Reg poked his head around the corner to read the serial number on the container and clip the seal, and AJ rose up to the top corner, feeding the end of the line through the holes. She tugged on the line and watched the excess stir up sand from the sea floor between herself and container one. As the rope became taut, it lifted off the bottom, and AJ looped it through the holes one more time and tied it off, creating a lifeline between the two. It missed the bommie by at least ten feet so she was glad they'd not let it damage any of the coral.

She checked on Reg, who'd repositioned himself at the end of the container, hanging on again with his left hand while he fumbled with the combination padlock with the other. After a minute, the lock was in his harness pocket, and he reached up to hold the line AJ had just secured. He pointed to container one, indicating they needed to return.

"No kidding," she garbled into her regulator.

As their line to the surface was attached to the first container, they didn't have much choice. She held up an okay sign and waved for him to go first. Hauling themselves hand over hand along the rope at over 100 feet down into the raging current was strenuous and slow going. When they reached their starting spot, AJ noted twenty-one minutes of bottom time. Their computers would calculate exactly where they stood based on the time they'd spent at each depth, but she was still aiming to be leaving the bottom at thirty minutes, or a little earlier due to the extra depth they'd been to.

Reg tugged on AJ's fin and she turned around. He pointed to

the container, then patted himself on the chest. This container was his, which meant the other two contained the tyres. He pointed to the container again then pantomimed opening the doors. AJ quickly thought it through. Working at the doors would put them below 130 feet again so they should certainly shorten their bottom time if they planned to make another dive today. She held up five fingers then pointed to the surface. Reg checked his own computer, then held up six fingers. AJ returned an okay sign. It wasn't often that AJ was more conservative than Reg, but it did happen occasionally. She agreed six minutes would be fine.

The next problem was how to work on a container, tipped on its side, exposed to hefty current. But apparently, Reg had already given it some thought. He had a third line with him that they'd brought along to connect the final container. But that was a project for another dive. He took the line, dropped down to the sand, and threaded it through the corner casting, and secured it by threading the length through its own loop as they'd done before. It took several minutes.

Grabbing the lowest locking bar, Reg then hauled himself into the current. AJ peeked around the corner and watched as he made it to what was actually the top right corner of the tipped-over container but had now become the lowest point. Precariously hanging on to the locking bar with his left hand, he poked the end of the line through the holes, then reached back with the end loop in his hand. AJ figured out what he needed and slipped around the corner, holding on tightly to the locking bar. She took the end from him then slid back behind the lee of the container.

By the time Reg rejoined her, she showed 26 minutes of bottom time and they were now working at 135 feet again. She knew they had plenty of gas to meet the increased decompression obligation they would be accruing, but her concern was more about their next dive, which in theory would need to be deeper to the third container. But she trusted Reg and knew all the same thoughts and concerns would be going through his head.

A shadow moved over them and AJ looked up at the underbelly

of a seven-foot reef shark passing overhead. He circled back, no doubt curious about the noisy bubble-spewing creatures invading his world. His presence made AJ remember her GoPro underwater camera and she quickly pulled it from her harness pocket. Ignoring the shark, she filmed container one before turning and filming number two in the distance across the bank. When she tried to line up to shoot down the slope towards the third container, she caught Reg's eye. He'd threaded the line through his harness and now pointed around the corner. AJ returned an okay signal.

Pulling himself along the locking bar once more, he tugged more line through the D-ring on his harness until he reached the middle of the doors. He then secured the line so he was tethered like a spaceman to his craft. Held by the line, he had two free hands to work on opening the doors.

AJ realised he'd removed the padlock earlier, as he slid the handle retainer aside, pulled the handle away from the door, rotating the cams on either end, and opened the door. It swung down like a ramp beneath his legs, and several cardboard boxes, already soaked through and falling apart, tumbled out, dumping their contents down the slope.

Groaning into her regulator, AJ resisted the urge to dive deeper and begin retrieving the goods, which mostly appeared to be smaller pictures in frames, ornaments, and small lamps. Reg took his dive torch and shone the beam inside. AJ waited to see what his next step would be, glancing at her Perdix while she had a moment. Twenty-seven minutes and forty-eight seconds. She banged on the side of the container and Reg looked over. AJ pointed her thumb towards the surface and Reg nodded, taking one more look inside the large steel box. As he began unfastening the line, AJ reached around the corner and touched his shoulder. When he turned, she handed him her GoPro. Taking the hint, Reg shone his torch inside once more, and hit record.

Once he was done, Reg lifted the door closed, latched it, dropped the tether and the two of them manhandled their way up the end of the tipped-over container to the buoy line. Swiftly ascending the rope hand over hand while their bodies waved in the current like drying laundry on a windy day, they began their decompression stops. It would be another twenty-five minutes before they cleared their bodies of enough excess nitrogen to surface.

17

According to Marjorie McKinven in the operations room at White Waltham, there stood a good chance that the Lysander would need ferrying somewhere the next morning, so Dotty was told to stay in Tangmere overnight. The WAAF secretary in the airfield office arranged a room at Tangmere Cottage across the road from the airfield guard shack as there weren't any pubs, inns, or hotels close by. Dotty was in a daze after her out-of-character greeting for Sandy, and was relieved for others to direct her as long as she could have dinner with the pilot.

He had taken her rambunctious swoon in his stride and told her he'd be happy if she'd always greet him that way. Dotty, of course, had immediately shrunk back into a red-cheeked ball of self-conscious embarrassment, scurrying away once he'd agreed to have dinner with her.

Knocking on the door, Dotty admired the home as the setting sun bathed the red bricks in soft hues. It was anything but a cottage, appearing more like a terrace of five homes with one front door. The door swung open revealing an elegant lady with a pair of English springer spaniels trying to wriggle past her.

"Come in dear, come in," the woman offered enthusiastically with an English upper-class accent.

She stepped back ushering the dogs with her and seemed to either be expecting Dotty or any and all stray pilots overnighting at Tangmere.

"I'm Anne and these two beasts are Rollo and Truffles," she said as Dotty stepped inside the home.

"Pilot First Officer Dotty Parker, ma'am," she replied, trying to keep back the smile from being able to announce her new rank.

"There'll be no ma'am or ladyship in Tangmere Cottage, my dear. Anne will suffice. Follow me and I'll show you to your room."

Dotty had to hurry to keep up as the woman strode down a hallway with the dogs in tow, their nails tip-tapping along the wood floor. The room was larger than Dotty was used to and the queen-sized bed enormous compared to the single size she'd grown up in at home and her billet provided.

"This is lovely. Thank you for letting me stay in your home," Dotty said, dropping her flying helmet, parachute and small overnight bag on the bed.

Anne laughed. "I'm not sure who the house actually belongs to, my dear, but I'm simply the temporary host while my husband is posted here."

The idea that Anne's surname might be Harrington burned like a hot coal through Dotty's mind.

"He's on duty this evening," Anne added. "Bath is down the hall, dear. Supper was a few hours ago, but I'll have our cook put something together for you. I understand a gentleman will be joining you?"

Dotty's heart skipped and she forgot about whether 'on duty' referred to Wing Commander Harrington, the uniformed officer by the Lysander, or perhaps someone she was yet to meet. "Yes, ma'am. I mean Anne. Sorry."

Anne smiled. "I'd offer you a quiet meal alone, but I doubt you'll be that lucky. Twenty minutes sound alright?"

Anne was gone and the door closed before Dotty had a chance

to answer, so with very little time and no choice in evening wear, she set about making herself presentable for her first date with the RAF fighter pilot. Who was waiting for her when she walked to the dining room twenty-five minutes later, having fought her wind-tussled hair into some sort of order beneath her dark blue cap, worn tilted to the side. But as Anne had forewarned, they were not alone. A group of pilots noisily joked, smoked, and drank across the room at a larger table. One of them whistled when Dotty walked in.

"Cut that out," Dotty heard Anne admonish from behind a small bar in the corner, and the men all laughed.

"You look lovely," Sandy greeted her, pulling out a chair at a table for two.

The other men fell away into background noise as Dotty sat and looked across the table at Sandy as he took his seat. He was tall but not awkwardly so, and lean but not skinny. His assured-ness stood in contrast to his youthful looks. She felt a strong desire to gently touch every freckle on his face. Which of course made her blush.

"What would you like to drink?" he asked.

"A lemonade or water would be fine, thank you," Dotty replied.

She suddenly felt childish, realising most young women on a date would be ordering wine or a fancy cocktail, but Dotty had never really partaken in alcohol. She detested the taste of beer, and wine seemed like an odd form of fruit juice you couldn't guzzle down to quench your thirst.

"I'll be right back," Sandy said, and disappeared towards the other end of the dining room where she'd noticed the small bar.

She could hear his fellow pilots ribbing Sandy, although Dotty couldn't make out exactly what they were saying, and all of a sudden she felt very alone and self-conscious, wishing he hadn't left.

"Try this, my dear," Anne said, arriving beside her and setting a glass down on the table. "It's a gin fizz."

"Oh my," Dotty muttered. "I'm not really much of a drinker."

Anne laughed. "Many of us were not until this war started. Give it a try, dear, it'll calm your nerves."

Dotty picked up the tall glass filled with pale yellow liquid with a white frothy head. She took a sip and was surprised by the carbonated tickle and the refreshing taste.

"That's rather nice," she said, taking another sip.

"Slow down, dear," Anne chuckled. "They can sneak up on you if you get too eager. We don't want calm nerves becoming wild abandon."

Dotty quickly put the glass down. She did feel a bit of a rush to the head. Anne turned to leave.

"May I ask you something?" Dotty said, and the woman turned back.

"Of course."

"Who is your husband?"

"Major Philip Kensington. Why do you ask?"

"I believe I met him this evening," Dotty replied, relieved it wasn't the prickly wing commander. "I flew a Lysander here from Suffolk."

Anne nodded, her expression tightening. "That was for Philip and his men. That particular plane had something or other they needed for tonight's operation."

Dotty realised the woman carried a wadded-up knot of fear and concern below her jolly and sparkling exterior. A burden she herself may also carry if her date with Flying Officer Sandy Lovell led to something more. As she hoped it would.

"He's a nice man," Dotty said, thinking of Major Kensington's kind gesture. "I'm sure I'll see him again tomorrow."

"I'm sure we will," Anne replied, forcing a wider smile as she hurried away.

"I see our host has chosen a drink for you," Sandy said as he sat down, bringing a glass of dark caramel-coloured liquid with him.

"Yes, and I don't usually drink, but I might be starting as this is lovely," Dotty babbled.

Sandy grinned. "Bottoms up," he toasted, holding up his glass.

Dotty clinked hers to his. "Bottoms up."

"To many more evenings like this," Sandy said before taking a sip.

"Many more," Dotty agreed.

She wished she had her double, full-width gold stripes for her epaulets, signifying her new rank, but otherwise she wasn't sure the night could be more perfect. They talked casually about how they began flying, sharing similar stories about their fathers being pilots, and when the cook brought their dinner, they continued chatting between bites as they slowly got to know more about each other.

By the time the plates were cleared, a few more men had joined the group by the bar, and the drunken singing began.

"Care for a walk?" Sandy asked.

"That would be nice," Dotty agreed, and they managed to slip away without being noticed.

"It's a beautiful night," she said, looking up at the full moon.

"That's why your delivery was so important," Sandy said, gazing up at the sky. "For navigation over the channel."

"Who are those men?" Dotty asked. "Major Kensington and the other two. Why is an army officer flying an RAF plane?"

"SOE," Sandy replied, lowering his voice in the still night as they sauntered down the lane by the airfield.

"SOE?"

"Special Operations Executive," Sandy clarified. "Officially, they don't exist. We're not supposed to know about it, but with them being based here at Tangmere, it's hard to keep them a secret. I figure it's better you know than ask questions about them when you leave. Mum's the word, you understand?"

"Of course, I'll never mention them," Dotty assured him with a nervous tingle running through her at the responsibility she now carried. "I dread to think of the awful risks those men are taking. The risks all of you take."

"You flew through anti-aircraft fire today," Sandy pointed out. "We're all taking risks."

"But that's hardly the same," Dotty scoffed. "One trigger-happy gunner having a quick go at me isn't anything like going up against the Hun."

"That trigger-happy idiot almost killed you," Sandy said, stopping and turning to Dotty. "It only takes one bullet or one piece of shrapnel, no matter who made it or fired it. I wish I could ring that silly bugger's neck."

Dotty felt a warm sensation well inside her chest. This man was willing to fight for her. Shy little Dorothy Parker.

"I don't know how you do it," she said, moving the topic away from her incident. "Tearing off into the sky knowing you'll be meeting men whose job it is to shoot at you."

They resumed their walk.

"It's what we must do," he replied. "Better than seeing swastikas flying from every flagpole in England, right?"

"True," she agreed, "and that's easy for me to say, but you have to actually do the fighting."

"I'd rather be up there," he said, eyeing the stars above them, "than in a muddy trench somewhere, or being torpedoed by a U-boat in the Atlantic."

"Is it thrilling?" she asked. "Or simply terrifying?"

Sandy didn't answer right away, and Dotty feared she'd crossed some line or become too inquisitive and personal.

"I'm sorry. That's an awful question. I shouldn't have pried."

"No. That's alright," he said quietly. "I'm thinking of how to describe it. Mostly, we all try not to think too much about how it feels. We talk about the techniques and strategies. The physics. How best to outmanoeuvre our opponent in a 109."

Dotty didn't say a word, allowing Sandy time to think.

"The hard part is when we're waiting on the ground," he began. "It's nervous anticipation, I suppose. I know what's coming and part of you wants it to not happen yet, and part of you wishes we could just get it over with. In the battle itself everything happens so fast you're too focused and absorbed to feel much of anything except determination. A few dots in the distance become Messerschmitts in the blink of an eye and you're twisting, rolling, and banking to outwit and outmanoeuvre one another.

"You're trying to be unpredictable while figuring out what he'll do next so you can get into a firing position. Meanwhile you pray your wingman is keeping your opponent's partner off your tail. Then it's all over and if you're still alive, you were partly skilled and partly lucky. And then you find out who was not so lucky."

Dotty brushed her hand against Sandy's and felt the warmth of his gentle grip as he took her hand in his.

"Make sure you keep it that way, Flying Officer Lovell," she said, already sensing his loss would devastate her. Especially now.

She knew so little about the man, but he was still perfect to her. Losing him now, before they'd spent enough time around each other to see the cracks and flaws, would be losing everything her imagination could build him into being. The unachievable ideal that another person can never truly live up to. An idol.

Sandy paused, and before she knew it, his hands were on her waist and he eased her to him. He leaned down and kissed her. Not the desperate peck she'd given him after they'd bumped into each other, but a long slow embrace with their lips firmly pressed together. Consumed by the warmth of his touch, Dotty felt their breath blending as one as his nose brushed the top of her cheek. Beneath the slightly disinfectant smell of carbolic soap, she detected the familiar and comforting odour of aircraft petrol, oil, and exhaust fumes.

For once in her life, despite another human's intense focus on nothing but her, Dotty wasn't blushing.

18

AJ and Thomas tied in *Hazel's Odyssey* while Reg finished up his call to the tyre importer, George Cook. After a brief discussion topside, they'd headed home instead of diving again, choosing to put plans in place for a return visit as soon as possible. With the current as strong as either had experienced before on Twelve Mile Bank, the odds of it improving were good, which would make their tasks exponentially easier.

"He's still keen and offering to help with costs," Reg announced, coming down the steps from the fly-bridge. "Let me see what Damon's up to."

AJ held up an okay sign but she had her doubts. Damon ran a flat barge with a crane in local waters moving items around the coast, building piers, and on one occasion, lowering a bronze statue into the ocean for an underwater installation. Which was where AJ had met Damon and his crane operator, Bash. She was certain the man would balk at running his barge out to the bank in the open ocean.

AJ picked up a pair of empty tanks by the valves, carrying one in each hand and hauling them off the boat. The daily tank-switching workout saved on a gym membership and kept her tattooed arms lean and toned. Thomas followed with another pair which they loaded into the rack in the back of her van.

"When we gonna have time to get back dere?" Thomas asked.

AJ paused and stared west across the ocean to where they'd been diving an hour before.

"We only have morning dives tomorrow," she replied. "Not ideal, going out in the afternoon, but we could."

"Be calmer in da morning, for sure," Thomas noted.

AJ nodded. "But this is the fourth or fifth time this group have booked with us. It's Craig, that nice fellow who owns a dive shop in California. You remember him?"

"Of course," Thomas replied. "Dey always a fun crowd."

"Yeah, and they're expecting us to guide them, so it wouldn't be right to put them on one of Reg's boats, even if he has one open."

"You need to stay shallow in da morning if you going back to da bank in da afternoon, boss," Thomas reminded her.

"You do too as you didn't get to dive this trip," AJ pointed out. "Let me text Nora and see if she's working tomorrow."

Thomas raised his eyebrows.

AJ paused before typing. "I don't think Nora has met this group, has she?"

Thomas thought for a moment. "No, I'm tinkin' of dat group from Texas."

"That bloke was a plonker," AJ said, typing a text on her phone.

"He was, and den some," Thomas agreed. "And she let him know it."

AJ laughed. "Yeah, she missed the tact lessons in school. Craig always brings solid divers, plus we'll be on the boat with them, so it'll be fine. Anyway, the guys will like the scenery having her along."

AJ's good friend, Nora Sommer, was more like a little sister. She worked as a constable for the Royal Cayman Islands Police Service, and her usual schedule was four long days on shift, followed by three days off. She was also trained as a divemaster. Thomas's concern was based on the young Norwegian's propensity for bluntness and honesty without any form of filter. Customer service tended to rank lower on Nora's priority list.

A red two-door Jeep Wrangler with the top down pulled into the car park, and after AJ hit send on her mobile, she waved to Pearl. Reg walked up the pier and hugged his wife as she climbed out of the Jeep.

"Is it all ruined?" Pearl asked, once he released his embrace.

"A bit jumbled up," Reg replied. "The container's on its side."

"We have video," AJ offered. "I'll get my laptop and we can watch it."

Pearl clapped her hands together. "I can't believe you're doing this for me. Thank you."

Reg threw AJ a glance which didn't look so enthusiastic. Their discussion on the ride back had centred around logistics of raising items in the current, so they hadn't discussed what Reg had seen when he opened the container door. From the look on his face, AJ guessed it wasn't promising and he may have wanted to keep quiet about the video. But it was too late now.

While AJ set up her laptop and pulled the memory card from the camera, Reg and Pearl sat on a pair of tall director's chairs outside the hut eating sandwiches she'd brought from home.

"It's hard not to look back and wish I hadn't spent more time with my mum over the past twenty years," Pearl said, then sipped from the bottle of Strongbow cider Reg had grabbed from the fridge.

"You spent every other Christmas with her, love," Reg said. "Plus a summer trip every year. We offered for her to come live with us enough times."

Pearl smiled. "What would she have done here? No, I understood Mum's life was in London, even though she cried about how much it had changed over all these years. I just wish I could have seen her more."

Reg patted her hand. "You spent the best part of the five years with her after your dad passed until we moved here, love. I don't know what she would have done without you."

"I suppose," Pearl sighed, shaking her head. "All those pictures of Mum and Dad are in there, Reg. Their wedding, holidays, family. Me growing up. The lot. They'll all be ruined, won't they?"

Reg forced a smile and didn't reply. He squeezed her hand instead.

"Okay, want to take a look?" AJ said, desperately wishing she hadn't brought up the film.

"Brilliant. Let's see what we're dealing with, then," Pearl replied, dropping from her chair and pretending to be excited.

AJ hit play and they gathered around the screen inside the hut, away from the bright sun. The shaky video was too dim to make anything out in the dark interior of the container until Reg's torch illuminated the scene. After the camera adjusted to the brightness, Pearl gasped.

The back of the container had been packed mainly with boxes which now lay crushed and crumpled against the metal side. Much of the water-sodden cardboard had released its contents, leaving the scene resembling a tornado-ravaged storage unit. AJ caught glimpses of furniture deeper inside, but they'd be wading through masses of debris before reaching anything.

"Bit of a mess then, isn't it?" Pearl said, and AJ could tell she was gritting her teeth and putting a brave face on what had to be emotionally devastating.

"We'll get it sorted, love," Reg assured her.

"I'm sure it looks much worse than it is, Pearl," AJ added. "You'll be eating off your mum's dining table in no time."

But AJ wasn't sure at all. The interior looked like a treacherous nightmare at 130 feet under water.

Ten minutes later, with Thomas taking *Hazel's Odyssey* out to its mooring, AJ walked towards her van with Reg.

"I forgot to ask. What did Damon say?"

Reg looked at his watch. "He's on a job in the harbour. I told him we'd drop by this afternoon."

"He said he's interested?" AJ asked in surprise.

"He was interested in talking to us."

"I'm really surprised," AJ said, opening the driver's door.

"Well," Reg grinned, pausing by the front of the van, "I didn't mention what it was we wanted to talk about."

AJ rolled her eyes.

"Better to speak face to face," Reg added. "That way I can win him over with my persuasive charm."

"Charming like a grizzly bear in a fish market," AJ retorted, as she pulled herself into the driver's seat of the van.

As a formality, and with the help of Brian Watler at the port authority, AJ and Reg registered the containers with Edwin Neville, the Receiver of Wrecks, who also happened to be the port manager. Although they weren't strictly considered a shipwreck, it was important to officially lay claim to the salvage so no one else could legally take anything from the containers.

Leaving the office, they spotted Damon's crane on the Hog Sty Bay side of the port and walked that way.

A middle-aged local man looked up and wiped sweat from his brow, pausing from his efforts of fixing a strap around a pallet of old engine blocks. "Tell me whatever you got needs doin' is better dan dis, Reg. I'm too old for dis nonsense," he said in a local accent, then broke into a wide smile.

Reg laughed and scratched his thick scraggly beard. "I reckon it will be, but I don't wanna hear you whining about being old, Damon. You're a spring chicken compared to me."

A younger man walked over from behind the crane controls at the helm station.

"Hi dere, Miss AJ," he said, briefly lifting a grubby baseball cap from his head in greeting. "Don't let him fool you none, Mr Moore. Ol' Damon like a pup on a T-bone when he get da mind to be."

Damon shook his head and waved a hand at his younger helper before turning back to Reg and AJ. "What is it you couldn't ask me about on da phone, Reg?"

Reg glanced at AJ but there was no way she was letting him off that easily. He'd touted his own charm, now she wanted to hear his best pitch.

"You remember my wife, Pearl, don't you?" Reg began, and Damon nodded with a wider smile.

"Your wife is hard to forget, if you don't mind me sayin'."

"That she is," Reg acknowledged. "Well, see that container ship over there?"

He pointed, but Damon didn't need to turn to know the large ship was over his shoulder.

"Yes, sir."

"Pearl had a container onboard filled with her recently deceased mother's possessions. During the storm, three containers were lost over the side, and one of them was hers."

"Dat's terrible. I'm sorry, man," Damon sympathised. "I heard about da containers going overboard, but didn't know it was yours." His brow creased. "But how dat have anyting to do wit me and my barge, Reg?"

"We found where the containers went down. That's how."

"Dey gotta be 6,000 feet under," Bash said. "How d'you find dem tings?"

"Got lucky," Reg replied. "They fell on Twelve Mile Bank."

Damon shook his head. "Nope."

"They did, mate," Reg assured him. "We dived them this morning."

"I believe you, Reg. But I'm sayin', nope, I ain't takin' my barge out to da bank."

Reg put his hands on his hips. "Why the bloody hell not, Damon? The storm's long gone. She's smooth like a baby's bum out there."

Damon looked at AJ and raised his eyebrows. "Like hell it is."

"Maybe not a baby's bum," AJ admitted. "More like a..."

She stopped hunting her mind for a backside analogy for slightly choppy seas after the first three ideas which jumped into her thoughts made her cringe.

"It was one to twos this morning and it's laying down more each day," she said, giving him an accurate description of the wave action instead.

Damon looked down at the rusty engine blocks and sighed. "Nope. You'll send dat lovely wife of yours over to butter me up for a cheap deal and I'll end up losin' money." He looked up. "I gotta pass, Reg."

"Did I mention there are three containers down there?" Reg responded. "The other two belong to an importer in town here. He's gonna be footing most of the bill."

Damon's expression softened slightly. "We can't pull a shipping container up with this crane, Reg. You know that."

"Not the containers. Just the contents."

"What's in da udder two?" Bash asked.

"Tyres," Reg replied. "Piece of cake to raise."

"They would be," Bash agreed, until Damon glared at him.

"How many days?" Damon asked.

Reg shrugged his shoulders. "Whatever it takes. At a guess I'd say two or three."

"We can only dive half days out there, 'cos of our customers," AJ added. "But we could anchor the barge on the bank and save you motoring back and forth." She looked at the rectangular steel deck of the barge. "Might get everything we bring up on one load if we stack the tyres right."

Damon groaned. "Let me tink about it. I'll get back to you later today."

"Fair enough," Reg acknowledged.

"And it'll be a tree-day job with a daily rate if it runs long," Damon warned. "Can't do nuttin' here while da barge is stuck out dere."

"I understand," Reg replied. "Call me later with a price and I'll see about getting it approved. Can you start tomorrow?"

Damon looked at Bash, then the deck, then at Reg. "Should be done movin' dis junk by lunchtime tomorrow."

"Perfect," AJ said. "I can't leave until after morning dives anyway."

"I'll be waiting for your call, then," Reg said. "Appreciate it, fellas."

Damon and Bash gave them a wave, and AJ and Reg walked back towards the van.

"That was cheating," AJ said once they were out of earshot.

"What do you mean?"

"Using Pearl and her tragic woes to persuade Damon."

Reg grinned. "We silver-tongued charmers use all the arrows in the quiver, love. What did we wager on my powers of persuasion?"

"Nothing."

"That doesn't seem right," Reg said thoughtfully. "I reckon you should pay for the tank fills."

"Okay," AJ agreed.

Reg stopped walking. "Wait. What?" He narrowed his eyes. "You agreed to that far too quickly."

AJ laughed. "Yeah. Because it's my turn to pay for the fills anyway."

"Ha!" Reg laughed, walking on. "I forgot."

"You might be a silver-tongued charmer, old man," AJ said, slapping his broad back. "But you've got a Teflon-lined memory."

19

Dotty arrived at the airfield early, having not slept particularly well. She'd lain in the large bed, staring at the pitch black above her in the room darkened behind blackout curtains, reliving her evening with Sandy. Finally drifting off, she woke unsure of the time and peeked around the window covering to find the sun threatening to appear. The chance of seeing Sandy again before she had to leave drove her out of the house before breakfast was even ready.

The matte-black Lysander sat on the grass near the dispersal hut with the soft morning hues creating contrast on the plane's fabric-covered fuselage. Where she noticed a series of fresh holes indicated the overnight sortie had not gone undetected.

"Good morning," came a voice close by, and Dotty turned.

Major Philip Kensington's uniform was perfectly clean and pressed, but the face below the cap looked dog tired. He held a cup of tea in his hand.

"Good morning, sir," Dotty responded. "Did everything go..."

She hesitated, returning her eyes to the peppered holes.

"Ran into a bit of bother," the major said, saving her the awkwardness of finishing her sentence. "Got one man on the ground."

"But only one?" Dotty quizzed, before realising she was asking a question she probably didn't want to hear the answer to and the major would rather avoid.

He took a sip of his tea before responding. "Yes. Harkins got unlucky, I'm afraid."

They stood in silence for a moment and Dotty was glad she hadn't snooped around the plane for a closer inspection. Hearing of the loss was bad enough. Seeing evidence of the man's demise would be too much. The burning cockpit of the Hurricane was still lurking in the recesses of her mind, ready to pop in at any unsuspecting moment.

It was now the second time within a week that she'd met a human being who was subsequently no longer living and breathing. The war had truly come to Dorothy Parker in full force. The stark contrast of her elation in the arms of Sandy against the reality of people dying in violent and horrific ways felt like she was being torn apart inside then healed over in a turbulent circle of emotions.

"Anyway, dare say you'll be ferrying the Lysander out of here today," Kensington continued. "Between your shrapnel and the damage we picked up last night, she needs a bit more care than the ground crew here can handle."

"I must call our operations room and see what they've assigned me," Dotty said, and began walking towards the office.

"Keep doing what you're doing, Miss Parker," Kensington said, bringing Dotty to a stop.

"Sir?" she responded, unsure what the major meant.

"What you're doing for your country is vital," he elaborated. "The only way we'll win this war and keep Hitler from our shores is to never give up. If we all do our part, although it seems too difficult at times, we will prevail."

Dotty nodded. "You have my word, sir."

Buoyed by Kensington's words, she hurried to the office where the young woman put a call into White Waltham for her.

"The same Lysander to Yeovilton aerodrome in Somerset for repair," Marjorie McKinven told Dotty, once she was on the phone.

"Then a new Spit from the Westland factory to Biggin Hill. Taxi plane will pick you up from there later this afternoon."

Dotty had hoped for a Spitfire out of Yeovil, the Westland factory having shifted to manufacturing Spitfires instead of their own planes, but Biggin Hill on the outskirts of London was not the Tangmere destination she desired.

"Righty-ho," Dotty replied, with the major's words echoing in her mind.

This was no time to put her personal ambitions ahead of the war effort. Having only been to Yeovilton aerodrome once before, she pulled out her map while striding around the corner of the building to the field. She sensed another person the split second before crashing into them, sending tea, map, and everything else they were both carrying flying into the air.

"I'm so sorry," she gasped, certain from the tea spillage she'd knocked Major Kensington for six.

"We're making a habit of this," Sandy said, wiping hot, brown liquid from his tunic.

Relieved, embarrassed, yet overjoyed to see him before she left, Dotty took a head scarf from her pocket and tried mopping up the mess. "You do seem to stand in places I'm travelling through," she joked.

"And you do travel at a high rate of speed," he added, bending down to pick up her small overnight satchel and parachute.

They crouched beside each other and both smiled.

"Good morning, Pilot First Officer Dorothy Parker."

"Good morning, Flying Officer Richard Lovell," she replied.

He slowly leaned towards her until they both jumped when the scramble siren screamed from the dispersal hut.

"Oh, no," Dotty faltered, as they leapt up.

Sandy pulled her to him and kissed her lips. "I must be off," he said, then rushed away, leaving her standing on the grass amongst her items and his teacup.

She wanted to call out after him and wish him luck, but the words didn't come. Dotty didn't want to wish him luck. She wanted him to stay on the ground or fly in the opposite direction so he'd be sure to come back in one piece. War and bravery be damned, she wanted to be held in his arms and kissed. For everything and everyone else to evaporate into the background as they had last night while they'd walked together.

But instead, Merlin engines roared, men shouted, the siren wailed, and by the time Dotty had gathered up her stuff and made it to the Lysander, the squadron had already taxied across the airfield.

With Wing Commander Harrington on the prowl and the chance of the fighters returning any time, Dotty soon took off and headed west. She desperately wanted to stick around to make sure Sandy returned, but it simply wasn't an option. Glad of the Lysander's design with its high wing mounted behind the pilot, partitioning off the cockpit from the gunner's location farther back, she made a point of not looking back there.

The plane had been designed for one gunner to stand, but with the armament removed, two men could squeeze into the space, sometimes with one lying down on the floor with his legs extended towards the tail. Dotty wondered which of the two men she'd seen in civilian clothes the night before had been Harkins. *How could it be that the bullets found him and not his companion? Physics or divine intervention?* She hated the idea that a higher power would be picking and choosing those to live and those to die, or suffer in agony while others walked away. The complex yet explainable maths of angles and velocities seemed far more palatable.

With the English Channel in the distance off her port side, Dotty passed by the source of Southampton Water, the tidal estuary stretching ten miles inland from the Solent. The city of Southampton and its docks along the water were clearly visible on what was turning out to be a pretty spring day. Crossing Dorset she flew over the hills of Cranborne Chase, picking up Henstridge Airfield, a Fleet Air Arm training aerodrome still under construction, then on to Yeovilton.

With a circle of the field and seeing no other air traffic, Dotty dropped the Lysander down on the grass airstrip. Within half an hour, she was back in the air, this time in a Supermarine Spitfire Mk VC. With 1,500 horsepower capable of propelling the aircraft up to a top speed of 446 mph, she was soon whistling across the countryside, even at the safe, ATA-sanctioned pace.

Farmland and hills streaked by a few thousand feet below and Dotty's mind wandered back to Sandy's description of a dogfight. How quickly everything happened. She scanned the skies for signs of another plane, but picked up nothing. Her heart began to beat a little faster as she contemplated something she'd never done before.

In much slower aeroplanes, her father had taught her all the basic so-called stunt flying moves, but a slow roll in a Tiger Moth was a far cry from the same thing at four times the speed. Some of the other ATA pilots had talked about fooling around and testing the limits of the planes they delivered, especially the fighters, but Dotty had never been so bold. Until now.

Pulling back on the stick, she increased the throttle and the Spit roared upwards, pinning her into the seat. The aeroplane felt like an extension of her limbs, begging to go faster and turn harder, instantly reacting to her every demand. Adrenaline surged as she rolled the plane over, flying inverted above the fields north of Salisbury, eyes flicking between the horizon and the altimeter, locking in her bearings.

Rolling 90 degrees, Dotty pulled back on the stick, turning north with a force which drove her backside into the base of the seat. She forced her eyeballs to stay focused as the breath was crushed from her lungs. The stick was heavy in her grip and she knew a moment's lapse would mean a fiery crash into the ground below. Easing the control back, she rolled out of the turn and flew low and straight over Stonehenge which flashed past below like a set of garden ornaments.

Dotty screamed with joy inside the cockpit, climbing, turning, and banking once again, becoming more and more comfortable with the incredible g-forces. As a final test, she climbed almost vertically, then pushed the stick forward. The Spitfire started into an outside loop, lifting Dotty against her belts as the forces tried to crumple her into the canopy. For a moment, as all she could see was green pastures below, she became slightly disorientated, but trusting the aircraft and her father's training, she held the loop and levelled off, inverted, parallel to the ground.

Slowly rolling the aeroplane right side up, only 200 feet above the ground, she zoomed over a small village where a group of children waved from a school yard. Dotty waggled the Spitfire's wings before climbing again to a cruising altitude and looking around for a landmark. At well over 400 mph, she'd covered a lot of territory in a hurry, and for a moment had no idea which county she was in.

On her starboard side Dotty spotted an airfield and dipped her wing for a better look as she slowed. She'd delivered planes there many times and quickly recognised RAF Middle Wallop in Hampshire. She'd managed to stay on course for South London despite her acrobatics. Her heart began to settle, but she was still smiling from the excitement when she yelped in surprise as another plane pulled alongside.

The fellow Spitfire pilot gave her a thumbs-up, which she returned, and smiled. His brow creased as he stared across the distance between the two planes. Her long hair had given her away, and for a moment, Dotty was sure her tail number would be reported and traced back to the ferry pilot performing crazy stunts in a brand new fighter plane. But the man laughed, gave her another even more enthusiastic thumbs-up, before rolling away himself.

Dotty let out a long sigh. Hopefully, her tail number would remain a secret and the pilot would have a great story to tell at the pub that night. Which his fellow fighter pilots would likely contest and disbelieve as a tall tale. But just to be safe, Dotty flew steady and straight for the rest of the journey to Biggin Hill.

20

AJ looked across the calm blue water towards North West Point. One private boat was moored to a dive buoy; otherwise they had the ocean to themselves.

"They're on Big Tunnels. We'll stay a couple of sites away from them," she said to Nora, who stood next to her on the fly-bridge.

Nora didn't reply, but took out the *Reef Smart Grand Cayman Guidebook* which lived on the dashboard shelf and thumbed through the pages.

"We could go past to Orange Canyon, or stop short at In Between," AJ said, intimately familiar with every location on the west, south, and north sides. "Got a preference?"

"In Between," Nora replied, her English tinted with a Norwegian accent. "I don't remember that one."

AJ laughed. "You'd prefer to guide the group on a dive site you don't know?"

Nora shrugged her shoulders, showing a hint of a grin. "Sure. Might as well see something new. How hard can it be? Go along the wall, turn around. Move on top of the wall. Come back to the boat."

AJ laughed again. Her friend was right, navigation on Cayman's wall dives was about as simple as guiding could get, yet most people would still prefer familiar ground when responsible for others. But Nora wasn't *most* people.

"Do you want to come out to the bank this afternoon?" AJ asked. "We could use all the extra hands we can get."

Nora looked at her hands.

"It means extra help," AJ clarified. "We'll take all of you, not just your hands."

"Oh. Then I'll come with you," Nora replied, putting the dive guidebook back on the dashboard shelf. "But aren't all Pearl's things ruined?"

AJ cringed. "Much of it will be, but we're hoping to save a few pieces of furniture, ornaments, stuff like that. Her mum's best china is in there."

Nora frowned at AJ. "The container fell off the side of a ship in a storm, then sank to the sea floor, and you think her china is okay?"

"Not when you put it like that."

Thomas appeared on the bow and looked up at AJ.

"In Between," AJ called down over the sound of the wind, waves, and diesel engines.

He held up an okay sign and moved to the pulpit with a boat hook in hand. AJ began slowing the Newton, aiming for a large white buoy bobbing on the surface ahead. With well-practised timing, she shut down the throttles, coasting to within a few feet of the marker, allowing Thomas to scoop up the tie line with the boat hook. He quickly threaded their mooring line through the loop and tied it off to a second cleat, securing them to the site.

"Want me to do the briefing?" AJ asked Nora as she switched off the engines.

"Always," Nora replied.

AJ grinned as she made for the ladder. Her friend was notoriously frugal with her words, preferring to stick with verbalising only the absolute necessities. AJ laughed to herself, recalling Nora's last dive briefing; 'There's the reef, here's the boat. We swim around for a while, see stuff, and come back. Signal me if something is wrong. Let's go.'

The deck was buzzing with divers performing final checks on their gear, so AJ settled them down and gave them a more thorough briefing of what they could expect, plus a few key safety items.

"Anything to add?" she asked Nora once the speech was complete.

"No," Nora said, standing by the ladder, ready to go.

"Okay. Pool's open," AJ declared, and one by one she and Thomas helped the divers move to the stern and giant-stride into the water.

After watching the last of their guests disappear beneath the surface, AJ moved to the shelter of the deck area below the flybridge and retrieved her mobile phone from her backpack.

"Should be calmer on da bank today," Thomas commented, staring at the horizon line to the west.

"Surface will be," AJ agreed, calling Reg's phone. "Just hope that current has mellowed."

"What?" Reg answered. "You only left here twenty minutes ago, and you're already bothering me?"

"Cracking the whip, mate," AJ quipped in return. "Figured you'd be sitting on your arse if I didn't."

"I just finished my list and was about to hop in the Landy until you interrupted me."

"I had an idea."

"Can't wait."

"It's a good one."

"Doubtful, but tell me anyway."

"We run a second line from the container to the boat and send the tyres up the line with a lift bag," AJ explained, having chewed over the idea on the ride out to the dive site. "The tricky part will be handling the line while we load the tyres and unload them at the top. It has to be untied each time."

"Hmm," Reg grunted.

"Connect at two points each end," Thomas said, turning from the gunwale.

"Hang on a sec," AJ said, and put her mobile on speaker phone. "Say that again, Thomas."

"I was tinking, if da rope were tied in two places, it can always stay connected."

"Now that's a great idea, Thomas," Reg responded cheerily. "Good thinking, mate."

"Hey, hey, hey!" AJ complained. "I had the idea, Thomas just added a final touch. A good one, I must say, but an addition to my brilliant plan."

"No," Reg said. "You came up with a harebrained scheme that wouldn't work, and young Thomas turned it into a perfectly crafted plan. I have to give ninety percent of the credit to him."

Thomas laughed, and AJ groaned.

"You'll need 200 foot of line," she added, getting back to the logistics.

"On it," Reg replied, and before she could say anything more, he hung up.

AJ tucked her mobile in her backpack and thought for a moment.

"If we tied a loop in the line, we could clip it to the other end of the container," she said, looking at Thomas. "That way the line is still tethered and we could untie the very end, pop the tyres on the line, then tie it off again."

Thomas nodded. "Need to string the tyres together and use one lift bag."

"Exactly. Unclip the loop and a wagon train of tyres should run up the line."

"Yup," Thomas agreed. "Could do the same along the side of the barge."

AJ frowned. "One problem."

"What's dat, boss?"

"How do we clip the loop in again? The boat will be tugging on the line."

"Not if we keep dat second line ten or twenty feet longer dan da mooring line you already set. It should be a little slack."

AJ pointed at Thomas. "That's why you make the big wedge. Always thinking."

After forty-minutes of dive time, the group began surfacing and climbing up the ladder. AJ and Thomas helped the customers back to the bench as *Hazel's Odyssey* gently swayed in the mild swells. From their enthusiasm, AJ figured the dive had gone well and they'd seen plenty of cool critters.

"An eagle ray?" she enthused to Nora who brought up the rear.

Nora grinned and held up two fingers.

"You saw two?" AJ groaned, keeping a steadying hand on Nora's tank until she'd lined it up with a rack and sat down on the bench.

"And a beautiful turtle up close," Craig added. "A green."

AJ's shoulders slumped. Hawksbills were more common on the west side than the green sea turtles who had smoother shells and less pointed beaks.

"Sounds like I'd better have my cool fish radar working over-time for the second dive," AJ joked. "I have my work cut out for me."

Craig laughed. "I'm sure whatever you show us will be fantastic, but yeah, that was kinda special."

AJ moved slightly north and shallower for the second dive, and after an hour's surface interval, she led the group through Bonnie's Arch, a large natural window in the coral reef. After spending ten minutes taking pictures and admiring the splendid colours of sponges, fans, and fish life around the arch, AJ took the divers on a tour of the neighbouring reef.

Feeling the stresses of the storm and Pearl's loss melt away, AJ soaked up the healing ambiance of the reef, leaving her troubles on the boat for an hour. She excitedly pointed out a tiny juvenile spotted drum with its long willowy dorsal fin and was soon consumed by the underwater world, gently finning from one inter-esting find to the next. The time whistled by so fast, she was surprised to see 50 minutes on her Teric, and realised they were still a long way from the boat.

Craig's group were all experienced divers and good with their air consumption, so running long wasn't an issue and she led them back at a leisurely pace. Last on the boat, she pulled up the ladder and let Thomas tie it in for the ride back.

"Thought you were takin' em home witout da boat," he kidded. "Lost sight of your bubbles you went so far."

"I was looking for an eagle ray," she quipped back, lining up her tank with the rack and dropping onto the bench.

"See one?" Nora asked.

AJ frowned at her friend.

"Maybe next time," Nora said, grinning.

AJ stuck two fingers up at her. "Get the mooring line before I make you swim home."

Nora grinned a little more before heading to the bow.

"I don't think she'd mind if you made her swim, boss," Thomas laughed.

AJ shook her head. "And she'd probably beat us back."

"Two fantastic dives, AJ. Thank you," Craig said, backed by enthusiastic cheers from the group. "You're really under the gun to top that tomorrow."

"Challenge accepted," AJ replied, but her mind had already shifted to the technical dives she faced that afternoon.

One step at a time, she reminded herself, and scaled the ladder to the helm.

AJ closed the door on the van Craig's group had rented and waved goodbye to them as they drove away. Turning around, she looked at the mostly organised chaos raining down on the dock. Two of Reg's boats were refilling tanks for afternoon trips, and *Hazel's Odyssey* was being topped off with diesel from five-gallon jugs and loaded with a pile of gear Reg had assembled. AJ took a deep breath and started down the little sloped car park when a white

SUV with fancy custom wheels and tyres pulled in behind her. She paused, ready to redirect the customer to the public car park across the road.

"Hello, I'm looking for Reg Moore," the man said, stepping from the vehicle.

He had an English Home Counties accent and AJ placed him at mid-forties. He was dressed in cotton shorts, boat shoes, and a golf shirt from a country club she couldn't read the name of. He looked ready to go sailing rather than diving. A second man exited the passenger side, gathering something from inside the SUV.

"He's down at the boats," AJ replied. "Are you on one of his afternoon trips?"

"I am, yes," the man replied.

"Do you have any of your own gear, sir?" AJ asked, already gauging his wetsuit and BCD size.

"Do I need it?"

"If you're planning on diving you'll need something, but we have everything available for rent."

He took a few steps towards her and stopped, looking confused. "I don't know how to dive."

AJ wasn't sure how to respond.

"George?" came Reg's voice from behind her.

"You must be Reg," the man responded, extending a hand. "This is Raúl," he added, nodding towards the Hispanic man who smiled their way with a what looked like a shopping bag in his hand.

"Hello," Reg said, shaking both men's hands. "I see you've met AJ." Seeing the nonplussed look on AJ's face, he continued. "This is George Cook, the tyre importer. He's agreed to cover Damon's bill if we take care of the diving."

"Oh, right. That's brilliant," AJ laughed awkwardly, feeling embarrassed. "Sorry. I thought you were a customer."

George shook AJ's hand. "That's okay, I thought you were a man."

AJ frowned and looked down at herself. She was without make-up, as usual, but in her dive leggings and tank top she didn't feel unfeminine. She was no Pearl, but her shape certainly wasn't masculine. George held up both hands.

"I'm so sorry, you misunderstand me," he said, his cheeks blushing. "Reg talked about him and AJ tackling this project, and I mistakenly assumed by AJ he meant a man. Which you are most definitely not."

Now AJ blushed more, and they stood in uncomfortable silence for a few moments.

"Is it okay if Raúl comes along?" George asked. "He's my right-hand man at the company."

"And I come bearing gifts of burritos," Raúl offered.

"Sold," AJ announced. "Anyone with tacos or burritos is always welcome."

"Shall we head to the boat and get going?" Reg suggested, chuckling behind his beard. "If you three men are ready?"

AJ poked him in the ribs as they walked down the pier.

21

Dotty had never flown a Bristol Beaufighter. In fact, she'd never even sat in one before. But such was the life of an ATA ferry pilot, and with her new advanced twin-engine rating, she expected plenty of challenges ahead. With pilot notes in hand, her first problem was getting inside the aeroplane, and she was glad the ground crew had placed a stepladder underneath the fuselage as a clue. Dotty pulled herself up through the hatch before spending several minutes trying to figure out how to get the seat to fold down so she could access the single-seat cockpit.

Bigger, broader, and heavier than the Spitfires and Hurricanes, the Beaufighter was originally developed as a lightweight bomber before being modified into a night fighter with a crew of two or three. A pilot, an optional navigator and wireless operator, and a gunner in a turret farther back along the fuselage. Dotty would have neither aboard for her flight. Reading the notes, she followed the starting sequence for the two Bristol Hercules radial engines and while they warmed up, she found information on taxiing, take off speed, and stall speed.

After a quick check around the cluttered cockpit full of gauges and controls, she identified everything she'd need to fly the plane, then gave the ground crew a thumbs-up and eased away. The engines roared on either side of her as Dotty accelerated down the grass at White Waltham, reminding herself how much more room the bigger plane needed to lift off the ground. Every vibration, creak, groan, and engine growl was new and slightly different from anything she'd flown before. But the basics of flying an aeroplane remained the same, so once airborne, Dotty relaxed and picked out her navigation references on the ground and followed the map unfolded on her lap.

RAF Hibaldstow was 140 miles away in Lincolnshire, not far from Scunthorpe. Very much in the opposite direction of where Dotty wished she could be, but Marjorie couldn't send her to Sussex every day. It was another nice day with high cloud and low winds, making the trip a relatively easy one, giving Dotty's mind time to wander. She thought of Sandy and the way his eyes seemed to draw her to him as though they were the only two souls in a private world, void of war and misery.

But when could she see him again? A desperate urge to be near him reached far beyond the pangs of a new love. He was a fighter pilot, risking his life every day above the southern counties and English Channel. She knew they may never see each other again, and the very idea made her gasp. They had so much to share and discover. It seemed crazy to be contemplating a future together after just one date, but the war accelerated everything. *Would he turn her away if he knew she had little desire for children?* Dotty wanted to fly aeroplanes, not change nappies and have supper dutifully on the table. It was something he needed to know yet words she was scared to express.

Looking out the window at the northern English countryside, Dotty quickly realised she'd completely lost track of time and her location.

"You silly girl," she muttered to herself, and scoured the terrain for a prominent landmark.

In the distance ahead, she spotted water. A broad inlet running from west to east. An estuary into the North Sea. It had to be the

Humber, which meant she was over or beyond her destination. Banking to port, Dotty began a sweeping circle, searching below for the airfield. She'd flown right over the top of it and could now see it thousands of feet below. Dotty thanked her lucky stars for good visibility and coming to her senses before she'd found herself in Scotland.

Fifteen minutes later, she set the Beaufighter down at RAF Hibaldstow and taxied to where a ground crewman waved her into a line-up of similar aircraft. Slipping from the hatch, Dotty dropped to the grass before the men had time to bring over a ladder.

"In a hurry, sir?" the man asked in a thick northern English accent.

She hadn't realised it until the man said something, but her thoughts of Sandy and their ticking clock must have had her moving quickly.

"Bit of a long flight," Dotty replied, making up a reason, although it wasn't a complete lie. "I could use the nearest lady's room if you'd point me in the right direction."

The mechanic did a double take, picking up her voice. "Stone the crows. Had one of you Attagirls in here a few weeks back. They got you flying everything these days?"

"Some of us do, yes," Dotty responded. "Where would I find the loo?"

"Oh, sorry, love," he said, pointing to a building next to the first hangar. "You'll find one in there."

After using the facilities and a quick clean-up, brushing her hair and straightening her uniform, Dotty found a young lady at the reception to help her and called Marjorie.

"There should be an Anson waiting for you," came her next instruction. "One of the other girls dropped her last passenger there two days ago and then ferried a damaged Beaufighter, leaving the Anson behind. You'll have pick-ups at a handful of stops on your way back here."

"Alright," Dotty replied, having never been *the* ferry pilot for the *ferry pilots* before. "I have a pencil if you'd like to give me the stops?"

A smile crept over her face as she jotted down the airfields, which zig-zagged a path south towards White Waltham.

"Got it," she said once Marjorie had given her all five locations and the names of seven pilots.

Once outside, Dotty tracked down the Avro Anson and made sure it had been fuelled and cleared by the ground crew. It was nearing lunchtime, but she was too keen to get airborne to heed the growl in her stomach. First jaunt was a relatively short 30-mile hop to RAF Winthorpe in Newark, where Dotty picked up an older male pilot who sat in the right-hand seat and didn't say a word to her. A grunt or two seemed to be the extent of his critique when she sat the twin-engined Anson gently down on the runway at their next destination.

Which was RAF Burnaston outside Derby, where a female pilot from Poland had delivered a Tiger Moth to the RAF training school. Dotty knew Irena as she was also based at White Waltham. A bold but friendly woman and an accomplished pilot who had escaped her home country shortly after the Germans had invaded.

"Take the right seat," Dotty urged after scrounging a sandwich from the mess at the small airfield and walking back to the plane with Irena, where the male ATA pilot stood smoking a cigarette.

"Two weeks straight with no days off," the Polish woman replied. "I sleep in back."

"Please," Dotty begged, whispering and chewing quickly. "He just stares and grunts and oozes disdain for female pilots. Just until we make the next stop."

"Where is next stop?"

"Spitfire factory at Castle Bromwich. Not even 30 miles."

"Fine. I do this," Irena replied. "But maybe I grunt and stare too."

Dotty came to a stop by the door to the plane and turned to Irena, unsure what to say. The Polish woman gazed blankly back. Until her lips curled into a smile. They both burst into laughter and climbed aboard before Grunting Man had a chance to stub out his cigarette.

At Castle Bromwich, Dotty picked up another male pilot. A younger man who she recognised but hadn't spoken to before. He'd likely failed the RAF physical for some reason, but the 'Ancient and Tattered Airmen' must have deemed him fit for ferry duty. He greeted them pleasantly as he climbed in the back. Irena stayed upfront after all and the two women talked flying over the headsets as the Anson's Armstrong Siddeley Cheetah engines droned on. And with Dotty getting more and more excited as their next destination soon loomed ahead.

"Toilet break," she announced once they'd landed and taxied to a large hangar where ground crew awaited.

"I'm good," the grumpy older pilot announced. "Let's get home."

"I must pee," Irena said, to Dotty's relief.

The younger man jumped out as well, so Dotty quickly ran towards the airfield office, but a voice stopped her short.

"What a lovely surprise."

Dotty swung around to see a man in a neatly pressed RAF uniform.

"Flight Lieutenant Parker," Dotty greeted him with a salute.

"Pilot *First* Officer Parker," he responded, emphasising her new rank. "Come here, my girl."

Dotty gave her father a big hug.

"You flying the Anson?" he asked.

"I am," she replied as he held her at arm's length and examined his daughter. "And it's all been short hops so I haven't pulled the landing gear up once."

Patrick laughed. The Anson landing gear was manually cranked up and down and notoriously laborious.

"You look well, love," he said. "Time for a cuppa?"

"Not really, but we'll have one anyway," she said, and they hurried to the hangar where the ground crews kept a teapot.

"How was training?" he asked as they heated the water.

"Fine. Although I didn't like riding along with the others. One of them almost dropped us out of the sky in the Blenheim."

"Let me guess; emergency fuel cut-off?" he asked.

"Yup. If the instructor hadn't been on the ball, we'd have been scattered all over Berkshire."

"I'm glad he was then," Patrick grinned. "These kids they're sending us here now are so wet behind the ears we have to show them the nose from the tail. Losing too many still, although it's not like it was in '40."

Dotty's face dropped as she thought of Sandy and the awful odds he faced every day.

"What else is going on with you?" her father asked. "Billet alright?"

"They're very nice," Dotty replied as they waited for the tea to brew. "Worried about their son in North Africa, same as half of the country."

"Good job I'm surrounded by girls," he said, and squeezed her shoulder.

"How are they?" Dotty asked.

"Your mum's doing fine. Volunteering for everything she can get involved in. Your sister is growing up too fast. Don't think she's leaning towards flying anytime soon, but she's top of her class in school."

"Good job one of us is," Dotty joked.

"You'd have been too if you weren't gazing out the classroom windows looking for aeroplanes all day."

Dotty poured them both tea and found a drop of milk and sugar.

"Right then," Patrick said, as they stepped from the hangar with cups in hand. "What is it?"

Dotty looked at her father. "What do you mean?"

"I mean you've got something flying around inside that noggin of yours, so how about you tell me what it is."

Dotty felt her cheeks redden, but not nearly as much as they usually did.

"I've met a fella."

"Oh, you have now?" Patrick responded sternly. "Would I like this fella?"

"He's a pilot," she announced cheerily.

"That's promising. ATA?"

Dotty took a moment.

"He's not ATA," her father guessed. "RAF?"

She nodded.

"Blimey, girl," he breathed, and a silence fell between them.

Dotty could normally read her father, but for once she had no idea how he was about to react. His expression looked pained, and she didn't expect anger, but hoped for understanding. He'd always been understanding. But, of course, her previous love had been aeroplanes. The anticipation felt like the planet had stopped spinning and life itself was on hold, waiting for the next words to be spoken.

"When can I meet him?" he finally asked, and Dotty's world rotated once more.

"He's based at Tangmere in Sussex," she replied, knowing the distance from the Cotswolds was only a twenty-minute flight away yet could have been Australia with petrol rations and neither men having much leave available.

Patrick nodded. "Fighters, then."

"Hurricane squadron."

Her father swallowed. "I don't need to tell you the odds, then, do I love."

"No," she murmured. "No, you don't."

He reached his arm around her shoulders and pulled her to him. "Best be careful, love. That's all I ask. You be careful."

Dotty leaned her head against his shoulder and tried her best to ignore the ferry pilots all standing by the Anson wondering why they weren't already on their way home. She also tried not to think about the chances of her father never meeting the man she was falling in love with.

22

AJ stood alongside Reg at the back of the fly-bridge. They waved to Pearl, who returned the gesture from the end of the dock as she watched them leave. She was smiling, but AJ knew it was pasted on for their benefit. All the effort on her behalf was weighing on Pearl's mind. In typical English fashion of her generation, Pearl was uncomfortable with a fuss being made around her, despite her love of performing on stage. Which, in her mind, was about the music and not about her. In reality, the majority of her audience would argue that it was *all* about her.

Once clear of the sandy-bottomed shallows, Thomas opened up the engines, and AJ handed everyone a sandwich from the bag Pearl had brought them. They ate in silence as the Newton rode through the light chop brought on by the afternoon winds. Holding a steady 16 knots, the trip took forty minutes, and as AJ tied into the buoy they'd fastened to the mooring line the day before, she could see Damon's barge approaching.

The Caymanian had thrown out a price which AJ guessed he'd hoped would be too rich for the project, but George Cook had agreed when Reg relayed the deal.

"Both boats on this one line might be a bit much," AJ said to Reg when she returned from the bow.

"I brought enough rope to reach from here to bloody China, so I figured we'd hook the barge to container two. We can start unloading the tyres and running 'em up a second line. You know, like Thomas came up with."

"Like I came up with!" AJ protested. "He added the loop business."

Reg grinned and shrugged his shoulders. "Right, like I said, the dumb idea you had that Thomas turned into a workable plan."

Reg leaned closer. "Figured we needed to make a start on the tyres, seeing as Georgie Boy is footing the bill."

"Yeah, fair enough," AJ agreed. "Let's see how the current looks. I'm thinking you and Thomas start work on container two, and I'll string a line down to the deep one. Dive two, we'll start into Pearl's container."

Reg nodded. "I'll sort the lines out."

AJ went to work organising everyone. Over the radio she arranged with Damon to wait close by once he arrived, and Nora would call him when she saw an SMB surface with a line attached.

George Cook stayed out of the way, looking green around the gills. It appeared that his boat shoes were his only nautical attribute. Raúl on the other hand seemed right at home on the water and endeared himself to everyone with his tasty burritos, which he swore were homemade. He even had a vegetarian version for AJ.

In short order, Reg and Thomas geared up, using twin 28% nitrox tanks, while AJ chose 26% for her deeper dive. Loaded with extra SMBs, lines, and stainless-steel carabiners, the three of them splashed in and hauled themselves along a wreck line Thomas had strung from the mooring buoy to the stern. With something to hang onto, they performed a final surface check before dropping below and descending the line.

The surface current had been similar to the day before, tugging the Newton against the mooring, but as AJ dropped through 60 feet, she was optimistic the waters had calmed at depth. Reg must have observed the same thing, as at 80 feet, he waved to AJ, then he and Thomas released their grip on the mooring line and aimed for container two. AJ watched them as she continued hand over hand down the line. With minimal effort, Reg and Thomas were able to fin west while a far gentler current drifted them south.

AJ reached container one, and once she'd seen Reg safely contact his destination, she picked up the line they'd left on the slope and headed over the edge. The current had certainly subsided, but it was still present, and she worked to kick against it while descending. She reached the top of container three at 154 feet, and quickly realised it was upside down. She tied the line into the corner casting, then dropped over the end to examine the doors.

Quickly snipping the customs seal, she stuffed it in her harness pocket. Using the code George had given them, she tried rolling the tumblers on the lock. After only a few days submerged in saltwater, the mechanism was already seizing up, and for a moment AJ thought she'd be returning with a bigger cutting device of some description. But she wiggled, jiggled, and persuaded the tumblers to roll, and finally the lock came free.

She checked her Perdix. Five minutes into her twenty-two-minute planned dive if she remained at the deep location. AJ pock-eted the lock and released the handle, which took her three tries as she forgot the container was upside down, requiring her to push down instead of pulling up. Carefully releasing the cams, she immediately felt a force trying to swing the door open. Grabbing another locking bar for leverage, she heaved the door closed and secured the handle again. Looking past her deco tank, she stared down the steep slope into the darkness below. They wouldn't be retrieving anything that tumbled down there.

The other concerning element she noticed was the container's precarious perch on the slope. Pulling herself down the door, AJ shone her torch underneath the big metal box. From the marks on the slope above and the fact that the container was now inverted, she guessed it had rolled to its current position, arrested by a small coral outcrop illuminated in her beam. They'd need to be especially careful when removing the tyres from inside as it wouldn't take much at all to topple the container from its tentative grasp on the side of the underwater mountain.

With little more to accomplish at container three on this dive, AJ let go and gently finned while the current swept her up the slope to container one. Flipping over her wrist slate, she checked the alternate dive plan she'd written out on the boat, having suspected she wouldn't need to spend the whole dive at container three. The alternate plan had 10 minutes at 160 feet, then another 15 minutes at 132 feet before beginning her ascent. Her Perdix would track her exact changes of depth, then calculate a new deco plan, but she needed to know an outline of what to expect. With 7 minutes of bottom time showing, shaving 3 minutes off her alternate plan time at 160 feet, AJ figured she could extend her stay at the current depth by 4 minutes as it was 28 feet shallower. Which meant leaving at 26 minutes to meet approximately the same deco obligation.

Having watched Reg open the right-hand door, which had dropped like a ramp as the container was on its side, sprinkling contents down the slope, they'd discussed another idea: opening the left-hand door and holding it up, created a letterbox-shaped window leaving the lower door trapping the debris. AJ tied a short piece of cord around the latch handle and moved on top of the container. Standing with her fins against the metal, she used the cord to slowly haul the door open, tying it off to the mooring line.

Dropping back down, she shone her torch inside for a better look at the carnage. Having only seen the video, AJ wasn't sure if she was encouraged or shocked by what she saw. Another twenty-four hours underwater and the boxes had deteriorated further, making her glad she'd opened the top door. A rapidly crumbling pile of sodden brown filled her view behind the lower door, with signs of the contents poking through all over the place. How they'd sort through the mess, she had no clue. But beyond, some of the furniture had been revealed, and while it was tipped over with packing blankets hiding the identity of some items, she could see how most of the pieces could be retrieved.

AJ moved up to the line and held on with one hand so the current didn't ease her away. Unclipping her deco tank, she attached it to the line, ready to collect as she exited. Pulling a mesh bag from her pocket, she kicked to the opening and pulled herself inside.

The container seemed a whole lot bigger from the outside than the cramped, dark interior. For the first six feet where the boxes had fallen, crumpled, and come apart, AJ had a few inches below her while her tanks scraped along the metal above. Once she reached the furniture, all access was blocked. There'd be no way to remove any items without first clearing a path through the cardboard mash.

Carefully rotating, AJ felt better looking at the open door instead of the confined interior. She searched the boxes with her torch, looking for anything retrievable. There were so many photo albums it made her want to cry. All those memories lost forever. She realised at least half the boxes were full of books and wondered how many first editions and classics handed down through generations were now destroyed.

Something metal protruded from the pile and she reached down, tearing the soggy box away. AJ laughed into her regulator, before digging out the objects and placing them in her mesh bag. As with many daunting tasks, making the first move kick-started the process, and AJ now continued working her way across the boxes, trying to use a systematic process.

One problem quickly became evident. *What to do with anything unsalvageable?* Which appeared to be a larger quantity than items worth surfacing. It wasn't like she had a skip outside to toss the junk into, and there was no way she would discard the non-organic waste outside onto the reef. Which left her with the dilemma of separating good from bad with no room to truly make two stacks. The best solution she settled on was to begin going through the mess on one side by removing anything saveable and depositing the rest on the opposite side. When she got to the bottom, she'd shovel the mess back into the void she'd created, and begin going through the second side. It was imperfect and AJ knew it, but they'd only be able to make so many dives in their spare time, so she needed to make the most of each opportunity.

She checked her Perdix. Bottom time showed 19 minutes of her allotted 26 and her mesh bag was half full. Six minutes later, the bag would only just close, and AJ was happy to get out of the container which felt a little too much like a metal cave on the sea floor. Carefully placing the mesh bag on top of the container, she retrieved her deco tank, clipping it to her Dive Rite harness. As she picked the bag up again, AJ looked across Twelve Mile Bank to check on Reg and Thomas. What she saw made her smile.

Thomas had just released the second clip from the east end of container two, and a lift bag began hauling a wagon train of tyres up the line towards the surface. AJ grabbed the mooring line and began ascending, watching the delivery package gain speed as the gas expanded in the lift bag on its way up. The barge was nothing more than a shadow at the surface, and the tyres disappeared into the murk at such a distance, but she hoped they were ready for what was about to arrive. She hadn't considered the issue of letting the lift bag fly on its own. A diver would usually accompany the process, bleeding off air from the lift bag to control the ascent as the water pressure lessened.

After 30 minutes of decompression stops, AJ handed the mesh bag to Nora and climbed the ladder. Reg and Thomas had also left the bottom shortly after AJ, and with less deco obligation they'd surfaced before her, but on the barge. Nora had let a buoy on a line drift from the Newton to the barge, which the two divers now used to haul themselves back to *Hazel's Odyssey*, where they'd need to switch tanks.

"Were you able to reach the second container?" George asked as AJ slipped from her harness.

"We're calling it container three, but yeah. It's upside down and a bit dodgy where's it's perched on the slope, but hopefully we'll be able to unload it."

"That's amazing," George enthused. "I see they were able to send quite a few up already."

Raúl slapped his boss on the back. "You guys are incredible. I'll keep making burritos if you keep bringing up our tyres."

AJ laughed. "Might be a chance we can finish getting everything from the first one today, but we'll see what Reg says," she replied, moving to the stern.

"Looked like that worked swimmingly," she said, taking Reg's deco tank from him, making it easier for him to step up the ladder.

"Put a bit too much gas in, I reckon," Reg grinned. "Damon said he thought a kraken was attacking the boat when that lot surfaced."

Nora helped guide Reg to the bench while AJ took Thomas's deco tank.

"How was Mrs Moore's container?" Thomas asked as he scaled the ladder. "Saw you filled a bag with someting."

"Yeah, not bad," AJ answered, helping Thomas to the bench. "I sent Pearl a picture of all the stuff I brought up."

"What did you get?" Reg asked, looking at the mesh bag sitting under the fly-bridge.

"Your Land Rover parts," AJ replied, and waited.

"Blimey, that's mega," Reg replied, then whipped around to look at AJ. "Wait. You sent Pearl a picture of my Landy parts as the first thing we brought up? She'll bloody kill me."

AJ grinned. "That's what I figured too."

23

"Call me once you're on the ground in Brighton," Marjorie said, handing Dotty her chit for the morning. "I dare say we'll have something else to bring north."

"Alright, thank you," Dotty replied and read the chit as she walked through the offices to the field.

A new Boulton Paul Defiant to deliver from the factory in Wolverhampton to RAF Shoreham near Brighton in Sussex. Two other ATA pilots had the same assignment, she learned once they were aboard the Anson taxi, replacing Lysanders with the newer Defiants for 277 Squadron. Except the other two pilots were scheduled to fly Lysanders out of Shoreham instead of checking in with the operations room.

Brighton wasn't Tangmere, but it was Sussex, and only around 30 miles away by car, so there was a chance she'd be assigned an MU from the fighter base. All Dotty could do was hope. Which struck her as absurd that she'd be craving a mechanically unfit aeroplane to fly.

With a stop on the way, it was nearing ten in the morning by the time the three pilots were dropped at the airstrip beside the Boulton Paul factory. Three glistening new Defiants sat waiting, and Dotty quickly climbed into the cockpit of the first in line and familiarised herself with the controls. From the outside, the Defiant slightly resembled a Hawker Hurricane, with the exception of a gun turret behind the cockpit. Designed to attack bombers, for which it was quite effective, the plane was unfortunately vulnerable to fighter attack from the front as it lacked any forward firing guns. In the cockpit, many of the controls and gauges for the Rolls-Royce Merlin engine were familiar to Dotty, so within a few minutes she was warmed up and ready to taxi.

She quickly realised her eagerness to head south came with added responsibility. As the ground crew waved her away, the other two pilots appeared happy to fall in line, leaving Dotty out front in charge of navigation. All three were soon in the air and with 150 miles to cover, she had her map on her lap and eyes keenly following landmarks below.

Skirting Birmingham, Dotty spotted Stratford-upon-Avon, with the larger city of Worcester in the distance off their starboard side. Over Moreton-in-Marsh, she picked up the A44 and followed the road to Oxford where the landscape became more familiar. Dense but high cloud had been building all morning, leaving fleeting glimpses of the sun, occasionally highlighting the fields and villages. As midday neared, Dotty noticed more cloud beginning to form, lower and darker in the skies ahead. The three planes briefly flew through a rain shower over the Chilterns before the weather remained in check for the duration of their flight south.

Landing at RAF Shoreham, they handed over the Defiants and made a quick stop in the loos before Dotty called the operations room at White Waltham.

"Have one of them drop you at Tangmere in a Lysander where you'll pick up a damaged Spit to fly up to Castle Brom," Marjorie said. "How's the weather looking?"

"Thank you," Dotty replied, acknowledging the woman's manoeuvring to get her another visit, albeit brief. "It's closing in, but a 2,000-foot ceiling so we should be fine as long as nothing sweeps in from the channel."

"Safe travels," Marjorie said, and hung up.

The other two ferry pilots tossed a coin to see who won the extra stop, and a nice man in his late thirties who called heads when he should have called tails became the taxi. Dotty was often surprised by how friendly and amiable a few of the male ATA pilots could be towards the women, treating them simply as fellow pilots doing their bit.

Ground crew waved the Lysander to a stop halfway between the Hurricane and Spitfire squadron's dispersal huts. Dotty hopped out, thanking the pilot, and looked around. Both squadrons had to be airborne as only a handful of fighters remained on the field, several being worked on by mechanics. As the Anson took off once more, Dotty walked to the Spitfire side in search of her plane to ferry.

"They said they were sending a pilot, but she's not ready, miss," a mechanic explained, wiping his hands on a rag. "I'm not sure I can make it ready, if truth be told. She was shot up pretty bad."

"Oh," Dotty faltered. "I suppose I'll wait and you'll let me know?"

"Laces, miss," he replied.

"I'm sorry?" she questioned.

"Everyone calls me Laces, miss."

"Oh, I see. Why Laces?" she asked.

He smiled. "On account of me being able to string most things together with baling twine and shoelaces, miss."

"Well, it's nice to meet you, Laces," Dotty said, offering her hand. "Although it sounds like this one might need more than a pair of laces."

"I'm a bit grubby, I'm afraid," he said, holding his oil-stained hands up.

Dotty kept her hand extended. "I'm a pilot, Laces. I'm not afraid of a little oil and grease."

He grinned and shook her hand.

Dotty's eyes raised to the sky. "How long have the lads been up?"

The man glanced at his wristwatch. "Half hour, I'd say. Third sortie today and all. Huns have been busy."

While she was flying all over England, Dotty's fear for Sandy hung like an imminent, yet distant, threat. But now, standing at the airfield waiting for the pilots to return, her stomach twisted into a knot and her palms felt clammy.

"Give me an hour or so, miss, and I should have a better idea," Laces said, which Dotty heard but didn't really process.

"Of course, I'll be close by," she muttered, and began walking towards the Hurricane dispersal hut.

In the distance, she thought she detected a dark speck beginning to appear against the backdrop of grey cloud, which shaded the farmland between the airfield and the English Channel. Just as Dotty was beginning to think her mind was playing tricks, two more dark spots grew bigger. Wing Commander Harrington stepped from the hut and held field glasses to his face. Dotty crossed her fingers on both hands.

"Please be alright, please be alright," she whispered over and over as the dots became planes, lining up to land on the grass runway.

Several Spitfires touched down first, then a Hurricane trailing smoke from the engine cowl. It wasn't Sandy's tail number, unless he'd been switched. Three more Spitfires arrived safely, followed by another Hurricane. Soon, the sky was full of RAF planes, landing two or three at a time and hurriedly taxiing across the field. In the middle of them all, Dotty spotted the tail number she'd been searching for and she let out a long sigh of relief.

She stayed out of the way, keeping well away from Harrington as the men climbed from their planes.

"Forchester?" Harrington asked, and one of the pilots shook his head.

"In the Channel, sir."

"See a chute?"

"No, sir," the man replied. "I think Longman got out though, sir.

But it was a bit confusing. For a minute or two it seemed like there were more chaps under silk than planes still flying."

Sandy looked over and saw Dotty. He forced a smile before turning away and walking to the pilot climbing out of another Hurricane. Sandy placed his hand on the man's shoulder and said something to him which Dotty couldn't hear. The pilot nodded and finally looked Sandy in the eye. The two men stared at each other for a long moment, sharing whatever needed to be noted between two warriors after the fight.

"Debrief, men," Harrington called, waving everyone into the hut.

Sandy walked towards Dotty and broke into a more relaxed smile.

"How long are you here?" he asked.

"Until a Spit is ready. They're working on it now," Dotty replied.

"Tell them to slow down," Sandy said with a mischievous grin. "We have a dinner date."

"We do?" Dotty played back.

Sandy put a hand on her arm and leaned in to kiss her.

"Debrief, Lovell," Harrington barked. "Now."

Sandy clenched his teeth. "Please stay," he said, and strode away as ordered.

Dotty watched him go, then caught the look on the Wing Commander's face, standing by the dispersal hut door, staring back at her. Daggers flew from the man's expression before he followed Sandy inside.

Dotty couldn't decide if Harrington hated all women or just female pilots. Her relationship with one of his fighter pilots seemed to have heightened his disdain, but he'd been intolerant of her from the first moment they'd met. In the male-dominated world it was by no means the first time she'd been treated as a second-class citizen, but the wing commander was carrying his contempt to new levels.

Diligent to her duty despite her desire to find any way to

remain at Tangmere for the evening, Dotty called the operations room and reported the delay to Marjorie. She was told to stand by, and waited for fifteen minutes in the office, chatting with the young woman at the desk.

"There are two Spits who landed at the emergency satellite field at RAF Westhampnett that are ready to be flown back to Tangmere," Marjorie explained when she called back. "Find a ride over there and pop them across the hedge, dear. I'm told the patch-up job on the original Spit should be done by the time you've finished."

"Okay, will do," Dotty replied, pleased to be staying in the area a little longer.

The drive was a whopping two-and-a-half miles between airfields, winding around the lanes, so Marjorie hadn't been kidding: the flight was little more than a skip over a handful of fields. Dotty waited for the driver to return then repeated the process, and within an hour, both planes were lined up ready for their next sortie.

She checked with Laces once again, who reported the Spitfire she'd been supposed to ferry still wasn't safe to fly. Dotty took a walk around and could see why. The plane had been peppered with enemy fire from a Messerschmitt Bf 109's 20 mm cannons. The shells had left a series of three-quarter-inch holes through the fuselage and wings, luckily missing the pilot. But several of the control cables had been severed along with damage to the engine, cable pulleys, and aileron flaps.

As afternoon became early evening, with Laces still pessimistic about repairs, Dotty took it upon herself to walk across the road to Tangmere Cottage, where Anne greeted her with enthusiasm.

"Dinner will be at seven," her host announced as she showed Dotty to the same room she'd slept in before. "And I don't suppose you brought anything to wear, did you?"

Dotty looked down at her uniform, which needed a clean and press after a day of jumping in and out of various aeroplanes. "Perhaps I could borrow a damp cloth and a brush?"

Anne frowned with a smile on her lips. "That won't do at all, dear. I'll loan you a dress for the evening."

"Oh, I couldn't," Dotty immediately responded, looking at the woman's slender figure and imagining the designer outfits she undoubtedly owned. Fancy numbers at home in swanky private London clubs and exclusive restaurants, not dresses appropriate for having a bite to eat at overnight digs by the airfield.

"Nonsense, I have just the thing," Anne insisted. "Clean yourself up and I'll be back in twenty minutes."

Anne swooshed out of the room leaving Dotty with her mouth open before she could offer any further resistance. She hadn't seen Sandy again all afternoon and was hoping the message she'd left with the WAAF in the office had reached him. She'd feel incredibly stupid sitting at a table alone in the dining room wearing a dress which likely cost more than she made in half a year.

Dotty did her best with her tangled hair and washed over the sink as there wasn't time for a bath. Walking back down the hall from the bathroom, she met Anne carrying several outfits over her arm.

"Come along, dear. Let's see what works best with your shape and colour."

Dotty had never given an awful lot of time to considering her shape or colour before. She was shaped like an average woman as best she could tell. Only having a much younger sister, she'd never spent time with girlfriends trying on dresses and make-up. None of those things had anything to do with flying planes. Colouring wise, her face was mostly more tanned than her pale English body. Mostly, except for the large circles where her goggles screened out the sunshine pouring into the cockpit.

Why, Dotty had no idea – perhaps she missed the London life – but Anne was on a mission. Holding one dress after the other up to Dotty, who was clad in a dressing gown she'd found hanging in the wardrobe, Anne hemmed and hawed over each choice, never giving Dotty time to comment. Not that Dotty had much to say on the matter. She was relieved the choices were day dresses rather than evening gowns, and after two rounds of holding up and comparing, Anne chose a light sea green number with an off-white floral print which came just below the knee.

Slipping the dress on, Dotty blushed to be down to her underwear in front of someone, but was pleased to find it fit her perfectly. Anne cinched the accompanying belt a notch tighter than comfortable, but Dotty let it be, figuring she'd loosen it at her first opportunity alone.

"Oh, you have adorable legs, my dear," Anne swooned. "And you fill that dress out up top better than I do, that's for sure."

Dotty looked at herself in the mirror, and apart from her hair being unwilling to cooperate, she was pleasantly surprised by the image in the glass.

Fifteen minutes later, after Anne insisted on making an attempt at wrestling Dotty's hair and then speedily applying foundation to even out her skin tone, Dotty walked into the dining room. With a self-conscious hesitation, but feeling more feminine than she'd ever experienced in her life, she beamed when she saw Sandy waiting at the table.

He stood and watched her walk over. "Good Lord," he stuttered. "You look simply amazing."

Sandy held her chair while she sat, then retook his seat and looked her in the eyes as though they were the only two people on the planet. For a moment, Dotty was sure she was about to burst. No overtightened belt which she'd forgotten to loosen could contain her joy.

"I hope I'm not making a big blunder here and reading this all wrong," Sandy began in a soft tone. "But this bloody war tends to put things in perspective and hurry what would usually have more time."

Dotty held her breath, unsure where this was going and afraid he'd met someone else and was politely brushing her aside. He reached over and took her hand.

"I know this is frightfully unfair of me," he continued and she felt the tip of a dagger begin piercing her heart.

All the hope, optimism, and feelings she'd been trying to keep under control were about to be destroyed with a handful of simple words. Her father's caution echoed in her head and she felt foolish for having told him anything at all. But then Sandy finished his sentence.

"Dorothy Parker, will you marry me?"

24

AJ looked at her Teric for the umpteenth time. The watch-sized dive computer was her backup and had recorded her dive alongside the larger Perdix, which now hung from her harness while they were on their extended surface interval. She groaned seeing they still had another fifteen minutes before their second dive on the containers.

"Do you always get your tyres from Mexico, George?" Reg asked, relaxing on the bench under the shade of the fly-bridge.

"Mostly," George replied. "I have them shipped there from America and the Far East. Makes it easier to consolidate the shipments before bringing them here. Cheaper than doing it through Miami."

"You have a warehouse there?" AJ asked.

"I have the use of a portion of a warehouse when needed," George replied, and AJ noticed the Dramamine had finally seemed to work as he didn't look quite so green anymore. "We try to fill containers from origination, so it's simply a case of waiting for other shipments to arrive, then putting them all on one ship. Raúl is key in handling everything in Mexico for us."

"Do you always use this freight company?" AJ asked, peering over the side at the water.

George and Raúl both laughed. "First time, actually."

"Dat's some bad luck right dere," Thomas added.

George shrugged his shoulders. "Part of the international shipping business, unfortunately. Containers fall off ships more often than you might think. Of course, when you take into account that 250 million containers are shipped internationally each year, the 700 or so that plop over the side are a tiny percentage."

"Like the odds of winning the lottery," Reg grinned.

"Exactly," George agreed with a laugh. "Lucky old me."

"Let's gear up – it'll be two hours by the time we're in," AJ announced, unable to stand the wait any longer.

Reg and Thomas looked at each other and shook their heads. Nora opened one eye from where she lay on a bench, but didn't bother moving.

"Come on then," AJ urged. "Chop, chop, you lazy bums."

Shifting roles, Reg descended to his wife's possessions in container one, while AJ joined Thomas on tyre duty at container two. The current had died even more, so they were able to leave the line early and angle across, while Reg continued to his destination.

On the boat, Thomas had run through all they'd learnt on the first dive, so when they reached the container, they were ready to start working. With the doors already tied back and what they were now calling the 'tyre line' clipped into the corner castings at each end of the container, the task was relatively simple. In theory. In practice, it was awkward, hard labour.

The tyres were shrink-wrapped in bundles of four, and while they were slightly denser than seawater, their size made them difficult to manhandle. They'd also been shaken like a snow-globe inside the metal box, so the stacks which had left Mexico in neat rows were now more like a jumbled mess. AJ and Thomas, took off their fins, dropped their deco tanks, and let most of the gas out of their wings, so they could walk around inside the container. Which was more like a wobbly stagger.

Looking like spacemen on the moon, it was easy for the heavy tanks on their backs to pull them off balance, and AJ wished she had a pair of lead shoes to keep her feet down. After getting a couple of bundles to the doorway, she waddled back in slow motion, but froze when she saw movement. The doors had been open between dives, and curious fish had already gathered around the new object on their turf, but she hadn't noticed any deep inside yet. She looked over at Thomas, but he held up his hands, asking why she'd stopped.

Hoping it wasn't a moray eel, AJ pressed on, and the two of them dragged the next bundle to the doorway. On the list of things to bring next trip, magnetic torch holders and headlamps were at the top. As they couldn't really rest their torches anywhere, and certainly couldn't hold them while working, AJ and Thomas had resigned themselves to dealing with the dim light from the open doors. As they moved deeper into the container, the visibility was becoming more challenging, and wasn't helped by the fact they were dealing with black objects.

AJ took hold of a tyre bundle and began walking it away from the others, wiggling it side to side while pulling backwards. Something moved quickly from the stack she was holding, shooting over to another bundle. AJ jumped back, bumping into Thomas who was about to join her. Fumbling for her torch, she shone the beam on the floor, rather than directly at the creature.

"Ooooooh…" she crooned into her regulator, spotting the Caribbean reef octopus wrapped around the edge of a bundle.

They stared at each other for several moments with the octopus changing colour to blend in as best he could with the now slightly illuminated tyre. AJ glanced at Thomas to make sure he'd seen their new friend. Thomas nodded and she could see the smile in his eyes through his mask.

Forcing herself back to their task, AJ dragged the bundle clear of the others, then tipped it over and rolled it towards the entrance where Thomas stood it back up. She gave him an okay sign as a question, and he returned the same as a positive answer. Now they were deeper into the container, the tip and roll method made more sense than trying to awkwardly walk the bundles. Thomas then waved her over.

With enough tyres for their first load to the surface, Thomas unclipped the end of the line from the corner casting. The next part was like threading beads on a string on a far larger scale. The tyre bundles had to be manhandled onto the rope, and although their effective weight underwater was much lighter than on land, it was still going to be difficult. AJ had an idea, and tapped Thomas's arm before he started.

She held up a hand, telling him to wait, donned her fins, and kicked to the other end of the container where the line was still attached to the upper corner casting. Releasing the carabiner, AJ dumped all the gas from her wing, and sank to the sand. By connecting the carabiner to the lower corner casting, which was barely accessible in the sand, they wouldn't be trying to shove the bundles along a line that was above them. Thomas gave her an enthusiastic okay sign when he realised her intention, and they began working the bundles down the rope.

With six bundles on the line, Thomas had a tricky time of it, but was able to reconnect the carabiner by the container door. AJ returned to the other end of the container, threaded a new line through the stacks, looped it outside the tyres and returned to where she'd started. The two ends of the new line were then fixed to a lift bag. She added just enough gas from her backup regulator so the bag tugged a little tension on the wagon train of bundles. When AJ disconnected the tyre line from the corner casting, she then blew more gas into the bag, which began pulling on its payload.

Still tethered from Thomas's end, the tyre line was held, while the package attached to the lift bag slowly ascended, gaining more speed as it travelled up the rope. Thomas and AJ didn't wait to watch the 120-foot journey. Time was an enemy and they shucked their fins once more and re-entered the container, ready to start the process all over again.

The tyre bundles were stacked two high and three bundles across each row. George had told AJ he had 168 tyres in each 20-foot container, so she did the maths. Forty-two bundles meant five more wagon trains to the surface. She checked her Perdix: 16 minutes. Their plan was 38 minutes of bottom time, so they'd need to speed things up if they stood a chance of emptying the first container. AJ tumbled the next double-stacked bundle down then rolled them towards Thomas, who manhandled them outside, queuing them up in the sand. AJ grinned behind her reg. Thomas was on the same page as usual.

She grabbed the top of the next double stack and was about to pull it over, when she yanked her hand back in surprise. The octopus shot across to the next stack.

"You silly sod," AJ breathed into her mouthpiece. "I know this looked like a cool new home, but it's going to be a big empty metal box soon."

The octopus appeared to be watching her in the gloom from his new spot atop the next stack.

"Listen, Smudge," she garbled. "Don't look at me like that. I've got work to do. Can't hang about chatting with you."

Giggling to herself, AJ went back to tipping over the next set of tyres, and as she rolled a bundle towards Thomas, he looked at her quizzically. She showed him the hand signal for an octopus and pointed. Thomas just shook his head and dragged the tyres outside.

Despite Smudge continuing to distract her, AJ and Thomas soon found a rhythm, and the process went much faster. With four minutes of planned bottom time left, they watched the last wagon train leave the sea floor on its way to the barge. Thomas began untying the first of the short lines they'd used to hold the doors back, but AJ waved at him. She made the octopus signal again, cupping her hand upside down and wiggling all her fingers. She pointed inside the container. Last seen, Smudge had squished himself into an upper corner after the last of the tyres had been removed. Thomas nodded and left the line in place.

AJ looked towards the edge of the bank and was surprised to

see Reg still labouring at container one. He would have plenty of gas to handle the dive as they were using a very safe margin, but his deco obligation having spent all the time at 135 feet would be a lot longer. He was affixing one of the large net bags to the mooring line via a loop which would slide up the rope. Below the mesh bag she noticed what looked like a piece of furniture.

Thomas tapped AJ on the shoulder and pointed to their mooring line to the barge. AJ thought for a moment before pointing to the original line leading to the Newton. She figured they could fin into the lighter current and save themselves the surface swim in the choppy waves. They picked up their deco tanks, clipped them to their harnesses, then set off, angling up and to the north on an intercept course.

Looking down, AJ watched Reg blow gas into a lift bag until the payload slowly rose from the sea floor. By the time she and Thomas reached the Newton's mooring line, the package had passed by on its way to the boat, allowing them to hold the rope.

Reg quickly ascended in its wake, but held at 70 feet for his first deco stop. AJ and Thomas continued to 40 feet where her Perdix indicated they'd begin their stops, opening the valves for their 50% oxygen nitrox mix tanks on the way. Levelling off, they switched to the regulators for the new tanks, and AJ looked up at the hull of *Hazel's Odyssey* above them.

She watched Nora swim to the bow and for a moment wondered what she was doing. It soon became clear as her friend disconnected Reg's loop from the mooring line and began towing the lift bag behind her towards the stern. The mesh sack of Pearl's mother's possessions and a small wooden cupboard dangled in the water, trailing along behind.

AJ and Thomas moved up to 30 feet, where they'd spend four minutes. They both looked up and AJ laughed into her regulator, watching Nora, George Cook, and Raúl struggling to drag the cupboard from the Caribbean Sea onto the swim step of the Newton. AJ could only imagine how it was going with Nora barking orders to the island's tyre importers.

25

Pilot First Officer Dorothy Parker awoke engaged to be married. To say she was delighted to be so would be a vast understatement. The evening had been perfect, full of talk of the wedding, how they'd tell their families, and when they'd be able to have a ceremony. Soon, they agreed, without mentioning the reasons why. But with the dawn came the reality that the war didn't stop for anything, especially love.

She dressed, ate a quick breakfast, and thanked Anne profusely for her seemingly telepathic ability to prepare Dotty for the best evening of her life. Making the short walk to the airfield, it was too early for the secretary to be in the office, so Dotty started towards the Spitfire squadron to see if the plane was ready.

"It's time for you to leave," came a voice from the Hurricane squadron's dispersal hut as Dotty passed by the door.

She spun around, recognising Harrington's voice. "Heading there now, sir," she replied, a shiver running through her as the man stepped into the light, looking her over from head to toe.

"I'll see if they have it ready," she added.

"It's ready," he replied. "It flew here, didn't it? Isn't that what you told me the other day?"

Dotty gritted her teeth hearing her own words thrown back in her face. The situations were completely different, but the fact that he'd retained what she'd said spoke volumes about how the wing commander regarded her.

"You're an unwanted distraction. You know that, right?" he said, casually walking away from the door and exhaling cigarette smoke as he spoke. "We have a war to win. Everything else must wait. One moment he's thinking about a girl who's pretending to be a real pilot when he should be focused on the enemy, and the next he's dead. Which would be because of you."

Dotty raged inside, but somehow kept a cork in the bottle. Somewhere amongst the roiling emotions of fury, humiliation, and fear that the man was correct, a little voice told her to stay silent. He was baiting her. All he needed was a hint of insubordination, and although the ATA was a civilian organisation, he'd land her in big trouble. At a minimum she'd be barred from his airfield, and if he really pursued the issue, she suspected he could have her kicked out of the ATA.

"Sir," she blurted, then strode away without looking back.

Her legs shook and quivered with every step, but Dotty kept going. She desperately wanted to see Sandy before she left, knowing his smile would untwist the knot in her stomach, but the wing commander would never allow it. By the time she reached the broken Spitfire, Dotty had convinced herself the best thing to do was leave. Marjorie would find a way for her to return to Tangmere, and she'd try calling Sandy this evening from wherever she ended up.

"Ready?" she asked Laces, struggling to keep a tremor from her voice.

The mechanic scratched his head. "Done the best we can, miss," he replied.

Between his tentative words and the look on his face, she didn't get the impression he placed much confidence in the plane.

"Is it fit to fly?" she asked.

"Wing Commander says it is, miss."

Dotty glanced back across the field where Harrington leaned against the dispersal hut doorframe, watching from a distance.

"What do you say?" she asked, turning back to Laces.

"I think you should be careful, miss, and I'd fly above 1,000 feet if I were you."

Dotty knew what the man meant. One thousand feet was considered the minimum height from which to bail out and survive. That was a thousand feet above the ground, so the height of the terrain above sea level had to be added to one thousand to give the number on the altimeter. Pilots had lived from less, but between clearing the tail safely and getting the cord pulled and the chute filling out to arrest the fall, the odds diminished immensely. She looked at the overcast skies. Low cloud had closed in overnight, and while the conditions were currently flyable, she doubted the ceiling would allow her the safety margin over the South Downs. Which meant taking a greater distance to duck through the valley over Arundel.

For a brief moment, she thought about calling Marjorie and explaining the situation, but quickly disregarded the idea. Harrington had told the ATA that the plane was ready to be ferried, and Marjorie was in no position to question him.

"What should I be on the lookout for?" Dotty asked, wondering in which manner the aircraft would attempt to drop from the sky.

"Watch the temperature," he said with a pained expression. "I think we have all the surface controls reliable, but the engine took a few hits. We've patched her as best we could."

"Is it holding pressure?" she asked, knowing the Merlin engine relied on a pressurised coolant system containing a mixture of water and glycol.

"It is this morning," he replied with little confidence. "Welding dirty tubes back together isn't easy, miss."

Dotty nodded. "I dare say it's not." She climbed onto the wing. "Thank you and the lads for all your effort. Hopefully I'll see you again to tell you what a bang-up job you did."

"I hope so too, miss. You can buy us a pint before you're a married woman," he said, managing a grin.

"Word gets around fast," Dotty laughed, setting her parachute in the cockpit.

"It does, at that," he agreed. "And if I may say so, Lovell has done well for himself, miss."

Dotty slipped into the seat then looked down at Laces in surprise.

The man continued. "Can't say I much understood the whole concept of having women flying these fighters all over, but you've changed our view of all that, miss."

"I have?" Dotty said. "I mean, thank you, but I haven't done anything different from any other ATA pilot."

"I suppose that's the point, ain't it, miss?"

Dotty wished she'd seen Sandy for a multitude of reasons, but at least the Spitfire mechanic's words had washed away her feeling of angst over Harrington's comments. Somewhat replaced with a new angst over the airworthiness of the plane, but she'd rather face a mechanical failure than the idea she'd be the cause of Sandy's death.

Before she could talk herself out of it, Dotty fired up the engine and taxied to the grass strip with two mechanics on the tail. When the Spitfire briefly came to a stop, the men dropped to the ground and Dotty rumbled down the field until the aeroplane lifted off. Immediately, the controls felt different. It took a few turns for Dotty to figure it out, but the cables to the ailerons weren't even side to side, which she tried adjusting with the trim controls. That helped, but the controls required a different amount of effort to bank left versus right. Something was tight, bent, or hanging up. That was fine, she decided; she could adapt. Every plane had its idiosyncrasies, and these were just a bit more amplified on the damaged Spitfire.

Choosing shorter distance over altitude, Dotty headed north over the downs and breathed a sigh of relief when the fields of West Sussex and Surrey were below her. Flying just below the grey clouds at an altitude of 1,200 feet put her about 1,000 feet above the ground most of the time. Close enough to the guideline that she felt bailing out might be survivable. Whether she would leave the disabled Spit to crash wherever fate chose was another matter. She'd never live with herself if the plane hit someone's house, or God forbid a school. That thought left Dotty determined to stick with the Spitfire until it was on the ground. However that may occur.

She kept a careful eye on the gauges as she continued north, the engine temperature running slightly higher than normal but holding steady. Over Oxfordshire, rain began reducing visibility, and water streaked over the windscreen. Dotty dropped altitude, making sure she didn't get caught in the cloud, and pounded on, running the Merlin at well below its capabilities in the hopes of nursing it to her destination.

Passing over Royal Leamington Spa with only 15 of the 125-mile journey to go, the temperature gauge began rising. It was hard to tell with water droplets flying over every external surface, but Dotty thought she could see a trickle of white vapour, which would indicate a coolant leak. She couldn't be sure, but the needle continuing to climb on the temp gauge suggested her eyes weren't deceiving her.

At 700 feet above the ground, her option to bail was removed from the equation, so what she needed now was somewhere to land before the engine seized. While she had power, she had choices. If she'd done her maths correctly in her head, gliding from 800 feet meant covering about two miles before the Spitfire would meet the ground. The rainy conditions didn't help that number.

Studying her map, Dotty then looked below, rolling the Spitfire one way and then the other to see the ground. RAF Honiley should have been close by but she must have been past it. Ahead, through the rain, the small training field at RAF Elmdon appeared, but now she was only seven or eight miles from her intended destination. With no hills to be concerned with, and a solid compass heading for

Castle Bromwich, Dotty broke one of the ATA's cardinal rules. She climbed into the cloud.

Running quick calculations in her head, she figured that at 200 mph it would take her a minute and a half to cover five miles. She kept an eye on her watch. At 1,500 feet, Dotty levelled off with fluffy grey murk rushing by outside, making her eyes unable to focus properly and her head began to spin. Focusing on the gauges instead, she maintained level flight on her compass heading, glancing at the temperature. She had just begun calculating a glide from her new altitude when the engine note laboured, then stopped. The Merlin had overheated and seized.

RAF Elmdon seemed like a far better option now, but that horse had bolted. She could berate herself for poor decisions later, but there was no time for it now. Bailing out was an option at this height, but she reminded herself how close she was to the city of Birmingham. Dotty checked her watch. It had been just over a minute. All her maths was now out the window as the speed and altitude were dropping.

Feathering the prop wasn't an option on a Spitfire, so it continued turning at the whim of the air Dotty raced through. She pulled out her ATA pilot notes. According to the text, the best glide speed for the Spitfire was 150 mph. Now came a balancing act which would determine whether she landed or crashed. Her speed was now controlled by her angle of descent and the key was to find the magic 150 mph. Dive too steeply and she'd give away precious altitude. Not steep enough and the Spitfire would be travelling below its most efficient speed for lift, meaning she'd still give away precious altitude. Or even stall.

The irony of her situation following so soon after the best evening of her life brought a lump to her throat. *Surely the world couldn't be this cruel?* A flash of anger flitted through her mind as she thought of Wing Commander Harrington. It was on his insistence that she was flying a plane unfit for the air. But those emotions also had to wait. If she was still alive in five minutes, she could hash them over at leisure.

Breaking through the cloud, Dotty searched the ground for Castle Bromwich airfield, looking for the factory buildings more than the fields themselves. The rain lashed down, making it hard to see out the cockpit and reducing visibility to only a few miles. Conditions were now below those deemed safe by the Air Transport Auxiliary for ferry pilots to take off.

Through the misty haze she spotted what she hoped were the large grey roofs of the Castle Bromwich Aeroplane Factory. Unable to spot the windsock, Dotty gambled on the wind direction based on experience and the feel of the plane being buffeted. She'd only have one attempt at landing, so she had to hope no one else was being silly enough to land or take off in this weather.

As she came gliding in, the field loomed ahead, the grass runway stretching away to her port side. Desperate not to give away altitude she'd never regain, Dotty flew straight until she was a few hundred yards from the farmer's fence at the edge of the strip, then banked while lowering the landing gear as late as possible. The extra drag slowed the plane and she dipped the nose to compensate, easing it back up as the wet grass raced towards her.

The tyres met the soggy earth with a firmer thud than she'd be proud of, but Dotty yelped in relief as she carefully braked and slowed, veering off the main strip before coming to a stop.

She slid the canopy back and let the rain pelt down on the top of her leather flying helmet. The fresh smell of soaking wet grass quickly became overwhelmed by the burnt stench of the fried engine. Dotty gathered her stuff and hopped out, sliding the canopy closed from the outside. Dropping to the ground, she looked up to the sky, feeling the raindrops pepper her face.

Dotty didn't much care for smoking, and rarely partook. But this seemed like a moment that required a cigarette, seeing as brandy wasn't on hand.

After a few minutes, a Standard 12 Tilly came bouncing towards her and stopped by the Spitfire.

"Couldn't taxi it over to us, then?" a ground crewman said as he stepped from the vehicle and raised an eyebrow at Dotty.

"I managed to land it without the engine," Dotty replied. "But I can't push it all by myself."

"You dead-stick landed in this?" the man questioned, pulling his collar up and wiping the rain from his face.

"Seemed like the better option once the engine seized," Dotty replied, and managed a very relieved smile. "Considering the alternative."

26

AJ gathered up merchandise strewn around the little hut and stuffed the garments back into the right boxes for their sizes. She'd worn her Peace Love Dive T-shirt on the boat and several of Craig's group had decided they couldn't go another day without one for themselves. Nora's long, slender build modelled the Mermaid Divers leggings and rashguards perfectly, so after following the Norwegian around as she guided the deep dive again, several of the women in the group had been sold on them too. The sales were great, but AJ was itching to start their trek back out to Twelve Mile Bank.

Pearl's smile when they'd returned to the dock the evening before with the first items from her container was fuelling AJ's enthusiasm. A freshwater wash and plenty of WD-40 on anything metal – which was mainly Reg's Land Rover parts – and they were optimistic they'd saved the pieces. AJ had chuckled when Pearl was surprised to see the Landy parts. Reg glared at AJ and shook his head. He'd fretted all the way back from the bank, but of course AJ had never sent Pearl a picture.

With tanks replenished, the crew finally got underway and were tying into the mooring buoy by 1:30pm. Reg had told George they'd be working exclusively on container one this afternoon, so the tyre importer had stayed on dry land with a promise his second container would be their priority on Tuesday. Reg, AJ, and Thomas had discussed the challenge of the greater depth, but still figured they could empty the unit in two dives despite the limited bottom time. They'd use Thomas staged at container one to shepherd the loads to the surface as he wasn't tech certified to dive below 150 feet.

AJ looked over at the barge still safely moored to its buoy. The tyre bundles were lashed down and all looked secure after a night on the open ocean. Damon and Bash had also skipped this trip as Reg felt they could fit whatever they brought up of Pearl's on the deck of *Hazel's Odyssey*.

"Should we turn the lights on the barge off until we leave?" AJ asked.

Reg shook his head. "Damon told me his battery was fine to run the lights for several days. He'll fire up the engine and recharge them tomorrow. I'd be more worried about us forgetting them when we leave."

"Won't be no good if a cruise ship hit dat ting in da dark," Thomas said.

AJ laughed. "I don't know. A cruise ship would make a great dive site out here on the bank."

Thomas frowned at her, stifling his easy smile.

"I mean as long as everyone got off safely," AJ quickly added.

"I think we'll have to settle for dat new bronze statue they gonna put on Soto's Reef," Thomas said, as he readied his gear.

"As long as no one tries to blow this one up," AJ replied, recalling all too well the disaster surrounding the Angels of the Deep statue they'd all been involved in trying to place on the sea floor.

No one had been hurt in the incident, but a disgruntled man had attempted to blow up members of the royal family who were visiting the island to witness the placement of their gift.

"Are you two planning on talking all day, or can we get on with it?" Reg grumbled.

"Oh hush up, you miserable old goat," AJ chided in return. "I'm ready."

"I'm ready, Big Boss," Thomas hurriedly agreed.

"Get off the boat and leave me in peace," Nora added, holding AJ's tank valve as she helped her waddle in the heavy gear to the swim step.

On Reg's wrist slate, he'd written Pearl's priority list which she'd made from the inventory they'd supplied to customs in the UK. The original list had been somewhat vague as they'd had little time to go through everything in detail, so boxes had been filled with only a brief description. But the major items Pearl hoped they could retrieve were the furniture, her mother's china, and the safe which they'd been unable to open in England, as Pearl's mother hadn't left the code. It could be empty, or it could contain important family papers as Pearl suspected; they had no idea.

Reaching the open upper door, the divers dropped their deco tanks on top of the container, and Reg eased himself inside. AJ and Thomas used magnetic mounts to secure torches to either side of the interior, filling the space with light. AJ noticed Reg had accomplished a lot of work the previous day. The pile of mushy boxes, papers, and books was now level and below the height of the lower door. A row of boxes in better shape than the rest sat atop the debris.

Reg was already farther into the container, his fins protruding from a mass of furniture wrapped in sodden blankets. He looked back and waved at AJ, who gently kicked her way forward to join him. Reg used his handheld torch to show her the tangled mess they'd be dealing with. Everything had been neatly and efficiently stacked for shipping, but the drop from the ship and subsequent trip to the sea floor, where the container now lay on its side, had created chaos.

The torch beam made a circle on a shape that was clearly a chair and AJ immediately understood Reg's plan. To remove any of the larger pieces, including the rectangular dining table, the eight chairs had to be pulled out. Most of the packing blankets had become dislodged and the chair legs were entwined with each other, along with everything else in the second half of the container. AJ back-finned to give Reg room, and he wiggled the first chair free, passing it to her. In turn, AJ handed the chair to Thomas, who set it on top of the container, using one of their deco bottles as ballast to hold it down.

The current had subsided further, making the environment far more workable, but they all knew that could revert at any time without warning. While their luck held, Thomas took advantage of the favourable conditions and used the flat metal surface as a staging area.

Reaching for the second chair, AJ squealed into her regulator.

"Smudge!"

An octopus, about the same size as the one she'd seen in container two, shuffled along the underside of the table. He stopped and peeked out at AJ. She was sure it was the same one.

"This one won't be much better, mate," she garbled into her mouthpiece. "But it's nice to see you again."

The leg of the chair waggled in AJ's outstretched hand, and she looked up to see Reg staring back at her. She responded to his questioning frown with the octopus hand signal and pointed to the table which was perpendicular to them. Reg shook his head, but once AJ had taken the chair, she saw him look under the table. Smudge eased away into the shadows.

The rest of the wooden dining chairs came out in short order, and apart from a few scratches and scrapes where the blankets had pulled away, appeared to be in remarkably decent shape. AJ noticed one or two crooked legs, but considering what they'd endured, it was a miracle they weren't firewood. The oak was slightly buoyant, so once the chairs were freed from the tangle, AJ felt like Superwoman moving living room furniture around as though it weighed nothing.

After passing the last chair to Thomas, AJ finned alongside Reg, and they both studied the table. Four large bookcases had been the first items loaded, filling the back wall. In front of them was an oak desk and then the dining table. The chairs, bedside tables, and a matching coffee and end table had begun the journey stacked atop the desk and dining table. With one bedside table and all the chairs removed, the smaller tables were next.

Reg circled the end table with his torch beam, and AJ reached down beyond the pile of box debris to grab one end. Reg's aluminium tanks bumping against the steel container made a subdued clank, dampened by the water, as he manoeuvred his large frame into position. Between them, they wiggled the tall square-end table free and shoved it behind them. It quickly disappeared in Thomas's grasp.

Smudge relocated again, and AJ was amazed the little creature hadn't inked in fear of the strange beasts making all the bubbles. He appeared to be more curious than concerned. She reached out her hand, resting it on a wardrobe which had unfortunately taken the brunt of the other furniture crushing against it. Smudge initially shrank back into the corner he'd found, but after a moment, cautiously extended a tentacle. AJ invitingly wiggled one finger and the octopus edged closer.

A grunting sound made Smudge retract and AJ turn. Reg's eyes were apologetic, but he pointed to the next piece of furniture. AJ scowled at him, but he was right. In the back of a shipping container at 130 feet underwater with a job to do was not the time to play octopus footsie. She gave Smudge a little wave, then helped Reg haul the second bedside table away.

By the time they'd cleared everything except the dining table and desk, AJ checked her Perdix then nudged Reg. At 27 minutes into their 35 minutes of planned bottom time, they needed to get out of the container and start the process of raising the furniture they'd removed. As they carefully manoeuvred to the door, Reg pointed at the sturdier boxes still to be opened. He mimicked tipping a cup to his mouth, and AJ returned an okay sign as acknowledgement. She understood the boxes were filled with Pearl's china, much dating back to her grandmother, and which AJ unfortunately expected to find in shattered pieces after the ordeal it had been through. It was devastating to think that plates and cups which had survived the London Blitz of World War II and all the years until now could be smashed to pieces before Pearl ever placed them on a shelf.

Outside, they used line to tie the chairs together in one bundle and a second grouping containing the other pieces. Using very little gas in the lift bags, they affixed the bundles to a loop on the mooring line, sending the first package to the surface. As Nora was alone on the boat, they gave her a few minutes to get the chairs unhooked from the line and moved to the stern as they began ascending with bundle two. Pausing at 40 feet to switch gases, Reg looked up and, seeing that the line was clear, released the second bundle.

While performing deco stops on the line was far more relaxing without a current whipping them like flags in a strong wind, hauling the furniture aboard *Hazel's Odyssey* was a chore. With gravity back in full effect, even the chairs were awkward, and the soaking wet blankets made them extremely heavy. Things went far more smoothly once they removed the blankets in the water before handing up the items.

"That desk is going to be a bugger," Reg commented, plonking himself down on a bench once they were done.

"The dining table won't be a walk in the park, either," AJ added. "And first, we have to get them out of the container."

Reg shook his head. "They're old, dense oak, and maybe it's metal hardware or perhaps the water has soaked into the wood already, but they're not floating like you'd expect."

"Maybe everything got all discombobulated when it fell off the ship," AJ suggested. "Once we un-wedge them from those book-cases and wardrobe, they should be somewhat buoyant like the chairs were."

"True," Reg agreed. "Just awkward, I suppose. The table almost fills the full width of the container."

After a break to get their breath back, they busied themselves switching tanks in preparation for the second dive, while the Newton bobbed and swayed in the gentle swells. After a while, the person who usually stayed quiet broke the silence.

"What about the safe?" Nora asked. "Wasn't there a safe on Pearl's list?"

AJ looked at Reg, who stopped what he was doing.

"Yeah," Reg acknowledged, sitting on the bench as he thought about it. "I'm trying to remember where we put it."

"I haven't seen a safe," AJ said. "How big is it?"

Reg held up his hands about two feet apart. "You know, normal household safe size."

"Wouldn't it float?" Thomas said, more as a statement than a question.

"Should," Reg responded.

"As long as it hasn't let the water in," AJ pointed out.

Reg looked up at her. "I think it's one of them fireproof and floodproof types."

AJ winced. "Rated to 130 feet?"

Reg grunted. "I dare say we're the first ones to test that."

27

The shared bathroom didn't offer much time for a soak, but a hot bath still felt good after the damp, dreary day filled with drama. Dotty quickly towelled herself dry, hearing impatient feet pacing outside, and hurriedly threw on her trousers and shirt. Clutching the towel and her underwear to her chest, she swept past the man in the hall and disappeared into her room.

The small overnight bag held little more than her toiletries and a nightgown, so after stripping down and finishing drying herself properly, it was back on with the uniform. She rather missed the feel of Anne's floral dress she'd borrowed the evening before, but her uniform was far more appropriate amongst the pilots, all male, who were also staying in the guest rooms above the local pub.

Heading downstairs, Dotty waited for the payphone in the reception area to become available. Getting a call connected was always a chore and often impossible, but when the phone was free, she asked the operator to reach her family's billet in Little Rissington.

"Parker residence," her father answered and the operator clicked off the line.

"Daddy, it's me."

"Hey, love. That's two smashing surprises in a matter of days. Everything all right?"

"Yes. Well, I did have to dead stick a Spit into Castle Brom today, but all's well that ends well."

"Blimey, girl. Lose the engine?"

"Coolant leak. Seized up. But I was close enough to glide in."

"I hope that was this morning before the weather closed in. Pea soup around here this afternoon," he said.

"Umm, it was after the morning. Spot of rain, but it all turned out alright," she replied, trying to make it sound less perilous than it had actually been.

Patrick grunted his displeasure. "S'pose flying the dodgy ones is part of the job."

"Afraid so," Dotty replied. "But that's not why I called, Daddy."

"Alright, love," he said, his voice a mixture of concern and curiosity.

"Sandy asked me to marry him last night."

The line quietly crackled and Dotty held her breath.

"Didn't give me much chance to meet this fella, did you?" her father said.

"I'm sorry about that, but it's all been a bit of a whirlwind."

"I'd say."

"You'll really like him, I promise."

"If he passes muster with you, I suspect he's probably alright," Patrick said, and Dotty couldn't tell across the line if her father was putting on a brave face or truly being accepting.

"I said yes," Dotty said, realising she hadn't clarified that part.

"I'd assumed that much, love. Didn't think you'd called to tell me you'd sent him down the road."

Dotty laughed.

"Besides, I already knew," Patrick said.

"What?" Dotty gasped.

"Sandy called this morning and apologised for not asking my permission."

"You let me squirm and be all scared to tell you?" Dotty fumed, and it was her father's turn to laugh.

"You were squirming around a bit there, but I hope you're never scared to tell me anything, love."

"Well, not scared. Apprehensive perhaps," she said. "So you're alright with this, Daddy?"

"Hard to say I'm completely alright with it, my love, seeing as I've never met the bloke and you barely know him. But I could see the happiness in your eyes when you stopped by. If he can keep that look on your face, then I'll be pleased as punch about the whole thing."

"Thank you," she whispered. "Does Mum know?"

"Oh yes. She'll have your guts for garters for not bringing him around and talking to her about it, but she's already fussing about dresses and telling family and what have you, so she'll be fine."

"You can tell her I won't need a dress."

"Then maybe she won't be fine," he responded with a laugh.

"I'd like to get married in my uniform," Dotty explained.

"I'll be the proudest father a wedding ever had, but we'll have to put in a bit of work to bring your mum around to our way of thinking. Your sister just wants to be sure that she gets a new dress to wear, so that might get us off the hook."

"She can wear any dress she wants," Dotty chuckled.

"I take it this wedding is going to happen rather sharpish."

"That's what we talked about, but I don't even have a ring yet," Dotty confessed. "And his CO isn't keen on female pilots, especially this female pilot, so we have to see when Sandy can get leave."

"He mentioned about the ring," Patrick replied. "The lad has a plan there which sounded good."

"He did? What is it?" Dotty asked.

"I can't tell you that," her father chuckled. "He told me in confidence."

"Great. You haven't even met him and you're already conniving together."

He just laughed, which made Dotty feel wonderful after a challenging day.

"Tell Mum and Sis I said hello, Dad. I'd better go before I run out of coins."

"Alright, girl. Congratulations."

Dotty thanked him and hung up. A man was waiting to use the telephone, so she slipped into the pub and ordered something to eat from their meagre wartime menu. For a moment, she considered ordering herself a gin fizz, but decided she'd better keep her wits about her and settled for a lemonade.

After dinner, the telephone was free and she tried getting through to Sandy's billet near Tangmere. The village was so small, many of the pilots had to stay in other nearby houses. It took a while, but the operator finally connected her, and a woman answered.

"Lawrence residence."

"Is Flying Officer Lovell there, please," Dotty asked.

"One moment," the woman said, and Dotty heard footsteps and her call out to Sandy.

After several moments there were more footsteps. "Flying Officer Lovell."

"It's me," Dotty responded, overjoyed to hear his voice.

"I hoped it was," he replied. "I've been so worried. Did you make it alright?"

"Worried about me?" she questioned, perplexed over the madness of a fighter pilot's concerns over her ferrying planes.

"The lads told me the Spit wasn't airworthy, but the Wing Commander insisted. I was ready to wring his neck."

"Oh, don't do that, Sandy, I'm fine. Please don't land yourself in trouble because of me."

"I don't know what his problem is," Sandy said, still agitated. "In times like these, airworthy is subjective sometimes, but Laces knows his stuff, and this was to ferry the darn thing. It could have waited a day."

Dotty couldn't help but beam although she was glad Sandy

couldn't see her face. She didn't want him to mistake her elation at her man defending her for amusement at his anger.

"The trip went fine," she lied. "How was your day? Can I ask that? I'm sure they're never good, so maybe I shouldn't."

"It's okay," he said, his tone lightening. "If I come home then that's something good, but it's hard to feel great when some of your chums weren't so lucky."

"I'm afraid I have a more selfish view when I know you made it home."

Sandy laughed. "And I hope you get to feel that way every day." His voice became serious again as he continued. "Today wasn't bad. Bruce was hit over northern France, but we saw him bail out, so hopeful he made it. Nice chap from Dorset. Other two sorties we missed them. Flew around over the channel and came home. Happens sometimes."

Dotty wasn't sure whether to ask anything more, which she was burning to do, or to let it go. If they were together and she could look into his eyes, she figured she'd know, but over the telephone was different.

"You spoke with my father," she blurted, remembering her prior call. "He let me prattle on about you like a little schoolgirl, all nervous and butterflies, before he finally told me you'd spoken with him."

Sandy laughed again. "He sounds like a top-shelf fellow. He was very kind and understanding considering the situation. I did feel awful having not asked his permission."

"I think he understands. My mother will have quite a time over me not wearing a dress, but Daddy was all for me getting married in uniform. Are you sure you don't mind?"

"I'll be proud to stand next to you as two people serving their country," he replied. "Besides, you can wear a top hat and tails as far as I'm concerned, as long as you say 'I do'."

Dotty smiled from ear to ear. "I challenge anyone to try and stop me."

"Hopefully no one does," Sandy replied.

"Your wing commander might," Dotty said, thoughts of how he might intervene flashing through her mind. "Have you asked for leave?"

"I'll ask tomorrow. I wasn't sure if I could ask him today without grilling him on why he sent you up in that Spit."

"Well, if he had a nefarious plan," Dotty replied. "I foiled it with a bit of luck and a good glide."

The line went quiet for a moment and Dotty realised her blunder.

"That doesn't sound like your trip went fine, Dotty. What happened?"

She sighed. "The engine seized, but I was only a few miles out and I'd already picked out alternate airfields if it had happened earlier. It really *was* fine."

"What was the cloud ceiling?" he asked.

"About 1,000," she said. "Maybe a touch less."

"Dotty," he breathed. "Please don't tell me fibs. It's my job to worry about you."

"I am sorry," she said, and surprised herself that she wasn't nervous of having offended him. Exactly what she was feeling wasn't clear, but she liked it. "I'll tell you if something like that happens again."

"Thank you, my dear," he replied softly.

"But that means you have to be honest with me too," she said firmly. "It's also my job to worry about you."

"That's fair," he responded.

So many subjects and points were yet to be discussed and considered between them, Dotty suddenly felt slightly overwhelmed as she realised she was about to run out of coins.

"I'm not certain I want to have children," she said, launching the words into the telephone before she could stop herself.

The line was silent again for several moments and she began to think her money had run out and they'd been disconnected.

"I don't care," he finally said. "There's nothing we can't figure out as we go, my love."

And then the line did indeed go dead.

28

AJ shrugged off the aches in her shoulders and back as she finned her way into the container once more. The work at the surface was physically demanding, but the underwater labour required a lot of awkward bending and twisting, using muscles which didn't usually get strained.

Placing a mesh bag down on the messy pile of debris, AJ carefully attempted to lift the first box of china. The cardboard felt like soggy bread to the touch and began falling apart in her grasp. Reg wiggled the mesh bag underneath the box, causing sugar lump-sized pieces of brown cardboard to waft away like a mini slow-motion explosion. A chunk of white and blue china tumbled down the debris pile and a knot formed in AJ's stomach.

Reg enveloped the crumbling box in the mesh bag and lifted it from the pile. Turning, he handed it to Thomas, who delicately pulled the package from the shipping container. AJ took a long breath through her regulator and refocused on the task, lifting the next box as best she could off the pile so Reg could slide a bag underneath. They continued until all four boxes of china had been removed from the container and they turned their attention to the remaining furniture.

The bookcases they could see had been damaged and the wardrobe had taken the brunt of the other pieces crushing against it, so Reg had made the call to leave them. Which left the desk and the dining table. With the container on its side, both items were on end, sitting on the wardrobe, which in turn was being covered with debris spreading from the pile of boxes. Visibility inside the container had also noticeably diminished as particulate scattered from the crumbling cardboard and other buoyant items floating around the divers.

Reg pointed to the top of the desk, indicating for AJ to lift that side, so she slipped off her fins, setting them aside, and manoeuvred herself into position. She was now standing on the wardrobe with what looked to be old newspaper clippings and the now ever-present disintegrating cardboard around her feet. Together, they tried lifting the desk, but it was caught on something. Reg held up a hand, telling her to wait while he looked around to identify the snag.

Pointing towards the doors, he signalled for them to slide the desk that way before lifting, and after a few wiggles, the desk came free. AJ laughed into her regulator. It was strange, moving what would normally be a very heavy object as though it were an inflatable toy instead of an oak desk. They paused for a moment to pull the shipping blankets back into position, but the tape securing them had already lost its stickiness and nothing would stay in place. The blankets were now more of a hindrance than a protection, and Reg shook his head, slipping them away from the desk.

With the covering cleared, AJ saw the real beauty of the desk in the torch beams and light spilling through the one open door. It was sturdy, with a rich tone to the stain, and AJ wondered how many letters had been written on the inlaid top. The drawers were held closed by a shrink-wrap around the base, which fortunately had held up so far. The desk began moving again, and AJ realised Reg was ready to get on. They helped Thomas move the desk to the top of the container, where he used a pair of their deco bottles as ballast to stop the wooden desk drifting away.

AJ and Reg ducked back inside after a check of their computers. The plan was for 30 minutes of bottom time, shortening it by 5 minutes over the first dive as they thought it would be enough to finish the job, and it added another step of conservativeness. Always a good idea when doing multiple decompression dives. AJ had a backup plan for 40 minutes, but as they were 16 minutes in and over halfway done, she was confident they'd be ascending early rather than late. Although they still had to move the large table, and were yet to see any sign of a safe, so any hiccup could derail their timing.

Lowering themselves either side of the table beyond the debris pile, AJ and Reg both looked around to see what might be stopping the dining table from floating. AJ soon saw the problem. She waved at Reg then pointed to the bookcases on the back wall of the container. What AJ presumed were the shelves had been wrapped in a blanket and placed on the base of each bookcase. When everything had been tipped over, they'd become wedged and tangled with the broken frames of the cases and the table.

After much jiggling, shoving, and pulling, they freed the interference and cast the bundles of shelves aside. The table, whose blankets had remained more securely in place, became a toy in their hands, and after carefully turning and twisting it from the back of the container, they moved it towards the doors. Before they reached the opening, a waft of murky water overtook them, and AJ turned around.

The torch beams reflected off a brown, mucky cloud, much like a car's headlights in fog. She looked at Reg and nodded towards the exit. He picked up his side of the table and they guided it into Thomas's arms, helping him manoeuvre it atop the container alongside the desk and mesh bags. Reg pointed to the desk and threw a thumb towards the surface. He wanted to send it up. Thomas began affixing a small lift bag as it wouldn't need much help floating, so AJ left them to it and quickly pulled herself back inside the metal cave.

The disturbance was beginning to settle. Given a few months, everything left behind would decay, rot, or fall apart, leaving the inside of the container a treacherous place that would silt out in the waft of a fin. Although the hinges and latches would have rusted by that point, so entry would require a cutting torch if someone was keen enough to want inside.

They'd discussed at length their concerns about the materials they'd be forced to leave in the container on the ocean floor, as it went against the divers' rule of only taking pictures and leaving bubbles. It would be decades, but coral would slowly grow over every surface where a hint of light reached down from above, and eventually the steel would rust through. In some cases, coral would create a cocoon-like shell, but more likely, the contents would eventually be open to the ocean.

Fabrics, cardboard, paper, and metal would decompose, and china, glass, and pottery would become part of the reef without causing ill effects. The problem would be plastics. Reg and Pearl had racked their brains trying to remember what they'd come across during packing, and were confident there wasn't much. They'd deliberately used cardboard boxes instead of plastic tubs, as they didn't want to bring more plastic to the island. They hadn't kept any regular household goods or consumables, taking them to a charity instead. Reg and AJ had kept an eager eye out for anything they'd overlooked, but so far the shrink-wrap on the desk was all she'd seen, and it was on its way to the surface.

The back of the container was finally visible once more, but the lens effect of her dive mask underwater, which made everything appear 25 percent larger and much closer, made it hard to tell if the bookcases were leaning forward. Something had moved to cause the disturbance but it took AJ a minute to realise that one of the bookcases had toppled to the floor, or what was the side of the container before it tipped over. It now covered most of the wardrobe.

AJ played her torch beam around, and caught movement in the lower corner. Smudge slid around the broken wood and appeared to look up at her. AJ lowered the light so she didn't blind her little friend. As the beam fell on the spot the octopus had just left, it shone on a smooth, dull black surface. Something about the texture made AJ take a second look and at first she thought it might be the metal of the container. Except it didn't have a corrugated shape.

Dropping to the remains of the bookcase, she reached down to feel the surface of the object. Smudge backed up but kept an eye on her. AJ cheered into her regulator and wiggled her hips in glee. She'd found the safe. The next problem was how to dig it out without disturbing the other bookcases. Rising up and away from the broken wood, she realised the safe had been pinning down the wardrobe. Which made no sense as the safe should float. If it was full of air. Which likely meant the seal had succumbed to the water pressure, allowing seawater in and ruining any documents inside. AJ's elation soon switched to disappointment.

She spotted metal wall brackets attached to the bookcase, which explained why it had fallen instead of floating, and she guessed the other cases would likely have the same brackets.

She turned to Smudge, who was still peeking around a section of wardrobe. "Move, little fella, I'm going to make a mess."

The octopus didn't budge, but she knew he'd be nimble enough to deal with what she was about to do. Reaching up, AJ pulled another bookcase away from the last two. Slowly, it toppled, and as she predicted, sank on top of the first one, putting the safe farther out of reach. Dancing shadows and a deep grunt from behind told her Reg was back inside the container, and she wasted no time pointing to one side of the bookcase she'd pulled over.

Reg moved into position and looked at her with a questioning expression. AJ pointed towards the exit. Reg waggled a finger, shaking his head, then pointed a thumb upwards. He didn't want to take the bookcases to the surface. AJ rolled her eyes and pointed more vigorously at the doors. Reg shrugged his shoulders, but followed her lead, and they moved the bookcase over the pile of debris, setting it down against the closed lower door.

Returning to the back of the container, AJ pulled another book-case away from the wall, revealing the corrugated metal. Reg helped her place it next to the first one, creating a relatively flat surface over the debris pile. AJ looked up when Thomas banged on the steel to get their attention. He tapped a finger on his Perdix computer and AJ checked hers. Twenty-five minutes. She held up an okay sign and hurried back to the broken bookcase on top of the wardrobe. Pulling pieces up, some floated in the water as though suspended from puppet strings now they'd been freed from the mess.

Reg joined her, and they made quick work of the loose sections of wood. Smudge had wisely retreated out of sight to a safer spot as they tugged and pulled the broken doors of the wardrobe from their hinges, casting them aside. Yanking another large piece of wood away revealed the safe and AJ had reason to be optimistic once more. Shrink-wrapped to the safe were a pair of old army ammo boxes, which Reg enthusiastically pointed at.

AJ held her hands up and shrugged her shoulders. Reg tapped the waistband of his Dive Rite harness where weight pockets would live if he needed them – which he didn't with the hefty tech diving set-up. He then ran his hand across the top of the ammo cases and safe. From what AJ could determine from his hand signal explanation, he'd forgotten he'd put ammo cases of lead weights with the safe, forming a flat surface on which to stack the furniture.

Shaking her head, she frowned through her mask, made a balloon shape with her hands and pointed at her friend. She could see him chuckling behind his regulator as he left to retrieve a lift bag as ordered.

29

Dotty walked around the brand-new Spitfire, running her hand along the sleek fuselage and wing edges. She was always stunned by the beautiful lines of the aircraft designed for such a terrible task. A light dew made the grass underfoot glisten and little droplets hung to the shadowed surfaces of the aeroplane while the sun, rising above the hedges surrounding the field, slowly evaporated the moisture it touched.

The morning was beginning with high, scattered cloud and the promise of a pretty day, but Dotty knew that could all change, especially near the coast. English weather was many things, but reliable and predictable were not amongst its favoured traits.

Climbing aboard, she settled into what was by now the familiar surroundings of the fighter's cockpit and ran through her pre-flight checks with her pilot notes on her lap. With the steps committed to memory, she didn't need the notes, but scanned the procedure after she was done to double-check herself. Yesterday's landing had worked out, but she was acutely aware that she'd been terrifyingly close to becoming the subject of an accident report.

Dotty felt embarrassed by her poor decision making. If her father knew all the details, he'd have put a hand on her shoulder and asked what she thought she should have done. The answer was land at one of the optional airfields approaching Castle Bromwich. Once the engine temperature had risen dangerously high she could have landed safely before the Merlin had seized. Not doing so was cavalier. All the ferry pilots felt pressure to deliver their aircraft to their destinations, but Amy Johnson had proven that even the best could meet their match when wishful thinking and optimism led them into insurmountable situations.

"Ready?" the ground crew shouted up. "We've got a bunch to get to, miss."

"Yes. Sorry!" she called back, realising they were waiting on her. "Clear?"

"Clear," he called out, waving a hand in the air.

Dotty started the Spitfire and watched the temperature gauge rise off the stop in a minute or so. After a short taxi and a pause to let the two men off the tail, she was humming down the airstrip then rising from the earth into the blue skies of the crisp dawn.

The men making decisions for the ATA had insisted the female pilots wear a uniform skirt. It was ridiculously cold and inappropriate for flying planes, so Pauline Gower had negotiated for women to wear uniform trousers while ferrying and on base. Dotty was glad. She'd chosen not to wear her Sidcot suit lately as summer neared, but the morning flights could be quite chilly in trousers and tunic.

Her flight south was diametrically opposed to her previous day's stress-filled jaunt. Fair conditions and a new aeroplane which had been test flown, tuned, and approved by the pilots at Castle Bromwich meant plenty of altitude, easy navigation, and balanced controls. Nearing the coast, she'd expected conditions to deteriorate with the common morning fog or cloud from the English Channel, but instead they remained clear.

Flying at 5,000 feet above the South Downs, Dotty spotted an aircraft ahead, climbing steeply. A bright flash from the ground caught her attention, drawing her eyes to where she suspected Tangmere and Westhampnett to be, ten miles away. Another bomb blast made her gasp, and she realised dark silhouettes of planes peppered the backdrop of the countryside. At least thirty or forty of them. She startled as a flash raced by and she swung around to see a Hurricane streaking down to meet the German fighters.

The Baedeker raids were at night with hundreds of bombers, but Dotty knew this had to be what the RAF had nicknamed 'tip and run' attacks. Messerschmitt Bf 109s equipped with single bombs under their fuselages raced across the Channel and unleashed their ordnance on the English airfields located near the coast. Fast and effective, the enemy sneaked under the RAF's early warning systems, sending the Allied fighter squadrons scrambling to catch up with the Luftwaffe as they fled back to occupied France.

Unsure what to do, Dotty watched chaos reign before her eyes. The Hurricanes and Spitfires which had managed to get airborne now engaged the 109s as the last few dived at the airfield, dropping their bombs. Tracer bullets drew lines through the sky in all directions as dogfights erupted over the fields of West Sussex. By the time Dotty had halved the distance to Tangmere, the battle had become an air race with the RAF pilots giving chase across the sea.

In total shock, she quickly descended, gathering her wits. Hoping the ground crews would wave her off if the landing strip was too badly damaged, she circled the field and began her approach. Service vehicles were buzzing around and men inspected new craters in the dirt, but spotting a wide, clear path of grass, Dotty dropped in and landed, hurriedly taxiing to the Spitfire squadron's dispersal hut.

"You're a sight for sore eyes, miss," Laces called up as Dotty slid the canopy back. "But your timing could be better."

"Thought it best to nip in before the lads return," she explained, stepping out onto the wing. "Thought this one might be needed."

"Need every one we can get," the mechanic replied, and Dotty noticed several planes off to one side.

"Any of those ready to be ferried?" she asked.

"Both of them are in better nick than the one you flew yesterday, miss," Laces said, running a grubby hand through his hair. "I'm truly sorry about that."

Dotty hopped to the ground as planes began returning to the field landing one at a time while crews began patching the bomb craters.

"We made it there in one piece," she said, watching for the Hurricane tail number she'd memorised.

"I'll sleep better tonight knowing that, miss," Laces said, before calling out orders to other mechanics, directing them to arm the Spitfire Dotty had just delivered.

She walked towards the airfield office, which happened to take her past the Hurricane squadron's dispersal hut. Watching each plane land, she squinted to read the tail numbers. She finally spotted Sandy's plane, one of the last to land, and let out an audible sigh of relief. Being so early in the day, she knew her visit to Tangmere would be brief, but she hoped to at least say hello to her fiancé. Even thinking the word brought a smile to her face.

Rushing now she'd seen him land, Dotty nipped into the office where the WAAF girl put in a call to White Waltham.

"Word has it you pulled off some kind of miracle delivering yesterday," Marjorie said in way of a greeting.

Dotty groaned. The last thing she needed was chatter and fuss over yesterday's adventure. Questions would be asked and her explanations rightfully challenged.

"I'm sure it's being blown out of proportion," she replied and quickly changed the subject. "Bit of a mess down here at Tangmere this morning, so best to get on my way. I think they have a couple of Spits ready to take out for repairs."

"Yes," Marjorie confirmed. "I have another ferry pilot on their way who will take whichever one you don't. Both to Castle Brom."

"Righty ho. I'll be off in a bit, then."

"I have twin engines I need to have you ferrying as soon as I can free you up from this Tangmere-Castle Brom circle you seemed to be caught in."

Dotty laughed. "I don't mind making this circle at all."

Marjorie chuckled too. "No, I don't suppose you do. Fly safe."

Dotty thanked the secretary and walked outside. The Hurricanes had returned and were lined up being refuelled, the mechanics and ground crews frantically servicing the aeroplanes. She peeked into the side door of the dispersal hut and saw the pilots gathered in a group, most with cups of tea in their hands. From what she could hear they were discussing strategy of how to handle the tip-and-run attacks. She was about to move on when one of the pilots nodded her way and Sandy turned. He jogged over and met Dotty outside, giving her a quick kiss on the lips.

"You were almost caught up in that mess," he said, his hands on her arms and his sparkling blue eyes filled with concern. "I wondered if it was you when I saw the Spit above us."

"To be honest, I had no clue what was best to do, and before I could make up my mind, you were chasing the blighters off across the Channel," Dotty replied. "Did you get any of them?"

Sandy nodded. "A couple. They're staying low across the water so our observers don't see them until they're no more than a minute or two away. This time, one of our photography planes happened to spot them on the way over, so we managed to get airborne just as they arrived. Most of the time we end up chasing ghosts."

"A couple less ghosts next time," Dotty pointed out.

"Sure," Sandy conceded. "But they'll be back. Are you here for a while?"

"No. I wish I was. Two more to run up to Castle Bromwich. I'll take the first one and another ATA pilot is on their way for the second. But hopefully that will mean another Spit to bring down this afternoon. If I fly slowly maybe I'll have to overnight," she joked.

"Then fly very slowly," Sandy commented with a grin, before his expression turned serious. "Wait a bit before you take off now. The Hun have been sending a second wave sometimes, trying to catch us just after we've landed. Or rearming the same planes and sending them straight back to catch us napping. Safer to wait an hour or so."

"Okay, I will," Dotty replied. "But I'd better head that way before the wing commander sees me distracting you."

"Harrington can keep his pompous nose out of our personal business," Sandy whispered, and leaned in closer. This time his kiss lingered and Dotty closed her eyes and let the madness around them melt away for a brief moment.

"Be careful, my love," she said softly when they finally moved apart.

"Always," he replied with a smile. "You be careful too. Wait a while."

"Hopefully I'll see you again later," Dotty said, and forced herself to walk away.

"Fly slowly," he said as she rounded the corner to the field.

When Dotty arrived by the Spitfire dispersal hut, one of the two planes needing ferrying was being warmed up. Pilots sat around outside in a variety of chairs, drinking tea, reading, or playing cards. But they were fully geared up ready to scramble.

"Word is you're quite the pilot," one of the men said as she walked by.

Dotty was prepared to deal with wolf whistles and chauvinistic comments, but the complement threw her for a loop. She paused.

"Dead-Stick Dotty," a second man called out, and the pilots laughed.

Dotty blushed. Something she'd been doing less of in the past few days.

"I try to save petrol for you chaps whenever I can," she said, amazing herself for coming up with a witty retort.

The men all laughed some more.

"Attagirl!" the first man cheered, and the others joined in.

Dotty gave them a wave and moved on to the plane, which Laces had just switched off.

"I was told I should wait a bit in case another raid shows up," she said.

"That would be my advice too, miss, but the wing commander ordered me to get her ready."

A wave of nervousness flecked with anger made her breath catch. Why the man was taking such a personal interest in making her life difficult she didn't know, but he seemed hell bent on putting her in harm's way.

"I think I need to use the loo, Laces," she said. "I should probably check in with the operations room once more as well."

"That might be best, miss," the mechanic replied.

But then he straightened and raised his eyebrows at her. Dotty didn't want to turn around. She knew by the look in Laces' eyes that her excuses for holding off flying were about to be overruled.

"That plane won't fly itself, Parker," came Harrington's stern voice.

Her first reaction was to spin around and challenge the man, but she fought the urge. She would lose any confrontation with an airfield wing commander. Every time. No doubt. Instead, without acknowledging the man, she walked to the Spitfire and used the wooden box placed on the grass to step to the wing.

"What do I need to know about this one, Laces?" she asked as she stowed her gear in the plane.

"Flies fine, miss," he replied. "Had a problem with the ammo feed in the starboard wing since it came to us. We've tried all sorts to fix it but it still hangs up. Needs the wing pulled apart to see what's going on."

Relieved she wasn't stepping into another deathtrap, Dotty settled into the cockpit and quickly ran through her checks. Harrington leaned against the dispersal hut, smoking a cigarette and watching. She realised she'd forgotten to ask Sandy about his leave, but she guessed the subject was yet to be broached. *Surely the wing commander couldn't keep her fiancé on duty indefinitely?* She doubted he could, but was certain he'd try.

Laces and another mechanic hopped on the tail after Dotty fired up the Merlin engine, and she taxied slowly away from the dispersal hut. Once she reached the airstrip where workers were still busy shovelling dirt back into holes, she glanced back towards the buildings. Sandy was now standing by the wing commander, and from his stance and the way he was pointing, she guessed he was working on an insubordination charge.

Dotty groaned. Their idea of a short engagement could well turn into completely the opposite. With a sense of dread, she opened up the throttle and took off into the southerly wind coming off the English Channel, a mere five miles away.

Where the Messerschmitt Bf 109s of Jagdgeschwader 2 fighter squadron flew low across the water for their second raid of the morning.

30

Reg scratched his beard and stared at the safe on the bench in his garage. Pearl looped her hand through his arm and leaned against her husband.

"I'll call a locksmith tomorrow and see if they can do anything with it," she urged. "No point standing out here all night."

Reg nodded but didn't move. "What do you think she kept in there?" he asked.

"I think it's the missing jewels from the Antwerp diamond heist," AJ said with a grin.

Pearl laughed. "More likely it's her recipes for Christmas pud and mince pies."

AJ smiled even wider. "That's more valuable than the diamonds."

"Why did she have to buy a bloody safe from a company no one has ever heard of?" Reg complained. "No wonder they went out of business."

"Probably got it in a going out of business sale, knowing Mum," Pearl replied. "She had a nose for a bargain."

"No offence, love," Reg said, squeezing his arm around her, "but she wasn't the best at remembering things for the past decade or so. If she's been in there anytime lately, the number has to be written down somewhere."

"In there would be a *safe* place to keep it," AJ said in a serious tone.

Reg and Pearl both stared at her.

"Get it?" AJ chuckled. "*Safe* place..."

Pearl gave her a consolatory smile.

"You're a regular Dawn French," Reg groaned. "You should get a gig doing stand-up at the Holiday Inn."

AJ stuck her tongue out at him. "She probably wrote it down on something that's now papier-mâché in the container."

They stood and stared at the safe a little longer.

"Where was the safe?" AJ asked.

Pearl turned to her. "How do you mean? Like where in the house was it?"

"Yeah."

"Under the desk in one of the spare bedrooms," Pearl replied.

AJ turned to the oak desk, which sat next to the dining set in the garage where they'd thoroughly washed them with soapy fresh water. They'd removed all the drawers to wash every nook and cranny, and she began picking each one up and carefully examining every surface inside and out. Reg and Pearl joined her, searching all nine drawers for numbers.

"I don't see anything," Reg announced after they'd each looked at every drawer.

"It was a good idea though," Pearl said, placing the wide centre drawer back down on the concrete floor.

Reg walked back to the safe. "Mediocre idea, I'd say. Good would mean we found the numbers."

"Ignore him, love," Pearl urged, still managing a smile.

"Standard operating procedure," AJ replied as she found a torch on the bench and returned to the desk.

Shining the light around the drawer openings, AJ started at the top on the right side, and worked her way down. When she reached the lowest opening, she paused.

"Got a pencil?" she asked excitedly.

"What have you found?" Reg asked, handing her a carpenter's pencil.

AJ lightly ran the pencil back and forth over the wood. "Eight, thirty-one, sixty-seven, thirteen," she read from the slight indentions left by the faded digits handwritten on the wood.

"You're a bloody genius!" Pearl exclaimed, giving AJ a hug when she stood up.

"Genius is a bit strong," Reg muttered. "But not bad on that one," he added with a grin.

Using a guide they found online for the sequence and directions to turn the dial, Reg used the numbers, then paused before trying the handle.

"Stand back a bit," he warned. "I expect a boxful of seawater is about to come out."

The safe had been so heavy it had been hard to know if it was filled with water or made from extra thick steel, but Pearl and AJ stepped back all the same. Reg tried the handle, but it didn't budge.

"Wrong bloody code," he groaned.

"Bollocks," AJ exclaimed. "You must have buggered up the sequence. Try it again."

Reg reached for the dial, but Pearl stopped him. "Could it just be sticky from being in the water?"

"The water pressure would have gone in rather than air coming out," AJ thought aloud. "It's a solid vessel so unless it leaked, nothing changed inside."

"Unless..." Reg began, pausing his sentence to hunt around for a pry bar.

"Unless it's the temperature, not the pressure," AJ finished for him.

"Exactly," Reg agreed, returning and searching the door to the safe for a good place to use the pry bar.

"I think they design them so you can't use things like that, you plonker," AJ said. "Bet it won't open with a hairpin either."

Reg ignored her and pulled harder on the handle, but the door still refused to open.

"Get a heater," AJ suggested. "We need to warm it back up. It's been submerged in 78-degree water for days and it's 88 degrees outside here. The air inside is lower pressure than ambient."

"See, that fancy Sussex education of yours is finally paying off," Pearl laughed.

"Boyle's law," AJ beamed. "From my fancy diving education."

"More like Murphy's law," Reg chided, getting a heat gun from his tool chest, as like most people on the tropical island, they didn't own a heater.

"Glass of wine?" AJ asked Pearl.

"Don't mind if I do," she replied, and they walked to the door into the house.

"Oi," Reg barked. "How come I'm the one left out here?"

"Even heat there Reg," AJ replied, waving her hand back and forth to mimic the motion. "And it's a fireproof safe designed to withstand a bazillion degrees, so we'll check back after dinner."

"A bazillion degrees Fahrenheit or Celsius?" AJ heard him muttering as they left.

In the kitchen, Pearl poured them both a glass of white wine, while AJ looked over the china spread out across the dining table. From the eight full place settings, almost six complete sets had survived intact. They were one saucer short, but a quick internet search had found a couple of antique dealers with one available.

The two women weren't about to leave Reg on his own, despite their teasing, and were walking towards the door when he called out. They hurried to where he proudly stood next to the open door.

"No puddle on the floor," AJ observed.

"Did you look inside?" Pearl asked nervously.

"No, love," he replied softly. "I waited for you."

She gave him a smile, then leaned over and looked into the safe. Reaching inside, Pearl pulled out a stack of paperwork and placed it on the bench. Next, she retrieved an old, shallow wooden box with brass hinges and clasp.

"What do you think that is, love?" Reg asked, running a finger over the varnished surface.

"I'm really hoping it's something of my dad's," Pearl hesitantly replied, opening the delicate clasp.

The hinges creaked as she lifted the lid and Pearl gasped. Reg and AJ huddled closer to see. Six medals were a jumbled mess across a lining of cushioned dark purple velvet. Pearl carefully arranged them in order, smoothing out the folded ribbons and aligning the star- and circle-shaped medals.

"Blimey, Pearl," AJ whispered. "They're your dad's?"

Pearl nodded. "Yeah. This is only the third time I've ever seen them."

AJ rested a hand on her friend's shoulder. "Really? He didn't like them displayed?"

"He didn't like to talk about the war at all," Pearl explained. "I came upon them when I was a little girl, maybe eleven or twelve, and I asked him about them. He got really quiet, and for a moment I thought he was going to be angry with me, and he was the loveliest man, my dad, he never raised his voice. But this look came over his face like he was really sad, and he told me that he only did what any one of his mates would have done, except they didn't make it, and he did. Sheer luck, fate, whatever you want to call it, he told me. I've never forgotten the conversation. I don't ever want to be reminded of those days, he said, then took the box, closed it and I never saw it again until Mum had his medals out at his funeral."

AJ put her arm around Pearl and hugged her tightly. "When did he pass away?"

"Back in 1999," Pearl replied, sniffing back the tears. "I believe five of these are campaign medals, meaning they were awarded to anyone who was there for at least a certain period of time. But the Military Cross on the right is for gallantry."

"He was a good one, your dad," Reg said as softly as his deep voice would allow. "I'm glad these made it safe and sound."

"Me too," Pearl said, closing the lid. "Thank you both so much. I can't begin to tell you how much this means to me."

"What's all this stuff?" AJ said brightly, trying to lift the mood in typical British style. She pointed to the stack of papers.

"No idea," Pearl replied, wiping her eyes and picking up a few sheets from the stack. A memory stick slid from the pile and fell to the bench. "These look like papers for the house, but no clue what Mum would be doing with a thumb drive. She didn't even own a computer."

"Want me to see what's on it?" AJ asked.

"We should have a look, I suppose," Pearl replied. "If you get your laptop, I'll get our wine refilled. I need another drink for all these surprises."

Reg brought three bar stools into the garage from the kitchen counter, Pearl returned with fresh drinks, and AJ plugged the memory stick into her laptop. Opening Finder, she clicked on the thumb drive and found a folder labelled 'scans'. AJ opened it and the screen filled with a seemingly endless list of picture files. She opened the first one. It was a very old photograph of a man and a woman standing outside a terraced house.

"That's my nan and grandad," Pearl said, leaning closer. "Mum had the picture in her living room."

"She must have had all her photos scanned at some point," AJ suggested, scrolling down the list. "There's hundreds of them."

Stopping on a random file, she opened the image. It was a black and white picture of a little girl clutching a doll and smiling at the camera.

"Is that you?" AJ asked.

"It is," Pearl chuckled. "Chubby cheeks and all. That would be about 1964 or 65." Tears rolled down her face. "I thought they were all lost. I can't believe it. Mum never mentioned a word about having the photos scanned."

"What's the date on them?" Reg asked.

AJ looked at the filename, which was a series of digits, but next to it was a date.

"About a year ago," AJ said.

For the next hour, AJ peppered Pearl and Reg with questions as they scrolled through the photographs spanning generations of Pearl's family. When Pearl finally realised it was ten past eight and she hadn't even thought about dinner, she stood up and fussed over what to fix in a hurry.

"You keep looking at these," AJ suggested. "I'll find something to throw together. You probably have a pizza in the freezer. I'll warm it up."

As AJ slid from her stool, she peered into the safe. "Is there anything else in here? What's this old envelope?"

Pearl joined her and removed a faded document folder, held closed by a string around two circular bobbins. Turning it over in her hands, there didn't appear to be any markings or description, so she unwound the aged and discoloured string to lift the flap.

"Oh my," Pearl exclaimed, sliding a black and white photograph from the folder.

The image had turned sepia tone with time, especially around the edges, but the subject was clear.

"Who is that?" AJ asked, staring at the woman standing next to a World War II RAF Supermarine Spitfire.

"That's my aunt," Pearl replied. "Dorothy Pearl Parker. I was named after her. Except I'm Pearl Dorothy."

"She's a pretty lady," AJ commented. "And pretty amazing if she flew Spitfires in the war."

Pearl looked at the picture for another moment before turning to AJ. "She flew for the Air Transport Auxiliary delivering planes to the bases and taking damaged ones back to the factories and repair stations."

"I've never heard you speak about her," AJ said, surprised in all the years she'd known Pearl that her friend had never mentioned her aunt.

"She was quite a few years older than my mum," Pearl replied solemnly. "And mum didn't talk about her sister much. She just said how sad it was. Dotty was engaged to marry an RAF pilot, but then something happened."

"What? They didn't get married?" AJ asked.

Pearl shook her head. "Can't say I really know. Like I say, my mother wouldn't talk about her sister and I tried looking her up on the internet a few years back, but there's not much about her."

"Maybe there's more in that envelope then," Reg suggested, rubbing his wife's shoulder.

Pearl nodded. "Yeah. I hope so."

31

"Tell me why it was so important to send her up now instead of waiting?" Sandy shouted at the wing commander.

Every face was turned in their direction as the pilot confronted his senior officer. Sandy had begun in a controlled tone but the exchange had quickly escalated.

"May I remind you who you're talking to, Flight Officer," Harrington snapped, his face already red as his eyes flicked between Sandy and the other men all watching in amazement. "You will lower your voice, change your tone, and address me as sir!"

"I'm addressing you as a man and asking why you would possibly send..."

The rest of Sandy's words were lost to the wail of the scramble siren. He reached over and grabbed a fistful of the wing commander's tunic, pulling the man to him and yelling inches from his face.

"If anything happens to that woman, Harrington, I'll be coming for you. Stripes be damned, I'll be coming for you!"

Sandy shoved the officer away and ran towards the Hurricane squadron's dispersal hut as the Spitfire pilots climbed into their waiting planes. If Harrington had a retort, it was lost to the noisy chaos.

Climbing from the airfield, Dotty never saw the small, dark spots over the channel getting bigger as Jagdgeschwader 2 hurtled towards the English coast. She was banking east to turn away from Westhampnett in case there was activity over the satellite airfield when she heard an odd metallic ping. It took a moment for Dotty to process what was happening as streaks swept across the sky around the Spitfire. Tracer bullets.

By pure reaction, she turned hard to port, pushing the throttle all the way forward and pulling back on the stick to climb. The tracer streaks disappeared but Dotty kept turning one way and then the other as the Merlin engine pulled the fighter plane higher into the sky.

It felt like her eyeballs were being shaken in her head and everything became slightly blurry. She caught a glimpse in the rear-view mirror mounted above the canopy where another plane flashed across the reflection. She couldn't believe she was being chased by a Messerschmitt Bf 109. There was no time to see for sure, but the pilot must have left the squadron to pursue her, which meant he hadn't released his bomb yet. For an experienced Spitfire pilot that would mean a significant advantage and a mistake by the German, as the bomb made his plane more sluggish to manoeuvre. Dotty could only hope it would be enough of a difference to keep her alive.

Sandy accelerated down the grass runway as ordnance exploded off his starboard wing, rocking the Hurricane as it lifted into the air. The last 109 of the group flew towards him, releasing his bomb as Sandy fired a short burst with his four 20 mm Hispano Mk II cannons. The Messerschmitt exploded as Sandy's plane rose quickly from the Tangmere airfield leaving the stricken wreckage below him to plummet into the ground.

Jagdgeschwader 2 were already turning and running as hard as they could back across the water, scattered around the sky. Sandy saw one off his port side, turned, and gave him a burst from his cannons but either missed or didn't inflict enough damage to slow the plane. He swung around inside the cockpit, hunting for Dotty's plane, but there were too many Spitfires to pick hers out. Fierce dogfights were happening all around as RAF pilots singled out planes to attack as the German squadron attempted to flee.

A Messerschmitt had managed to turn the tables on one of the Hurricane squadron's pilots just overhead and to port, so Sandy raced that way to help. The Hurricane pilot dodged and weaved, but the German stayed on his tail with each move, trying to line up a shot.

"Turn for land," Sandy called over the radio, doubting the 109 would risk being caught alone over the English countryside.

Whoever was at the controls of the Hurricane either didn't hear or didn't process the instruction and kept heading out to sea while turning and twisting. Sandy gave chase but was too far behind to take a clean shot. When the RAF pilot climbed, the Messerschmitt saw a chance to fire and tracers ripped through the sky, clipping the Hurricane's port wing. Pieces flew from the British plane and Sandy knew the kill shot would be next. As both aeroplanes ahead climbed and turned to starboard, Sandy finally had a clear shot without risking his own man, and fired a quick burst.

A chunk of tail shredded on the Messerschmitt and the hit was enough to shake the pilot off the Hurricane's tail. The German banked to port, aborting his attack to save himself, and in the blink of an eye the skies around Sandy were clear with nothing more than small specks disappearing in the distance. He looked all around once more, turning back towards land. RAF pilots were regrouping and funnelling towards Tangmere, and the sky above the channel appeared to be clear. Except for two planes Sandy spotted over Selsey Bill, locked in a duel.

Dotty groaned against the lateral forces as she twisted, turned, and did every manoeuvre she could think of to shake the Messerschmitt. Focused on nothing but flying the Spitfire, she hadn't breathed since the attack had begun. Every comment, tip, and strategy she'd ever heard about surviving a dogfight was being channelled from her subconscious to her eyes, hands, and feet. There was simply no time for processing the situation and making decisions or a longer-term plan.

She had no way of knowing where the German plane actually was beyond a momentary appearance in the rear-view mirror and tracers flying past. Her eyes shot from one side to the other and up and down, trying to keep track of her position, annoyed by the impotent reflective gunsight in the windscreen. Both aircraft furiously zig-zagged around the sky and Dotty saw land, sea, and blue sky flash past, unconcerned with which way up or in which direction she flew. Until the notion hit her that she should get back to Tangmere. The RAF fighters would be there and the German would surely give up if she led him that way.

Pulling hard back on the stick, Dotty started into a loop, her backside forced into the base of the seat and her neck muscles screaming. Scattered clouds passed by her view and when the horizon appeared, she pulled out of the loop inverted. Unsure if the German had followed, Dotty rolled the Spitfire 90 degrees and banked hard to port. Her eyes flicked to the mirror then scanned the sky above out the side of the cockpit. Rolling to her starboard side, she banked again.

She could see no tracers or sign of the Messerschmitt. It was as though he'd vanished. Sandy's words about how quickly the dogfights were over echoed in her mind and she finally breathed. Shaking like a leaf, Dotty kept turning side to side and searching around her for signs of another plane, but she appeared to be alone. She eased the throttle back. Below her, the English Channel met the sandy beaches to the east of the headland known as Selsey Bill.

What now?

She wasn't sure what protocol dictated for a ferry pilot after surviving a dogfight with the enemy. *Should she land at Tangmere and kiss the ground, or carry on to Castle Bromwich and deliver the plane?* Her desire was to touch down and make sure Sandy had returned from the fray. The man she was going to marry.

Dotty couldn't believe she'd so nearly been robbed of the chance to ever see him again, and wondered if the Luftwaffe pilot ever realised he was trying to shoot down an unarmed female ferry pilot. Probably not. His job was to take Allied fighters out of the war in the same way Sandy's job was to shoot down Germans. Except her husband-to-be was fighting for good instead of evil. Remaining free rather than succumbing to Hitler's reign of tyranny.

Sandy ran the Rolls-Royce Merlin engine to its limit as he stormed towards the two planes in the distance. Halfway across the distance, the Spitfire made a loop, changing direction by 180 degrees. The Messerschmitt chased until he realised he was being drawn back to the coast, peeling off and choosing to follow his squadron across the channel.

The German had either caught the Spitfire after dropping his bomb or ditched it in preference of bagging a fighter, as the ordnance was gone from its undercarriage. Within a short moment the aeroplane was lost to the mid-morning sun as it sped away.

Sandy breathed a sigh of relief. He couldn't be sure the Spitfire was being flown by his fiancé, but his gut told him it was. From what he'd been able to see, whoever was piloting had done a mighty job fending off the German attack, and made the correct decision in forcing the fight to change direction. With no thanks to Wing Commander Harrington.

Anger rose inside, as post battle, Sandy's mind went back to the reason Dotty had been in the air during the second tip-and-run attack of the day. The Spitfire was still a mile or more away and appeared to be heading north, so Sandy directed his Hurricane towards Tangmere where he planned to wring Harrington's neck even if it cost him a court martial.

Incensed, he almost missed the aeroplane coming out of a high bank of cloud over the Sussex countryside, until sudden movement drew his eyes to a familiar silhouette.

Heading for Castle Bromwich was the right thing to do, Dotty decided. Her job for the war effort was to ferry planes, so regardless of the drama she'd experienced on the ground and in the air that morning, there was no reason for more delays. As much as she desired to see Sandy and kiss him one more time before leaving.

The metallic ping Dotty had heard earlier reached her ears a moment after the tracers streaked in lines through her starboard wing. Large-calibre bullets ripped the aluminium-copper alloy skin, sending shards of metal into the wake of the Spitfire. The Messerschmitt hurtled past as Dotty banked hard to starboard, praying the aileron was still functional. The Spit reacted, thrusting her into the seat as she pushed the throttle all the way forward once again.

She had no idea if this was the same 109 or another fighter looking for an easy kill, but it didn't matter. One of them had hung around after the others had left, letting all but the last one or two Allied planes land. Off to her port side, Dotty spotted a Hurricane coming to her aid, but he'd only be able to help if she kept herself alive long enough for him to reach her.

Tracers tore past her left side, forcing her to turn right and away from help. Dotty couldn't believe how quickly the German had got back on her tail and cursed herself for not diving for the ground instead of fleeing. Out her window was nothing but blue. Bright blue sky and a deep turquoise blue sea.

Pushing the stick forward, she dove, and in the few thousand feet between her current altitude and the waves, knew she needed to turn back to land once more. Flying straight offered her nemesis the opportunity to line up a shot, but banking gave him the chance of firing at her overhead profile if he could anticipate her move. She feigned starboard then cut to port, still diving and picking up speed. The stick felt like lead in her hand and the pedals resisted her movements. Water zoomed towards her as Dotty gritted her teeth and groaned at the effort.

The cockpit appeared to explode into a million shards of acrylic plastic as the canopy was torn apart. The vicious wind howled, buffeting her head, and the armoured glass windscreen shook and wavered on its decimated frame. Dotty couldn't breathe, the Merlin laboured, and the stick had lightened in her hand.

The English Channel filled all that remained of her view as the wounded Spitfire continued its dive at full speed.

32

Both AJ and Reg were keen to get the last container emptied. Retrieving the tyres was a monotonous and labour-intensive job, and the last batch were at a far more challenging depth. George was back on the boat along with Raúl, who brought along homemade tortilla chips for the ride out. AJ dipped gingerly into the spicy salsa that accompanied the chips, swigging plenty of water, but Reg and Thomas scooped merrily as the Newton ploughed through the Caribbean Sea. Damon and Bash were just as keen.

"This is the mild stuff," Raúl grinned, and Reg laughed at AJ, who frowned back.

"My mouth is numb," she complained, noticing George wasn't partaking, although he didn't say anything.

Reg and AJ's conversation kept returning to the treasure trove of documents and items retrieved from the safe the previous night. Pearl had been overwhelmed, and Reg had suggested she spend the day today going through everything in her own time while they were back on the water. AJ had been itching to check in with her at lunchtime before they'd left, but decided it was best to leave her friend in peace. She'd stop by tonight and see how she was doing.

When they reached the site, AJ dropped Damon and Bash at the barge before tying into the buoy from container one. Nora was back on police duty so Reg gave George and Raúl instructions on what to do, and more importantly, not do, on the Newton. Short of a major unforeseen catastrophe, the biggest issue would be if the boat came loose from the mooring or if one of the divers was swept away and needed retrieving. They strung a line between the two vessels, so in both cases the plan was to get Damon or Bash aboard as soon as they could.

AJ, Reg, and Thomas geared up and finalised their plan. Providing the current was workable, Thomas would sort out the lines while AJ and Reg began removing tyres from container three. If all went well, the rope AJ had strung from one to three would be the first leg of a line all the way up to the barge. The deeper divers planned on 24 minutes of bottom time, two of which they'd use getting down, so they would have to work fast to empty the container in two dives.

The first thing AJ noticed as she descended was the lack of current. Conditions were perfect, which boosted her confidence in them getting what they needed to get done in one afternoon. Thomas split off towards container two, where he'd begin consolidating the lines strung between locations, and AJ and Reg dropped down the slope on the edge of Twelve Mile Bank.

She'd warned Reg about the tyres trying to tumble out of the last container, so he waited at the ready while she pushed down on the handle then swung it out, releasing the cam locks. The door felt heavy as before, and Reg assisted in holding it from swinging open and allowing the contents to topple out.

Something else seemed to move and for a moment, AJ wasn't sure what was going on. The handle tugged her slightly downwards, and after a moment she realised the whole container had rocked on its precarious perch. Her eyes caught Reg's and he raised his eyebrows. AJ used a series of quick hand signals to her partner, who nodded his assent as his hands were too occupied.

The tyre stack trying to shove its way out the door was tipped over enough that when AJ dropped a length of line down the centre, she could reach underneath and grab the end. With a loop through the stack, she quickly fastened a lift bag and blew a small amount of gas into it from her deco bottle. Reg let the door open a little more, and bit by bit, AJ manoeuvred the tyres while Reg controlled the door, until the bag floated the stack out of the opening. Behind, more stacks were shoved up against the first row, but a few had fallen sideways, now holding back the rest, and Reg was able to open the one door.

AJ steered the first set to the top of the container and released some of the gas from the lift bag until the stack settled on the upside-down underbelly of the metal box. Looking up, she couldn't see Thomas yet, so she took a length of line she'd brought down with her and attached it to the far corner of the container. They'd use that as a staging line before sending up a wagon train of stacks like before.

Quickly dropping back to the opening, she found Reg heaving stacks around by the doorway, trying to make them accessible without sending any tumbling into the abyss. AJ was about to reach in and help when movement above her caught her eye. And for a second she worried her stack was falling over. It wasn't. The octopus slipped into the container and disappeared down the middle of a tipped-over stack.

"Hey!" AJ gasped into her regulator, then looked at Reg.

The questioning look in his eyes told her he hadn't seen Smudge on the move. AJ made the octopus hand signal and pointed to the stack. Reg rolled his eyes. AJ pointed again to her eight-legged friend's latest home. Reg shook his head, but moved towards Smudge's stack and began moving other tyres around so they could pull that one out. Once the stack was near the door and the filtered light from way above hit the shrink-wrapped bundle, AJ peered down the middle.

Smudge had spread his elastic body around the third tyre down, but AJ immediately noticed something different. Each tyre had been individually wrapped before the whole stack had been enveloped. Why, she had no idea, but it made it easier to throw a piece of line down the centre, and Smudge shrank back even more, trying to make himself disappear into the surroundings.

Attaching a second lift bag, AJ blew gas inside and the stack was gently dragged from inside the container. She kept an eye on Smudge as she manoeuvred the stack up to the top, where she released gas as before, and the tyres settled onto the belly of the container. AJ checked on her octopus buddy one more time and saw he was still nestled inside.

She was about to leave when something in the top tyre caught her attention. It was probably a trick of the light, but she unclipped her dive torch and turned it on, carefully aiming the beam so she didn't startle Smudge. Her eyes hadn't deceived her; there was something inside the tyres, which explained why they were individually wrapped. AJ remained still, moving nothing but the beam of light which penetrated the wrinkles and folds of the transparent shrink-wrap.

Unclipping her stainless-steel carabiner from her harness D-ring, she reached down and banged on the container. A few moments later, Reg's mask appeared over the end, and AJ waved him up. He threw his hands up then tapped his Perdix dive computer on his wrist to let her know they didn't have time for whatever game she was playing with the octopus. She waved at him more urgently, and with a disgruntled look, he finned up to join her.

Shining her light inside the tyre, she showed him what had caught her attention. He took the torch from her and looked more closely, moving the beam around to see past the shrink-wrap, which was torn open in a few spots. When the container had descended, the water pressure must have crushed the air trapped inside the individual tyres, stretching the shrink-wrap until the thin polyolefin tore, letting the seawater in.

Reg poked his fingers around inside the top tyre, opening a wider hole in the shrink-wrap. He shook his head and pointed his thumb towards the surface. AJ saw the look in his eyes. He was mad, which confirmed her suspicion of what she'd seen. AJ was about to blow gas into the lift bag when she remembered Smudge.

She leaned over the stack again and reached her hand down. The octopus remained absolutely still. AJ wiggled a finger. One, long tentacle moved over and touched her finger. The little suckers felt strange against her skin. Wiggling another finger, Smudge moved a little closer, his form effortlessly stretching and distorting at will.

AJ hummed into her reg with glee when the octopus eased over her hand and allowed her to lift him from the inside of the tyres. Moving to the first stack she'd brought up, Smudge slowly moved off her hand when she placed it on the stack and slipped inside. AJ gave him a smile and a wave before joining Reg, who'd blasted gas into the lift bag and was already on his way with their cargo.

Thomas had just arrived at container one when Reg and AJ joined him at 129 feet. He was surprised to see them. He was even more surprised when Reg thumbed towards the surface and waved Thomas off when the Caymanian began sorting the lines he'd configured. Reg shook his head and started up the buoy line which the Newton was tied to at the surface. AJ gave Thomas an okay sign, so he shrugged and followed them.

AJ and Reg had been at depth for only nine minutes, so their decompression obligation was far less than planned. Switching to their 50% oxygen deco tanks at 50 feet, they paused for one minute every ten feet until they were clear to surface after a final stop at ten feet. Before they broke the surface, Reg got AJ and Thomas's attention, putting his finger to his lips. They both returned an okay sign, knowing the big man wanted to handle things topside.

"That was quick," George commented as the three divers appeared at the stern with an inflated lift bag by their side. The tyre stack hung like a parachutist below.

"Got one lot up, but we need to adjust the plan to bring up the rest," Reg said. "Once we get up there, I'll explain."

George and Raúl aided the divers out of the water, AJ bringing up the rear where she kept hold of the tyre stack. Reg shed his gear and returned, grabbing the line looped through the stack. With a big heave, he dragged the first half of the stack onto the edge of the swim step, and the water began draining the shrink-wrap tears inside the tyres. As the load lightened, Reg and Thomas manhandled the stack onto the swim step where they rolled it around and tipped it back and forth to shed the seawater trapped inside.

AJ clambered out and waddled to the bench with Raúl lending her a hand. She quickly slipped out of her Dive Rite harness, keen to see how Reg handled the next part.

"So, George. These tyres of yours you're so keen on doing the right thing with and getting to your dealers," Reg began. "It's been bothering me about how this works out for you money wise."

"I'm sorry?" George questioned. "I don't get what you mean."

"What I mean is," Reg retorted, his deep voice booming across the ocean without him even trying, "with what you're paying the lads for the barge, there's no way there's any profit left on this lot. You have to be losing money."

George looked perplexed. "Well, I am, you're right. But the point is, I'm fulfilling my obligation to my customers. I'll lose a bit of money, but they'll get their shipment close to on time, and hopefully keep their business with me."

"Very noble," Reg commented.

AJ looked at Thomas, who was completely confused but knew better than to say anything. Across on the barge, Damon and Bash were both watching, and may well have been able to hear Reg's voice, even if they couldn't make out what George was saying.

"What do you mean by all this?" George asked indignantly.

Reg reached inside the tyre stack and pulled out a tightly vacuum-sealed package of white powder, holding it up in George's face.

"This is what I mean, mate."

AJ had to admit, George did an outstanding job of looking shocked.

"I've no idea what that is?" he stuttered.

"Seriously?" Reg responded.

"Well, I think I know what it is, but I have no idea why it's in my tyres."

AJ looked at Raúl, who appeared to be even more surprised.

"You can discuss that with the police," Reg grunted. "Sit over there you two," he added, pointing to the bench under the fly-bridge. "We're going in."

"Reg, I assure you I don't know anything about these drugs," George urged, but Reg glared at him and pointed to the bench again. George wisely complied and Raúl quickly followed.

AJ whistled at Damon and Bash, who looked her way. "We're heading in. You guys too!" she shouted across the water.

The two locals looked at each other then back at AJ. Damon shrugged and gave her a thumbs-up. AJ wondered about the buoys and lines still in the water, but decided now wasn't the time to ask Reg about them. She was sure they'd be addressed on another trip. Surely the police would want the rest of the tyres brought up.

Thomas and Reg rolled the stack onto the rear deck, securing the tyres with a strap, then Thomas moved to the bow as AJ warmed up Hazel's Odyssey's engines.

"Roy," Reg barked into the phone when he joined AJ up top. "Meet me at my dock, we've got a present for you. And bring a few lads with you, and whoever handles drugs for you lot."

AJ couldn't hear what their friend and detective for the Royal Cayman Islands Police Service, Roy Whittaker, said in return, but it must have been short, as Reg grunted and hung up.

Thomas waved from the bow to signify he'd released them from the mooring, and AJ looked over at the barge. Bash waved back.

"Haul bloody arse, love," Reg said. "I want these buggers off my boat."

"My boat," AJ corrected with a grin.

"Won't be if you don't haul bloody arse," Reg retorted. And grinned in return.

33

AJ glanced back. The barge with one container's worth of tyres was already well behind the Newton. Damon could only tickle along at eight or nine knots in the open ocean. *Hazel's Odyssey* was making over 20 knots with occasional slowing to crest a larger swell. Reg had moved to the deck to keep an eye on George, so AJ was alone on the fly-bridge.

As they got closer to the island, the boat traffic increased with local fishermen and deep-sea charters, and more and more of the newer higher rise buildings loomed larger. AJ regularly scanned the waters, keeping a clear picture of the other vessels and in which direction they were moving. Only one boat appeared to be crossing her path ahead, and it was a speedboat of some sort, racing across the water.

"Reg told Damon to follow us to our dock," Thomas shouted over the wind and engine noise as he arrived beside AJ at the helm. "He said best to have everyting together for Detective Whittaker."

AJ nodded, riding the undulations of the ocean by leaning against the helm seat and using her legs as shock absorbers.

"We're about fifteen minutes out," she yelled back, looking at the predicted arrival time on the GPS screen.

"Dis is crazy, man. How did you find da drugs?"

AJ laughed. "I didn't. Smudge pointed them out."

"Smudge?" Thomas asked.

"My sniffer octopus," AJ replied.

Thomas cracked up. "Da same one dat been in every container?"

"I'm pretty sure it's the same one," AJ shouted back. "We're buddies."

Thomas laughed again before returning to the ladder and climbing down to the deck. AJ scanned the waters once more. The speeding boat was closing but by her estimation, he'd pass her track several hundred yards ahead. Which would leave the Newton going through its wake. Coming from her starboard side, the speedboat had the right of way, so she'd have to slow and roll over the wake. Which Reg wouldn't be happy about, but it was better than launching everyone into the air and beating the heck out of the Newton.

AJ eased the throttles back as the other boat zipped along. It was a white 36-foot Contender centre console with four outboards. AJ whistled. She figured if the owner had enough money to buy the very expensive boat and have it brought to the island, he probably didn't worry about the cost of petrol. Evident by the wide-open speed at which he was flying across the ocean.

"Let's go!" Reg roared from the deck.

AJ grinned. "Hush up, or I'll jump his wake and see how you like that!"

She heard his deep-throated laugh over the idling engines.

The speedboat shot across in front so AJ slowed a little more as she approached their wake, which spread out in a broad vee. The Contender's engine notes changed and AJ watched in surprise as the powerful boat swung around and made a hard 180-degree turn.

"Go, bloody, go!" Reg shouted from below, and AJ, figuring something was up, pushed the throttles forward.

The Newton lurched ahead, bucking over the wake before settling on the other side where the propellers could bite into the water. A gunshot rang out and AJ turned to see the Contender dashing towards them with a man at the bow aiming what she guessed from the movies to be an AK-47 at them.

They were outclassed in speed and definitely outclassed in weapons as the best she had aboard was a dive knife. With no sensible alternative that didn't mean being shot to pieces, AJ set the throttles to idle and took the Newton out of gear. Quickly, she grabbed her mobile phone and, dropping into the helm seat to hide the device from view, she brought up the number for Detective Whittaker and typed a text.

"3 miles out. Pirates. Guns. Help."

Slipping the mobile back into the dashboard shelf, she raised her hands in the air.

"Get where I can see all of you!" the man in the bow of the Contender shouted.

He looked to be in his thirties with swarthy skin and dark hair, and spoke with an Hispanic accent. There were two others. The captain, who was older, and a third man about the same age, who had a handgun tucked into the waistband of his jean shorts and a large Tiger's head tattoo on his shirtless chest.

As the Contender pulled alongside, the man yelled something more in Spanish. AJ only understood one word. She looked down from the fly-bridge to see Raúl take a line from Tiger. The two men were clearly glad to see each other.

"Down!" AK-47 ordered AJ, waving the barrel her way.

She moved to the ladder and climbed down, taking in the situation on deck as she did. George was standing next to Reg and Thomas, all with their hands on their heads, and Tiger had hopped across to join Raúl now the two vessels were tied together. She was glad to see they'd used fenders, although scratches to the hull could well be the least of *Hazel's Odyssey*'s problems. She doubted international drug dealers liked leaving loose ends and witnesses behind.

"I told you I didn't know anything about any drugs," George

mumbled defensively as AK-47 waved his gun to indicate AJ should join the three other captives.

"I should have known he was trouble when he tried to kill me with his salsa," AJ muttered.

"Quiet!" the gunman barked. "No talking, and keep your hands on your heads."

The four of them staggered side to side as the boat swayed on the ocean swells while Raúl and Tiger cut the shrink-wrap from the tyres.

Everyone looked up when the captain shouted something in Spanish, and AJ tracked their stares. The barge was plodding along towards them, following the Newton's path to AJ and Reg's dock in West Bay.

Raúl turned and looked at Reg. "Call them and tell them to go into town."

"I can't," Reg replied.

"*Mierda*," Raúl said. "You called them when we left Twelve Mile Bank."

"Yeah, but I didn't have my hands on my head then, did I?"

Raúl glared at him. Gone was the amiable employee with bags of tortilla chips and tasty burritos.

"Don't test me, *amigo*. We'll shoot the woman first if you don't do as we say."

Reg moved slowly, letting them clearly see his movements, removing his mobile from his pocket. He hit redial then held the device to his ear.

"Careful what you say," Raúl warned.

"Damon, mate," Reg said, looking off the stern at the approaching barge. "Change of plans. You go back to town and we'll catch up with you later."

Standing next to Reg, AJ could just hear the voice on the other end of the call. It wasn't Damon.

"Okay, no problem. That should only take us a few more minutes."

"Thanks, mate," Reg said, and hung up.

Raúl and Tiger went back to work, pulling the vacuum-sealed bags from the tyres and handing them across to the captain. AJ couldn't believe the volume of drugs being brought into the Cayman Islands, and figured it had to be a link in a chain to a final destination elsewhere. The islands had their drug issues like everywhere else, but there was no way there was a market for that much cocaine.

"Hey," AK-47 said, looking behind the tethered boats. "What did you tell him?"

AJ looked to see the barge still heading their way and it was getting much closer.

"You heard what I told them," Reg said, shrugging his shoulders with his hands back on his head. "I don't know what they're up to."

"I don't see anyone," AJ added, which was true. She couldn't see either Damon or Bash.

"Call him back!" Raúl shouted. "On speaker. Tell him we start shooting people if they don't turn."

Moving slowly once again, Reg took out his mobile and AJ saw this time he was calling Damon's number. He put it on speaker. It rang and rang with no answer.

"He's gonna start by shooting her!" Raúl bellowed, and AK-47 swung his barrel towards AJ.

"What can I do?" Reg barked back. "Not my fault they're not answering. You've seen that barge – it's an old workhorse not really designed for the open ocean. They must have a steering problem."

"They're going to miss us, anyway," AJ added, although it certainly didn't appear that the barge would avoid both boats.

AK-47 pointed his gun into the air and fired off several rounds. He then pointed it at the barge and peppered the tyre stacks with bullets.

"Down," Reg grunted, and he, AJ and Thomas dropped to the deck.

AJ reached up and grabbed George, dragging him down with them.

"That way," AJ blurted, shoving Reg towards the port side of *Hazel's Odyssey*, which was tied to the Contender.

On the deck, they were hidden from AK-47's view, but by the sound of his gunfire, he was still focused on shooting at the barge. With more orders from the captain, Raúl and Tiger began scrambling to untie the Contender from *Hazel's Odyssey*, but they were too late. With an ear-splitting crunch of metal, the square bow of the barge crashed into the four, sleek outboard motors of the centre console.

Raúl had managed to free the stern tie, so the force drove the Contender spinning around, still held to the Newton at the bow. AJ peeked up to see Damon crouched behind the helm of the barge as it ploughed past. The bow line had either been freed or gave way, as the barge kept on going like a waterborne bulldozer, shoving the crumpled Contender towards the island. *Hazel's Odyssey* whipped around, tossing the four captives across the deck, before settling in the wake of the barge.

AJ was on her feet in a flash, and with Thomas's help, pulled Reg up off the deck. She scaled the ladder and waited for Thomas to give her a thumbs-up from the stern, where he made sure the stray lines and fenders weren't going to foul the props. Racing to the helm, AJ dropped the diesels in gear and sped after the barge which was now slowing with the Contender still pinned under its bow.

AK-47 had been thrown into the water, and AJ steered around him, guessing he'd dropped his weapon as he wasn't pointing it at them. As she pulled closer to the carnage, she saw Captain slumped over the console, but Tiger had his handgun drawn and was clambering from the crippled boat to the barge in search of the two Caymanians.

"Stay down!" AJ screamed although she doubted anyone heard her over the engines and churning water.

Reaching the stern of the barge, she pulled the starboard engine into neutral and then reverse, shoving the throttle forward, spinning the Newton around so the stern swung over by the barge. She then threw them both into neutral with the throttles back to idle.

Damon and Bash appeared from their hiding spots and leapt across to the dive boat, where Thomas helped grab them just as Tiger fired several rounds from the bow of the barge. The shots were errant from the swaying boat, so he ran past the tyre stacks for a closer shot.

"Hold on!" AJ bellowed and putting both engines in drive, she shoved the throttles forward and pulled away, leaving Tiger shooting wildly and screaming obscenities.

Once clear, AJ slowed and ran to the back railing of the flybridge to check on everyone.

"Okay down there?"

Thomas looked up from where he was helping Damon and Bash to their feet.

"All good, boss."

"Where's Raúl?" she asked, having accounted for the other three.

"He's asleep, boss," Thomas called back, grinning. "His head ran into Big Boss's fist."

AJ held up an okay sign as she heard the roar of powerful engines approaching. Moving back to the helm, AJ grabbed the microphone for the VHF radio and let the Joint Marine Unit boat know there was a man overboard and another with a gun.

From the bow of the Marine Unit boat, the three officers brandishing automatic weapons quickly persuaded Tiger to put his weapon down.

Over the radio, AJ heard the deep voice of her friend Ben Crooks reply.

"We gotta stop meeting like dis, AJ Bailey."

She shook her head and gave him a wave.

34

"So that was our day," AJ laughed when she and Reg finished relaying their chaotic afternoon to Pearl.

Most of it, at least. They carefully left out a few key details as they sat around the dining table eating takeout food Reg had picked up from the Fox and Hare. Like the gunfire. Pearl would likely hear about it in the news tomorrow, but they didn't see the benefit of having her fret over it tonight. They did explain how apparently they'd interrupted a major cocaine pipeline from South America though Mexico and the Cayman Islands on its way to Miami. Detective Whittaker guessed the men in custody were mid-level players, who would probably be replaced in short order, but at least the Cayman connection would be severed.

"Do you have to go back out there?" Pearl asked.

Reg nodded. "We'll bring the rest of the tyres up for the RCIPS, just in case there are more drugs in there."

"Gives us a chance to take a last look in your container, too," AJ added.

"It's amazing what you've been able to bring up for me," Pearl replied. "So I don't want you risking your necks any more on my account."

"I have to check in on a friend anyway," AJ said and grinned.

"A friend?" Pearl questioned.

Reg rolled his eyes. "She's in a relationship with a bloody octopus."

"Hey, Smudge isn't just *any* octopus," AJ protested. "He's a safe-finding, drug-sniffing best friend type of octopus."

Pearl laughed. "Sounds like you should check in on him then."

"But tell us how your day has been," AJ said. "I've been dying to know."

Pearl smiled. "I've learnt a lot about my auntie Dotty. Things I don't know that my mum even knew about her sister."

"Really?" AJ asked, finishing her fish tacos and wiping her hands on a napkin. "Like what?"

Pearl held up two envelopes. One appeared to be quite small and yellowed from age. The other newer and standard letter size.

"This one was posted to my grandfather, but was unopened," Pearl said, sliding the newer one across the table. "I opened it."

While Reg looked around for his reading glasses, AJ picked up the envelope.

"I got you covered, old man," she said, looking at the shaky handwriting on the envelope. It was addressed to Patrick Parker.

"The old letter was inside that," Pearl explained, holding up the yellowed envelope. "Read the one you have first."

AJ plucked a single page of cream-coloured letterhead from the envelope and flattened it out in front of her.

"From the office of Group Captain Robert Harrington, DSO, retired," AJ read aloud. "Do we know who he is?"

"I do now," Pearl replied. "Read what he says."

AJ returned her attention to the letter and strained to read the handwriting of what she assumed was an elderly person. The intention was for perfectly formed letters and punctuation, but she figured the man had been let down by ageing eyes and muscles.

Dear Flight Lieutenant Patrick Parker,

As I near the end of my days, I find myself regretful of very few things. I've been blessed with a life of meaning during years where one man's contribution was part of something far bigger and more important than himself. I take pride in having carried out my duties before, during, and after the war with this in mind. With one exception.

The enclosed letter from Flying Officer Richard 'Sandy' Lovell addressed to you, sir, was removed by me from his personal possessions on a fateful day in May of 1942. For decades I've told myself that I was protecting the Royal Air Force and the war effort, but as I face eternity in the hereafter, I believe I was in error. Both in my actions that day, and distorting the truth of what occurred. I placed myself before all else while using the excuse of duty.

My actions, sir, do not deserve your forgiveness, but you certainly deserve to know the truth. I hope you have always been proud of your daughter, despite the mistruth I created. ATA Pilot First Officer Dorothy Parker was an outstanding pilot, and should be remembered for her brave contribution to her country in its ulti-mate time of need.

Yours sincerely,
Robert Harrington

AJ sat speechless staring at the letter.

Reg reached his hand across the table and held Pearl's. "Blimey, love. What on earth is this bloke talking about?"

Pearl slid the older envelope to AJ. It was smaller, typical of personal correspondence from the wartime era. The seal had obvi-ously been broken many years before.

"How come your grandad never opened the letter?" AJ asked. "Or your mum?"

"I'm guessing my grandmother was too distraught to deal with it when it arrived. The postmark is January 1988. My grandfather died in December 1987. She wouldn't have known what it was about. Probably pure luck it ended up being kept with all this old paperwork. My mum may never have looked. Like I said, they never talked about Dotty. It was too hard for them."

"So, what happened to your aunt?" Reg asked.

"Officially," Pearl struggled to say. "She was lost over the English Channel on a clear day in a Spitfire which was supposedly in perfect flying condition. It was noted as unknown cause, but pilot error suspected."

Reg squeezed her hand.

"In the ATA records and on a few chat sites with comments, I found a couple of references about her crash landing a Miles Master a week earlier and narrowly escaping a crash in a Spitfire in poor weather. Pauline Gower, who headed up the female section of the ATA, was complimentary of Dotty, but there were comments that she had a reputation as a rule breaker and a pilot who pushed her luck."

AJ looked at the envelope. It too was addressed to Flight Lieutenant Parker. "But this tells the real story?"

Pearl nodded.

AJ pulled the letter from the old envelope and admired the flowing and precise handwriting. She began reading aloud.

Dear Mr Parker,

I write to you on what is undoubtedly the worst day of my life, and what I suspect will also be yours. As you'll already know by the time this letter reaches you, your daughter perished this morning while flying a Spitfire over the English Channel.

What I suspect you'll be told about the circumstances and cause of this tragedy, I very much doubt will be the truth. I was there, Mr Parker. I know the truth, and you should too. They may court martial me for writing this, and for my confrontations with Wing Commander Harrington before the incident, but the truth is more important than my own circumstances. I love my country, but I loved your daughter more.

Dotty should never have been sent up until later that morning. The Germans had been too often sending a second wave of tip and run attacks, and they had just hit us with the first of the day. Why the Wing Commander wanted Dotty to leave right away, I have no idea. He refused to offer me a reasonable explanation. But he insisted, and Dotty did as ordered.

Taking off to the south, she immediately met a squadron of Messerschmitt 109s approaching low across the channel. A German pilot singled her out and a dogfight ensued. I arrived at the end and ran as hard as I could to her aid, but she didn't need me. She flew valiantly. Brilliantly. The Hun gave up and retreated.

What happened next will haunt me for all my days and I apologise to you and your family for my grievous error in not recognising the German's ploy. Whether it was the same pilot, or another who had lain in wait under cover of the clouds, I could not say. But Dotty was pounced upon, and once again flew with the skill of a veteran fighter pilot. Before I could reach her, the German hit her Spitfire while Dotty was in a steep dive from which she was unable to recover.

I cannot say for sure whether the cannon fire was fatal or simply caused her to lose control, but I watched my darling fiancée crash into the water at a speed which left no doubt as to the outcome. A situation she should never have been placed in. A set of circumstances I will have brought to the attention of our Group Captain by the time this letter reaches you for I am convinced Wing Commander Harrington will not convey the true course of events. You and your family have my deepest sympathies, Mr Parker. If you would permit me the honour, I would like to visit you on my next opportunity for leave? I hope that can be before your daughter's services, which should not be our first opportunity to shake each other's hand.

Yours sincerely
Flying Officer Sandy Lovell.

AJ let out a long breath. "So the Group Captain bloke pinched this letter from Sandy's personal stuff?"

Pearl nodded. "He was a wing commander at the time, but he would have been responsible for dealing with them, yes."

"Dealing with them?" Reg queried.

Pearl nodded. "Dealing with his personal effects." She wiped tears from her cheeks. "Sandy was shot down and killed over France later that day," Pearl replied. "He died the same day as Dotty. He'd already written that letter, but hadn't had the opportunity to post it."

AJ gasped. "How absolutely awful."

"But you know what this means, love?" Reg said, tapping a finger on the letter AJ had set down.

"We have the chance to put history right," Pearl replied.

"Bloody right you do," AJ agreed.

I hope you enjoyed this story!
If you did, I've written something extra for those interested in
joining my newsletter.
Use this QR code for the exclusive bonus content!

For more AJ and Reg, grab the next book in series, *Cemetery Beach*

ACKNOWLEDGMENTS

My sincere thanks to:

My incredible wife Cheryl, for her unwavering support, love, and encouragement.

My family and friends for their patience, understanding, and support.

The Cayman Crew:
My lovely friend of many years, Casey Keller.
Chris and Kate of Indigo Divers for keeping Reg and AJ's dock in tip-top shape!

My editor Andrew Chapman at Prepare to Publish. I couldn't do this without him!
My advanced reader copy (ARC) group, whose input and feedback is invaluable. They had their work cut out on this one too, and came through with great feedback as usual.

The Tropical Authors group for their magnificent support and collaboration. Check out the website for other great authors in the Sea Adventure genre.

Shearwater dive computers and Dive Rite, whose products I proudly use.

Reef Smart Guides whose maps and guidebooks I would be lost without – sometimes literally.
My friends at Cayman Spirits for their amazing Seven Fathoms rum... which I'm convinced I could not live without!

Above all, I thank you, the readers: none of this happens without the choice you make to spend your precious time with AJ and her stories. I am truly in your debt.

LET'S STAY IN TOUCH!

To buy merchandise, find more info or join my Newsletter, visit my website at
www.HarveyBooks.com

Visit Amazon.com for more books in the
AJ Bailey Adventure Series,
Nora Sommer Caribbean Suspense Series,
and collaborative works;
The Greene Wolfe Thriller Series
Tropical Authors Adventure Series

If you enjoyed this novel I'd be incredibly grateful if you'd consider leaving a review on Amazon.com
Find eBook deals and follow me on BookBub.com

Catch my podcast, The Two Authors' Chat Show with co-host Douglas Pratt.

Find more great authors in the genre at TropicalAuthors.com

ABOUT THE AUTHOR

A *USA Today* Bestselling author, Nicholas Harvey's life has been anything but ordinary. Race car driver, adventurer, divemaster, and since 2020, a full-time novelist. Raised in England, Nick has dual US and British citizenship and now lives wherever he and his amazing wife, Cheryl, park their motorhome, or an aeroplane takes them. Warm oceans and tall mountains are their favourite places.

For more information, visit his website at HarveyBooks.com.

Made in United States
North Haven, CT
25 August 2024

56439133R00143